bird
box

ALSO BY JOSH MALERMAN

Bird Box

Black Mad Wheel

Unbury Carol

bird
box

josh malerman

ecco
An Imprint of HarperCollins *Publishers*

BIRD BOX. Copyright © 2014 by Josh Malerman. All rights reserved. Printed in the United States of America. No part of this book may be used or reproduced in any manner whatsoever without written permission except in the case of brief quotations embodied in critical articles and reviews. For information address HarperCollins Publishers, 195 Broadway, New York, NY 10007.

HarperCollins books may be purchased for educational, business, or sales promotional use. For information please e-mail the Special Markets Department at SPsales@harpercollins.com.

A hardcover edition of this book was published in 2014 by Ecco, an imprint of HarperCollins Publishers.

FIRST ECCO PAPERBACK EDITION PUBLISHED 2015.

FIRST ECCO MOVIE TIE-IN EDITION PUBLISHED 2018.

Designed by Suet Yee Chong
Tree branches by dimitris_k/Shutterstock, Inc.

Library of Congress Cataloging-in-Publication Data has been applied for.

ISBN 978-0-06-289571-4 (movie tie-in)

19 20 21 22 LSC   10 9 8 7 6 5 4 3 2

Sometimes I wish I were an architect, so that I could dedicate a building to a person; a superstructure that broke the clouds and continued up into the abyss. And if Bird Box *were made of bricks instead of letters, I'd host a ceremony, invite every shadowy memory I have, and cut the ribbon with an axe, letting everyone see for the first time that building's name. It'd be called the Debbie.*

Mom, Bird Box *is for you.*

bird
box

one

Malorie stands in the kitchen, thinking.

Her hands are damp. She is trembling. She taps her toe nervously on the cracked tile floor. It is early; the sun is probably only peeking above the horizon. She watches its meager light turn the heavy window drapes a softer shade of black and thinks,

That was a fog.

The children sleep under chicken wire draped in black cloth down the hall. Maybe they heard her moments ago on her knees in the yard. Whatever noise she made must have traveled through the microphones, then the amplifiers that sat beside their beds.

She looks to her hands and detects the subtlest sheen in the candlelight. Yes, they are damp. The morning's dew is still fresh upon them.

Now, in the kitchen, Malorie breathes deep before blowing the candle out. She looks around the small room, noting the rusted utensils and cracked dishes. The cardboard box used as a garbage can. The chairs, some held together by twine. The walls are dirty. Dirt from the feet and hands of the children. But older stains, too. The bottom of the walls in the hall is discolored, profound purples that have dulled to brown over time. These are blood. The carpet in the living room is discolored, too, no matter how hard Malorie scrubs. There are no chemicals in the house to help clean it. Long ago, Malorie filled the buckets with water from the well and, using a suit coat, worked on removing the stains from all over the house. But they refused to go away. Even those that proved less persistent remained, a shadow perhaps of their original size, but still horribly visible. A box of candles hides a blotch in the foyer. The couch in the living room sits at an awkward angle, moved there to shield two blemishes that look like wolf heads to Malorie. On the second floor, by the attic stairs, a pile of musty coats conceals purple scratches, embedded deep into the foot of the wall. Ten feet away is the blackest stain in the house. She does not use the far end of the home's second floor because she cannot bring herself to cross it.

This was once a nice house in a nice suburb of Detroit. Once, it was family-ready and safe. Only half a decade ago, a real-estate agent would have proudly showed it off. But this morning, the windows are covered with cardboard and wood. There is no running water. A big wooden bucket sits upon the kitchen counter. It smells stale. There are no conventional toys for the children. Pieces of a wooden chair have been whittled to play the part of little people. Small faces have been painted upon them. The cupboards are bare. There are no paintings on the walls. Wires run from under the back door into the first-floor bedrooms, where amplifiers alert Malorie and the children to any sounds coming from outside the house. The three of them live this way. They do not go outside for long periods of time. When they do, they are blindfolded.

The children have never seen the world outside their home. Not even through the windows. And Malorie hasn't looked in more than four years.

Four years.

She does not have to make this decision today. It's October in Michigan. It's cold. A twenty-mile trip on the river will be hard on the children. They may still be too young. What if one of them were to fall into the water? What would Malorie, blindfolded, do then?

An accident, Malorie thinks. *How horrible. After all this struggling, all this survival. To die because of an accident.*

Malorie looks at the drapes. She begins to cry. She wants to yell at

JOSH MALERMAN

someone. She wants to plead with anyone who might listen. *This is unfair,* she would say. *This is cruel.*

She looks over her shoulder, to the kitchen entrance and the hall that leads to the children's bedroom. Beyond the doorless frame, the children sleep soundly, covered by black cloth, hidden from light and sight. They do not stir. They show no sign of being awake. Yet, they could be listening to her. Sometimes, for all the pressure upon them to listen, for all the importance she's placed upon their ears, Malorie believes they can hear her think.

She could wait for sunnier skies, warmth, more attention paid to the boat. She could inform the children, listen to what they have to say. Their suggestions could be good ones. Only four years old, but trained to *listen.* Able to help navigate a boat that will be piloted blindly. Malorie would not be able to make the trip without them. She needs their ears. Could she also use their advice? At four years old, would they have something to say about *when* was the best time to leave the house forever?

Slumping into a kitchen chair, Malorie fights back the tears. Her shoeless toe still taps on the faded linoleum. Slowly, she looks up to the top of the cellar stairs. There she once talked with a man named Tom about a man named Don. She looks to the sink, where Don once carried buckets of well water, trembling for having been outdoors. Leaning forward, she can see the foyer, where Cheryl used to prepare the food for the birds. And between herself and the front door is the living room, silent and dark, where there are too many memories of too many people to digest.

Four years, she thinks, and wants to smash her fist through the wall.

Malorie knows that four years can easily become eight. Eight will quickly become twelve. And then the children will be adults. Adults who have never seen the sky. Never looked out a window. What would twelve years of living like veal do to their minds? Is there a point, Malorie wonders, where the clouds in the sky become unreal, and the only place they'll ever feel at home is behind the black cloth of their blindfolds?

Malorie swallows hard and imagines raising them by herself until they are teens.

Could she even do it? Could she protect them another ten years? Could she guard them long enough for them to guard her? And for what? What kind of life is she protecting them for?

You're a bad mother, she thinks.

For not finding a way to let them know the vastness of the sky. For not finding a way to let them run free in the yard, the street, the neighborhood of empty homes and weathered parked cars. Or granting them a single peek, just once, into space, when the sky turns black and is suddenly, beautifully, spotted with stars.

You are saving their lives for a life not worth living.

Malorie sees the drapes soften another degree through blurred, teary vision. If there is a fog out there, it won't be for long. And if it can help her, if it hides her and the children as they go to the river, to the rowboat, then she has to wake them now.

She slams a hand against the kitchen table, then wipes her eyes dry.

Rising and leaving the kitchen, Malorie takes the hall and enters the children's bedroom.

"Boy!" she yells. "Girl! Get up."

The bedroom is dark. The one window is covered with enough blankets so that even at its zenith, sunlight does not get through. There are two mattresses, one on each side of the room. Above them are black domes. Once, the chicken wire that supports the cloth was used to fence in a small garden by the well in the home's backyard. But for the past four years, it has served as armor, protecting the children not from what could see them, but from what *they* could see. Beneath it, Malorie hears movement and she kneels to loosen the wire that's fastened to nails in the room's wood floor. She is already pulling from her pocket the blindfolds as the two children look at her with sleepy, surprised expressions.

"Mommy?"

"Get up. Now. Mommy needs you to move fast."

The children respond quickly. They do not whine or complain.

"Where are we going?" the Girl asks.

Malorie hands her a blindfold and says, "Put this on. We're going on the river."

The pair take their blindfolds and tie the black cloth tightly over their eyes. They are well versed in the motion. Experts, if at four years old they can be experts in anything. It breaks Malorie's heart. They are only children and should be curious. They should be asking her why, today, they are going on the river—a river they have never been on before.

But, instead, they just do as they are told.

Malorie does not put on her own blindfold yet. She will get the kids ready first.

"Bring your puzzle," she tells the Girl. "And, both of you, bring your blankets."

The excitement she feels is unnameable. It's much more like hysteria. Stepping from one room to another, Malorie checks for things, small items they might need. Suddenly, she feels horribly unprepared. She feels unsafe, as though the house and the earth beneath it just vanished, exposing her to the outside world entirely. Yet, in the mania of the moment, she holds tight to the concept of the blindfold. No matter what tools she might pack, no matter what household object might be used as a weapon, she knows that the blindfolds are their strongest protection.

"Bring your blankets!" she reminds them, hearing the two small bodies ready themselves. Then she steps into their room to assist them. The Boy, small for his age, but with a wiry strength Malorie takes pride in, is deciding between two shirts that are both too large for him. They once belonged to an adult, long since gone. Malorie chooses for him and watches as his dark hair vanishes within the cloth, then sprouts again through the head hole. In her anxious state, Malorie recognizes that the Boy has grown some recently.

The Girl, average sized for her age, is attempting to pull a dress over her head, a dress she and Malorie sewed from an old bedsheet.

"There's a chill in the air, Girl. A dress won't do."

The Girl frowns; her blond hair is messy from her having just woken up.

"I'll wear pants, too, Mommy. And we've got our blankets."

Anger flares in Malorie. She doesn't want any resistance. Not today. Not even if the Girl is right.

"No dresses today."

The world outside, the empty malls and restaurants, the thousands of unused vehicles, the forgotten products on idle store shelves, all of it presses in on the house. It all whispers of what awaits them.

She takes a coat from the closet in the small bedroom down the hall from the children. Then she leaves the room, for what she knows will be the last time.

"Mommy," the Girl says, meeting her in the hall. "Do we need our bicycle horns?"

Malorie breathes deep.

"No," she answers. "We'll all be together. The whole trip."

As the Girl steps back into the bedroom, Malorie thinks of how pathetic it is, that bicycle horns are her children's greatest entertainment. They've played with them for years. All of their lives, honking from across the living room. The loud sound used to put Malorie on edge. But she never took them away. Never hid them. Even in the throes of early, anxious motherhood, Malorie understood that in this world, anything that brought the children to giggle was a good thing.

Even when they used to frighten Victor with them.

Oh, how Malorie longs for that dog! In the early days of raising the children alone, her fantasies of taking the river included Victor, the border collie, seated beside her in the rowboat. Victor would've warned her if an animal were near. He might've been capable of frightening something away.

"Okay," she says, her lithe body in the door frame of the children's bedroom. "That's it. Now we go."

There were times, placid afternoons, tempestuous evenings, when Malorie told them this day might come. Yes, she had spoken of the river before. Of a trip. She was careful never to call it their "escape" because she couldn't bear their believing their daily lives were something to flee from. Instead, she cautioned them of a future morning, when she would wake them, hastily, demanding they prepare to leave their home forever. She knew they could detect her uncertainty, just as they could hear a spider crawling up the glass pane of a draped window. For years, there sat a small pouch of food in the cupboard, set aside until it went stale, always replaced, always replenished, Malorie's proof, her evidence that she *might* wake them as she told them she would. *You see,* she would think, nervously checking the drapes, *the food in the cupboard is part of a plan.*

And now, the day has come. This morning. This hour. The *fog.*

The Boy and the Girl step forward and Malorie kneels before them. She checks their blindfolds. They are secure. In that moment, looking from one small face to the other, Malorie comprehends fully that, at last, the journey out has begun.

"Listen to me," she tells them, grasping their chins. "We're going to take a rowboat along the river today. It could be a long trip. But it's crucial that you both do every single thing I say. Do you understand?"

"Yes."

"Yes."

"It's cold out there. You have your blankets. You have your folds. There's nothing more you need right now. Do you understand me?"

"Yes."

"Yes."

"Under no circumstances will either one of you remove your blindfold. If you do, I will hurt you. Do you understand?"

"Yes."

"Yes."

"I need your ears. I need you both to listen as carefully as you can. On the river, you need to listen beyond the water, beyond the woods. If you hear an animal in those woods, tell me. If you hear anything in the water, you tell me. Understand?"

"Yes."

"Yes."

"Do *not* ask questions that have nothing to do with the river. You'll be sitting up front," she says, tapping the Boy. Then she taps the Girl. "And you'll be sitting in the back. When we get to the boat, I'll guide you to those places. I'll be in the middle, rowing. I don't want you two talking across the boat to one another unless it's about something you hear in the woods. Or the river. Understand?"

"Yes."

"Yes."

"We are not stopping for any reason. Not until we get to where we're going. I'll let you know when that is. If you get hungry, eat from this pouch."

Malorie brings the pouch to the back of their small hands.

"Don't fall asleep. Do *not* fall asleep. I need your ears more now today than I've ever needed them."

"Will we bring the microphones?" the Girl asks.

"No."

As Malorie speaks, she looks from one blindfolded face to the other.

"When we leave this house, we'll hold hands and walk along the path to the well. We'll go through the small clearing in the woods behind our house. The path to the river is overgrown. We may have to drop hands for a step, and if we do, I want you both to hold on to my coat or each other's. Understand?"

"Yes."

"Yes."

Do they sound scared?

"Listen to me. We're going somewhere neither of you has ever been. We're going farther from the house than you've gone before. There are things out there that will hurt you, that will hurt Mommy, if you do not listen to me, now, this morning."

The children are silent.

"Do you understand?"

"Yes."

"Yes."

Malorie has trained them well.

"All right," she says, her voice revealing a hint of hysteria. "We're going. We're going right now. *We're going.*"

She presses their heads against her forehead.

Then she takes each child by the hand. They cross the house quickly. In the kitchen, Malorie, trembling, wipes her eyes and pulls her own blindfold from her pocket. She ties it tight around her head and dark long hair. She pauses, her hand on the doorknob, the door that opens to the path she has taken for countless buckets of water.

She is about to leave the house behind. The reality of this moment overwhelms her.

When she opens the door, the cool air rushes in and Malorie steps forward, her mind's eye blurry with terror and scenarios too ghastly to speak of in front of the children. She stammers as she speaks, nearly yelling as she does.

"Hold my hands. Both of you."

The Boy takes Malorie's left hand. The Girl slips her tiny fingers into her right.

Blindfolded, they step from the house.

The well is twenty yards away. Small pieces of wood, once part of picture frames, outline the path, placed there for direction. Both children have touched the wood with the tip of their shoes countless times. Malorie once told them that the water in the well was the only medicine they'd ever need. Because of this, Malorie knows, the children have always respected the well. They never complained about fetching water with her.

At the well now, the ground is bumpy beneath their feet. It feels unnatural, soft.

"Here's the clearing," Malorie calls.

She leads the children carefully. A second path begins ten yards from the well. The entrance to this path is narrow, and it splits the woods. The river is less than a hundred yards from here. At the woods, Malorie momentarily lets go of the children's hands so she can feel for the scant entry.

"Hold on to my coat!"

She feels along the branches until she finds a tank top, tied to a tree at the path's entrance. She tied it here herself more than three years ago.

The Boy grabs hold of her pocket and she senses the Girl take hold of his. Malorie calls to them as she walks, constantly asking them if they are holding on to one another. Tree branches poke her in the face. She does not cry out.

Soon, they arrive at the marker Malorie has stuck in the dirt. The splintered leg of a kitchen chair, stuck in the center of the path, there for her to trip on, to stumble over, to recognize.

She discovered the rowboat four years ago, docked only five houses from their own. It has been more than a month since she last checked on it, but she believes it is still there. Still, it's difficult not to imagine the worst. What if someone else got to it first? Another woman, not unlike herself, living five houses in the other direction, using every day of four years to gather enough courage to flee. A woman who once stumbled down this same slippery bank and felt the same point of salvation, the pointed steel tip of the rowboat.

The air nips at the scratches on Malorie's face. The children do not complain.

This is not childhood, Malorie thinks, leading them toward the river.

Then she hears it. Before reaching the dock, she hears the rowboat rocking in the water. She stops and checks the children's blindfolds, tightening both. She leads them onto the wood planks.

Yes, she thinks, *it's still here.* Just like the cars are still parked in the street outside their house. Just like the homes on the street are still empty.

It is colder, out of the woods, away from the house. The sound of the water is as frightening as it is exhilarating. Kneeling where she believes the boat must be, she lets go of the children's hands and feels for the steel tip. Her fingertips find the rope that holds it first.

"Boy," she says, pulling the ice-cold tip of the boat toward the dock. "In the front. Get in the front." She helps him. Once he is steady, she holds his face in both her hands and says once again, "Listen. Beyond the water. *Listen.*"

She tells the Girl to stay on the dock as she blindly unties the rope before carefully climbing onto the middle bench. Still half-standing, she helps the Girl aboard. The boat rocks once violently and Malorie grips the Girl's hand too tight. The Girl does not cry out.

There are leaves, sticks, and water in the bottom of the boat. Malorie sifts through them to find the paddles she has stowed on the boat's right side. The paddles are cold. Damp. They smell of mildew. She sets them into the steel grooves. They feel strong, sturdy as she uses one to push off from the dock. And then . . .

They are on the river.

The water is calm. But there are sounds out here. Movement in the woods.

Malorie thinks of the fog. She hopes it has hidden their escape.

But the fog will go away.

"Children," Malorie says, breathing hard, *"listen."*

Finally, after four years of waiting, training, and finding the courage to leave, she paddles away from the dock, from the bank, and from the house that has protected her and the children for what feels like a lifetime.

two

It is nine months before the children are born. Malorie lives with her sister, Shannon, in a modest rental neither of them has decorated. They moved in three weeks ago, despite their friend's concerns. Malorie and Shannon are both popular, intelligent women but in each other's company they have a tendency to become unglued, as shown the very day they carried their boxes inside.

"I was thinking it makes more sense for me to have the bigger bedroom," Shannon said, standing on the second-floor landing. "Seeing as I've got the bigger dresser."

"Oh, come on," Malorie responded, holding a milk crate of unread books. "That room has a better window."

The sisters debated this for a long time, both wary of proving their friends and family right by erupting in an argument on their first afternoon. Eventually, Malorie agreed to a coin toss, which ended in Shannon's favor, an event Malorie still believes was somehow fixed.

Now, today, Malorie is not thinking about the little things her sister does that drive her batty. She is not quietly cleaning up after Shannon, closing cabinet doors, following her trail of sweaters and socks through the halls. She is not huffing, passively, shaking her head as she runs the dishwasher or slides one of Shannon's unpacked boxes from the center of the living room, where it's in both of their way. Instead, she is standing before the mirror in the first-floor bathroom, where she is naked, as she studies her belly in the glass.

You've missed a period before, she tells herself. But this is hardly consolation, because she has been anxious for weeks now, knowing she should have been safer with Henry Martin.

Her black hair hangs to her shoulders. Her lips curl down in a curious frown. She places her hands on her flat belly and nods slowly. No matter how she explains herself, she *feels* pregnant.

"Malorie!" Shannon calls from the living room. "What are you *doing* in there?"

Malorie does not respond. She turns sideways and tilts her head. Her blue eyes look gray in the pale light of the bathroom. She plants a palm on the sink's pink linoleum and arches her back. She is trying to make her belly skinnier, as if this might prove there could be no little life within it.

"Malorie!" Shannon calls again. "There's another report on television! Something happened in Alaska."

Malorie hears her sister, but what's going on in the outside world doesn't matter much to her right now.

In recent days, the Internet has blown up with a story people are calling "the Russia Report." In it, a man who was riding in the passenger seat of a truck driving along a snowy highway outside St. Petersburg asked his friend, who was driving, to pull over and then attacked him, removing his lips with his fingernails. Then he took his own life in the snow, using a table saw from the truck bed. A grisly story, but one whose notoriety Malorie attributes to the seemingly senseless way the Internet has of making random occurrences famous. But then, a second story appeared. Similar circumstances. This time in Yakutsk, some five thousand miles east of St. Petersburg. There, a mother, by all accounts "stable," buried her children alive in the family's garden before taking her own life with the jagged edges of broken dishes. And a third story, in Omsk, Russia, nearly two thousand miles southeast of St. Petersburg, sprouted online and quickly became one of the most discussed topics on all social media sites. This time there was video footage. For as long as she could, Malorie had watched a man wielding an axe, his beard red with blood, trying to attack the unseen man who filmed him. Eventually, he succeeded. But Malorie didn't see that part. She tried not to follow any more on the subject at all. But Shannon, always more dramatic, insisted on relaying the frightening news.

"*Alaska,*" Shannon repeats, through the bathroom door. "That's *America,* Malorie!"

Shannon's blond hair betrays their mother's Finnish roots. Malorie looks more like her father: strong, deep-set eyes and the smooth fair skin of a northerner. Having been raised in the Upper Peninsula, both dreamed of living downstate, near Detroit, where they imagined there were parties, concerts, job opportunities, and men in abundance.

This last item hadn't proved fruitful for Malorie until she met Henry Martin.

"Holy *shit,*" Shannon hollers. "There might have been something in Canada, too. This is serious stuff, Malorie. What are you *doing* in there?"

Malorie turns the faucet on and lets the cool water run over her fingers. She splashes some on her face. Looking up into the mirror, she thinks of her parents, still in the Upper Peninsula. They haven't heard of Henry Martin. *She* hasn't even spoken to him since their one night. Yet, here she is, probably tied to him forever.

Suddenly the bathroom door opens. Malorie reaches for a towel.

"Jeez, Shannon."

"Did you hear me, Malorie? The story is everywhere. People are starting to say it's related to seeing something. Isn't that strange? I just heard CNN say it's the one constant in all the incidents. That the victims *saw* something before attacking people and taking their own lives. Can you believe this? Can you?"

Malorie turns slowly to her sister. Her face carries no expression.

"Hey, are you all right, Malorie? You don't look so good."

Malorie starts crying. She bites her lower lip. She has grabbed the towel but has yet to cover herself. She is still standing before the mirror as if examining her naked belly. Shannon notices this.

"Oh shit," Shannon says. "Are you worried that you're—"

Malorie is already nodding. The sisters step to each other in the pink bathroom and Shannon holds Malorie, patting the back of her black hair, soothing her.

"Okay," she says. "Let's not freak out. Let's go get a test. That's what people do. Okay? Don't worry. I'll bet you more than half the people who get tests wind up not being pregnant."

Malorie doesn't respond. She only sighs deeply.

"Okay," Shannon says. "Let's go."

three

How far can a person hear?

Rowing blindfolded is even harder than Malorie had imagined. Many times already, the rowboat has run into the banks and gotten stuck for a period of several minutes. In that time she was besieged by visions of unseen hands reaching for the blindfolds that cover the children's eyes. Fingers coming up and out of the water, from the mud where the river meets the earth. The children did not scream, they did not whine. They are too patient for that.

But how *far* can a person hear?

The Boy helped get the boat loose, standing and pushing against a mossy trunk, and now Malorie paddles again. Despite these early setbacks, Malorie can feel they are making progress. It is invigorating. Birds sing in the trees now that the sun has come up. Animals roam amid the thick foliage of the woods that surround them. Fish jump out of the water, making small splashes that electrify Malorie's nerves. All of this is heard. None of it is seen.

From birth the children have been trained to understand the sounds of the forest. As babies, Malorie would tie T-shirts over their eyes and carry them to the edge of the woods. There, despite knowing they were too young to understand any of what she told them, she would describe the sounds of the forest.

Leaves crinkling, she would say. *A small animal, like a rabbit.* Always aware that it could be something much worse. Worse even than a bear. In those days, and the days that followed, when the children were old enough to learn, Malorie trained herself as she trained them. But she would never hear as well as they one day would. She was twenty-four years old before she was able to discern the difference between a raindrop and a tap on a window, relying only on her hearing. She was raised on *sight*. Did this then make her the wrong teacher? When she carried leaves inside and had the children, blindfolded, identify the difference between her stepping on one and crushing one in her hand, were these the right lessons to give?

How far can a person hear?

The Boy likes fish, she knows. Often Malorie caught one in the river, using a rusted fishing pole fashioned from an umbrella found in the cellar. The Boy enjoyed watching them splash in the well bucket in the kitchen. He took to drawing them, too. Malorie remembers thinking she'd have to catch every beast on the planet and bring it home for the children to know what they looked like. What else might they like if given the chance to view it? What would the Girl think of a fox? A raccoon? Even cars were a myth, with only Malorie's amateur drawings as reference. Boots, bushes, gardens, storefronts, buildings, streets, and stars. Why, she would have had to re-create the globe for them. But the best they got was fish. And the Boy loved them.

Now, on the river, hearing another small splash, she worries lest his curiosity inspire him to remove his fold.

How far can a person hear?

Malorie needs the children to hear *into* the trees, *into* the wind, *into* the dirt banks that lead to an entire world of living creatures. The river is an amphitheater, Malorie muses, paddling.

But it's also a grave.

The children *must* listen.

Malorie cannot stave off the visions of hands emerging from the darkness, clutching the heads of the children, deliberately untying that which protects them.

Breathing hard and sweating, Malorie prays a person can hear all the way to safety.

four

Malorie is driving. The sisters use her car, a 1999 Ford Festiva, because there is more gas in it. They're only three miles from home, yet already there are signs that things have changed.

"Look!" Shannon says, pointing at several houses. "Blankets over the windows."

Malorie is trying to pay attention to what Shannon is saying, but her thoughts keep returning to her belly. The Russia Report media explosion worries her, but she does not take it as seriously as her sister. Others online are, like Malorie, more skeptical. She's read blogs, particularly *Silly People,* that post photos of people taking precautions, then add funny captions beneath them. As Shannon alternately points out the window, then shields her eyes, Malorie thinks of one. It was of a woman hanging a blanket over her window. Beneath it, the caption read: *Honey, what do you think of us moving the bed right here?*

"Can you believe it?" Shannon says.

Malorie nods silently. She turns left.

"Come on," Shannon says. "You absolutely have to admit, this is getting interesting."

A part of Malorie agrees. It *is* interesting. On the sidewalk, a couple passes with newspaper held to their temples. Some drivers have their rearview mirrors turned up. Distantly, Malorie wonders if these are the signs of a society beginning to believe something is wrong. And if so, *what*?

"I don't understand," Malorie says, partly trying to distract her thoughts and partly gaining interest.

"Don't understand what?"

"Do they think it's unsafe to look outside? To look *anywhere*?"

"Yes," Shannon says. "That's exactly what they think. I've been telling you."

Shannon, Malorie thinks, has always been dramatic.

"Well, that sounds insane," she says. "And look at that guy!"

Shannon looks to where Malorie points. Then she looks away. A man in a business suit walks with a blind man's walking stick. His eyes are closed.

"Nobody's ashamed to act like this," Shannon says, her eyes on her shoes. "That's how weird it's gotten."

When they pull into Stokely's Drugs, Shannon is holding her hand up to shield her eyes. Malorie notices, then looks across the parking lot. Others are doing the same.

"What are you worried about seeing?" she asks.

"Nobody knows that answer yet."

Malorie has seen the drugstore's big yellow sign a thousand times. But it has never looked so uninviting.

Let's go buy your first pregnancy test, she thinks, getting out of the car. The sisters cross the lot.

"They're by the *medicine,* I think," Shannon whispers, opening the store's front door, still covering her eyes.

"Shannon, stop it."

Malorie leads the way to the family planning aisle. There is First Response, Clearblue Easy, New Choice, and six other brands.

"There's so many of them," Shannon says, taking one from the shelf. "Doesn't anyone use condoms anymore?"

"Which one do I get?"

Shannon shrugs. "This one looks as good as any."

A man farther down the aisle opens a box of bandages. He holds one up to his eye.

The sisters bring the test to the counter. Andrew, who is Shannon's age and once asked her on a date, is working. Malorie wants this moment to be over with.

"Wow," Andrew says, scanning the small box.

"Shut up, Andrew," Shannon says. "It's for our dog."

"You guys have a dog now?"

"Yes," Shannon says, taking the bag he's put it in. "And she's very popular in our neighborhood."

The drive home is torturous for Malorie. The plastic bag between their seats suggests her life has already changed.

"Look," Shannon says, pointing out the car window with the same hand she's been using to hide her eyes.

The sisters come to a stop sign slowly. Outside the corner house they see a woman on a small ladder, nailing a comforter over the home's bay window.

"When we get back I'm doing the same thing," Shannon says.

"Shannon."

Their street, usually crowded with the neighborhood kids, is empty. No blue, stickered tricycle. No Wiffle ball bats.

Once inside, Malorie heads to the bathroom and Shannon immediately turns on the television.

"I think all you gotta do is pee on it, Malorie!" Shannon calls.

Inside the bathroom, Malorie can hear the news.

By the time Shannon arrives at the bathroom door, Malorie is already staring at the pink strip, shaking her head.

"Oh boy," Shannon says.

"I've got to call Mom and Dad," Malorie says. A part of her is already steeling herself, knowing that, despite being single, she is going to have this baby.

"You need to call Henry Martin," Shannon says.

Malorie looks to her sister quickly. All day she's known Henry Martin will not play a big part in the raising of this child. In a way, she's already accepted this. Shannon walks with her to the living room, where boxes of unpacked objects clutter the space in front of the television. On the screen is a funeral procession. CNN anchormen are discussing it. Shannon steps to the television and lowers the volume. Malorie sits on the couch and calls Henry Martin from her cell phone.

He does not answer. So she texts him.

Important stuff. Call me when you can.

Suddenly Shannon springs up from the couch and hollers.

"Did you *see* that, Malorie? An incident in Michigan! I think they said it was in the Upper Peninsula!"

Their parents are already on Malorie's mind. As Shannon raises the volume again, the sisters learn that an elderly couple from Iron Mountain were found hanging from a tree in the nearby woods. The anchorman says they used their belts.

Malorie calls her mother. She picks up after two rings.

"Malorie."

"Mom."

"I'm sure you're calling because of this news?"

"No. I'm pregnant, Mom."

"Oh, goodness, Malorie." Her mother is quiet for a moment. Malorie can hear her television in the background. "Are you serious with someone?"

"No, it was an accident."

Shannon is standing in front of the television now. Her eyes are wide. She is pointing toward it, as though reminding Malorie how important it is. Her mother is quiet on the phone.

"Are you okay, Mom?"

"Well, I'm more concerned with you right now, dear."

"Yeah. Bad timing all around."

"How far along are you?"

"Five weeks, I think. Maybe six."

"And you're going to keep it? You've already made this decision?"

"I am. I mean, I just found out. Minutes ago. But I am. Yes."

"Have you let the father know?"

"I wrote him. I'll call him, too."

Now Malorie pauses. Then continues.

"Do you feel safe up there, Mom? Are you okay?"

"I don't know, I just don't know. None of us do and we're very scared. But right now I'm more worried about you."

On the screen, a woman, using a diagram, explains what may have happened. She is drawing a line from a small road where the couple's car was found abandoned. Malorie's mother is telling her that she knows someone who knew the elderly couple. Their last name is Mikkonen, she is saying. The woman on-screen is now standing in what looks like a patch of bloodied grass.

"*God,*" Shannon says.

"Oh, I wish your father were home," their mother is saying. "And you're *pregnant*. Oh, Malorie."

Shannon is grabbing the phone. She is asking if their mother knows any more details than the news. What are people saying up there? Is this the only incident? Are people taking precautions?

As Shannon continues to talk wildly into the phone, Malorie gets up from the couch. She steps to the front door and opens it. Looking up and down the street, she thinks to herself, *How serious is this?*

There are no neighbors in their yards. No faces in the windows of the other homes. A car drives by and Malorie cannot see the face of the driver. He's hiding it with his hand.

On the grass by the front walk is this morning's newspaper. Malorie steps to it. The front-page headline is about the growing number of incidents. It simply says: ANOTHER ONE. Shannon has probably already told her everything the paper has to say. Malorie picks it up and, turning it over, stops at something on the back page.

It's a classified. A home in Riverbridge is opening its doors to strangers. A "safe house" it says. A refuge. A place the owners hope will act as a "sanctuary" as the grim news mounts daily.

Malorie, experiencing the first real prickling feelings of panic, looks again to the street. She sees the door to a neighbor's home open, then close quickly. Still holding the paper, Malorie looks over her shoulder back to her house, where the sounds of the television still blare. Inside, at the far wall of the living room, Shannon is tacking a blanket over one of the room's windows.

"Come on," Shannon says. "Get in here. And close that door."

five

It is six months before the children are born. Malorie is showing. Blankets cover every window in the house. The front door is never left unlocked and never left open. Reports of unexplainable events have been surfacing with an alarming frequency. What was once breaking news twice a week now develops every day. Government officials are interviewed on television. Stories from as far east as Maine, as far south as Florida, have both sisters now taking precautions. Shannon, who visits dozens of blogs daily, fears a mishmash of ideas, a little bit of everything she reads. Malorie doesn't know what to believe. New stories appear hourly online. It's the only thing anybody talks about on social media and it's the only topic on the news pages. New websites are devoted entirely to the evolution of information on the subject. One site features only a global map, with small red faces placed upon the cities in which something occurred. Last time Malorie checked, there were more than three hundred faces. Online, they are calling it "the Problem." There exists the widespread communal belief that whatever "the Problem" is, it definitely begins when a person *sees something*.

Malorie resisted believing it as long as she could. The sisters argued constantly, Malorie citing the pages that derided mass hysteria, Shannon citing everything else. But soon Malorie had to relent, when the pages she frequented began to run stories about their own loved ones, and the authors of these blogs stepped forward to admit some concern.

Cracks, Malorie thought then. *Showing even in the skeptics.*

Days passed in which Malorie experienced a sort of double life. Neither sister left the house anymore. Both made sure the windows were covered. They watched CNN, MSNBC, and Fox News until they physically couldn't watch the same stories repeating themselves. And while Shannon grew more serious, and even grave, Malorie held on to a pinch of hope that this would all simply go away.

But it didn't. And it got worse.

Three months into living like shut-ins, Malorie and Shannon's worst fears came true when their parents stopped answering their phone. They didn't answer e-mails, either.

Malorie wanted to drive north to the Upper Peninsula. But Shannon refused.

"We're just going to have to hope they're being safe, Malorie. We're going to have to hope their phone was shut off. Driving anywhere right now would be dumb. Even to the store, and driving nine hours would be suicide."

"The Problem" always resulted in suicide. Fox News had reported the word so often that they were now using synonyms. "Self-destruction." "Self-immolation." "Hari-kari." One anchorman described it as "personal erasing," a phrase that did not catch on. Instructions from the government were reprinted on the screen. A national curfew was mandated. People were advised to lock their doors, cover their windows, and, above all, not to look outside. On the radio, music was replaced entirely with discussions.

A blackout, Malorie thinks. *The world, the outdoors, is being shut down.*

Nobody has answers. Nobody knows what is going on. People are seeing something that drives them to hurt others. To hurt themselves.

People are dying.

But why?

Malorie tries to calm down by focusing on the child growing inside her. She seems to be encountering every symptom mentioned in her baby book, *With Child*. Slight bleeding. Tender breasts. Fatigue. Shannon points out Malorie's mood swings, but it's the cravings that are driving her crazy. Too afraid to drive to the store, the sisters are stuck with the items they stockpiled shortly after purchasing the pregnancy test. But Malorie's tastes have changed. Standard foods disgust her. So she combines things. Orange brownies. Chicken with cocktail sauce. Raw fish on toast. She dreams of ice cream. Often, looking toward the front door, she thinks of how easy it would be to get behind the wheel of the car and drive to the store. She knows it would take only fifteen minutes. But every time she leans toward doing it, the television delivers another harrowing story. And besides, who knows if the employees show up to the stores anymore?

"What do you think people are seeing?" Malorie asks Shannon.

"I don't know, Mal. I just don't know."

The sisters ask each other this question constantly. It'd be impossible to count the number of theories that have been birthed online. All of them scare the hell out of Malorie. Mental illness as a result of the radio waves in wireless technology is one. An erroneous evolutionary leap in humankind is another. New Agers say it's a matter of humanity being in touch with a planet that is close to exploding, or a sun that is dying.

Some people believe there are creatures out there.

The government is saying nothing except lock your doors.

Malorie, alone, sits on the couch, slowly rubbing her belly, watching television. She worries that there is nothing positive to watch, that the baby feels her anxiety. *With Child* told her this would happen. The baby will experience the mother's emotions. Still, she can't look away from the screen. On a desk against the wall behind her, the computer is open and on. The radio plays softly. Together, it makes Malorie feel like she's in a war room. At the center of it all, while everything is falling apart. It's overwhelming. And it's becoming terrifying. There are no commercials anymore. And the newscasters pause for periods of time, shamelessly revealing their surprise as they receive updates on air.

Above this buzzing din of media, Malorie hears Shannon moving on the second floor.

Then, as Gabriel Townes, one of CNN's primary anchors, silently reads a sheet of paper just handed to him, Malorie hears a thud from above. She pauses.

"Shannon!" she calls. "Are you all right?"

Gabriel Townes doesn't look good. He's been on television a lot lately. CNN let it be known that many of their reporters have stopped coming in to the station. Townes has been sleeping there. "We'll go through this together" is his new slogan. His hair is no longer perfect. He wears little makeup. More jarring is the exhausted way in which he delivers the news. He looks sunken.

"Shannon? Come down here. It looks like Townes just got an update."

But there is no response. There is only silence from upstairs. Malorie rises and turns down the television.

"Shannon?"

Quietly, Gabriel Townes is discussing a beheading in Toledo. It's less than eighty miles from where Malorie watches.

"Shannon?! What are you doing up there?"

There is no answer. Townes speaks quietly on the television. There are no accompanying graphics. No music. No inserts.

Malorie, standing in the center of the room, is looking toward the ceiling. She turns the volume of the television even lower, then turns the radio off, then walks toward the stairs.

At the railing, she slowly looks up to the carpeted landing. The lights are off, but a thin ray of what looks like sunshine sprays upon the wall. Placing her hand on the wood, Malorie steps onto the carpet. She looks over her shoulder, to the front door, and imagines an amalgamation of every report she's heard.

She takes the stairs.

"Shannon?"

She is at the top now. Trembling. Stepping down the hall, she sees sunlight coming from Shannon's bedroom. Slowly, she comes to the open door and looks inside.

A corner of the window is exposed. A part of the blanket, having come loose, hangs.

Malorie quickly looks away. There is a stillness, and a faint hum from the television below.

"Shannon?"

Down the hall, the bathroom door is open. The light is on. Malorie walks toward it. Once there, she holds her breath, then turns to look.

Shannon is on the floor, facing the ceiling. A pair of scissors sticks out of her chest. Blood surrounds her, pooling into the tiles on the floor. It seems like more blood than her body could hold.

Malorie screams, clutching the doorframe, and slides to the ground, wailing. The harsh light of the bathroom exposes every detail. The stillness of her sister's eyes. The way Shannon's shirt sinks into her chest with the scissor blades.

Malorie crawls to the bathtub and throws up. Her sister's blood sticks to her. She tries to wake Shannon, but she knows this will not happen. Malorie stands, speaking to Shannon, telling her she's going to get help. Wiping blood from her hands, Malorie rushes downstairs and finds her phone on the couch. She calls the police. No answer. She calls again. No answer. Then she calls her parents. Still, no answer. She turns and runs to the front door. She must get help. Her hand clutches the doorknob, but she finds she cannot turn it.

Dear God, Malorie thinks. *Shannon would never do this willingly. Dear God, it's true! Something is out there.*

And whatever Shannon saw, it must be close to the house.

A piece of wood is all that separates her from what killed her sister. What her sister *saw.*

Beyond the wood she hears wind. There are no other sounds. No cars. No neighbors. Only stillness.

She is alone. Suddenly, agonizingly, she understands that she needs someone. She needs safety. She has to figure out how to leave this house.

The image of Shannon blazing in her mind, Malorie rushes into the kitchen. There, under the sink, she pulls forth a stack of newspapers. She manically rifles through them. Breathing hard, her eyes wide, she checks the back of each one.

Finally, she finds it.

The classified. Riverbridge. Strangers inviting strangers into their home. Malorie reads it again. Then she reads it another time. She falls to her knees, clutching the paper.

Riverbridge is twenty minutes away. Shannon saw something outside, and it killed her. Malorie must get herself and her child to safety.

Suddenly, her heavy breathing gives way to an endless flow of hot tears. She does not know what to do. She has never been this afraid. Everything within her feels hot, like she's burning.

She cries loudly. Through wet eyes, she reads the ad again.

And her tears fall upon the paper.

six

"What is it, Boy?"

"Did you hear that?"

"What? What did you hear? *Speak!*"

"Listen."

Malorie does. She stops paddling and she listens. There is the wind. There is the river. There is the high squawking of birds far away and the occasional shuffle of small animals in the trees. There is her own breathing and her heart pounding, too. And beyond all this noise, from somewhere *inside* it, comes a sound she immediately fears.

Something is in the water with them.

"Don't speak!" Malorie hisses.

The children are silent. She rests the paddle handles across her bent legs and is still.

Something big is in the water before them. Something that rises and splashes.

Malorie, for all the work she has done protecting the children from madness, wonders if she's prepared them enough for the old realities.

Like the wild animals that would reclaim a river man no longer frequents.

The rowboat tips to Malorie's left. She feels the heat of something touching the steel rim where the paddle ends rest.

The birds in the trees go quiet.

She holds her breath, thinking of the children.

What plays with the nose of their boat?

Is it a creature? she thinks, hysterical. *Please, no, God, let it be an animal. Please!*

Malorie knows that if the children were to remove their blindfolds, if they were to scream before going mad, she still would not open her eyes.

Without Malorie paddling, the rowboat moves again. She takes hold of a paddle and prepares herself to swing it.

But then she hears the sound of the water splitting. The thing moves. It sounds farther away. Malorie is breathing so hard she gasps.

She hears a fumbling among the branches at the bank to her left and imagines the thing has crawled onto shore.

Or maybe it walked.

Is a creature standing there? Studying the limbs of the trees and mud at its feet?

Thoughts like these remind her of Tom. Sweet Tom, who spent every hour of every day trying to figure out how to survive in this awful new world. She wishes he were here. He would know what made that sound.

It's a black bear, she tells herself.

The songs of the birds return. Life in the trees continues.

"You did well," Malorie pants. Her voice is caged with stress.

She begins paddling and soon the sound of the Girl shuffling her puzzle pieces joins in with the sound of the paddles in the water.

She imagines the children, blinded by their black cloths, the sun embarrassing them with visibility, drifting downstream. Her own blindfold is tight against her head, damp. It irritates the skin by her ears. Sometimes, she is able to ignore this. At others, all she can think about is scratching. Despite the cold, she regularly dips her fingertips into the river and moistens the cloth where it chafes. Just above her ears. The bridge of her nose. The back of her head where the knot is. The wet cloth helps, but Malorie will never fully get used to the feel of the cloth against her face. Even her eyes, she thinks, paddling, even her eye*lashes* grow weary of the fabric.

A black bear, she tells herself again.

But she isn't so sure.

Debates like these have governed every action Malorie has taken for the last four and half years. From the moment she decided to answer the classified in the paper and first arrived at the house in Riverbridge. Every noise she's heard since has delivered visions of things much worse than any earthly animal.

"You did a good job," Malorie says to the children, shaking. She means to reassure them, but her voice betrays her fear.

seven

Riverbridge.

Malorie has been to this area once, several years before. It was a New Year's Eve party. She hardly recalls the name of the girl who threw it. Marcy something. Maribel, maybe. Shannon knew her, and Shannon drove that night. The roads were slushy. Dirty gray banks of snow framed the side streets. People used ice from the roof for their mixed drinks. Someone got half-naked and wrote the year 2009 in the snow. Now it's summer's peak, the middle of July, and Malorie is driving. Scared, alone, and grieving.

The drive over is agonizing. Traveling no more than fifteen miles per hour, Malorie frantically looks for street signs, for other cars. She closes her eyes, then opens them again, still driving.

The roads are empty. Every home she passes has blankets or wood boards covering the windows. Storefronts are vacant. Strip mall parking lots are barren. She keeps her eyes immediately on the road ahead and drives, following the route highlighted on the map beside her. Her hands feel weak on the wheel. Her eyes ache from crying. She feels an unyielding flow of guilt for having left her sister, dead, on the bathroom floor of their house.

She did not bury her. She just left.

The hospitals didn't answer their phones. Neither did the funeral homes. Malorie covered her, partially, with a blue and yellow scarf that Shannon loved.

The radio comes in and out. A man is talking about the possibility of war. If mankind bands together, he says, but then it's all static. On the side of the road, she passes an abandoned car. The doors are open. A jacket hangs from the passenger seat touching the road. Malorie quickly looks ahead again. Then she closes her eyes. Then she opens them.

The radio is working. The man is still talking about war. Something moves to the right, and she sees it out of the corner of her eye. She does not look at it. She closes her right eye. Ahead, in the middle of the road, a bird lands and then takes off again. When Malorie reaches this spot, she sees the bird was interested in a dead dog. Malorie drives over it. The car bounces; she hits her head on the roof, her suitcase rattling in the backseat. She is shaking. The dog didn't just look dead, it looked bent. She closes her eyes. She opens them.

A bird, maybe the same bird, caws from the sky. Malorie passes Roundtree Street. Ballam Street. Horton. She knows she is close. Something darts on her left. She closes her left eye. She passes an empty mail truck and its letters are strewn on the concrete. A bird flies too low, almost hitting the windshield. She screams, closes both eyes, and opens them. When she does, she sees the street sign she is looking for.

Shillingham.

She turns right, braking as she rounds the corner onto Shillingham Lane. She does not need to check her map for the number 273. It has been on her mind the entire drive.

Aside from a few cars parked in front of a house on the right, the street is empty. The neighborhood is ordinary, suburban. Most of the houses look the same. The lawns are overgrown. Every window is draped. In her eagerness, Malorie looks to the house where the cars are parked and knows it is the one she's looking for.

She closes her eyes and slams on the brakes.

Stopped and breathing hard, the faint image of the house remains in her mind.

The garage is to the right. The garage door, beige, is closed. A brown shingled roof rests on white siding and bricks. The front door is a darker brown. The windows are covered. There's an attic.

Steeling herself, eyes still closed, Malorie turns and grips the handle of the suitcase. The house is maybe fifty feet from where she stopped. She knows she is not close to the curb. She does not care. Attempting to calm herself, she breathes deeply, slowly. The suitcase is beside her in the passenger seat. Eyes closed, she listens. Hearing nothing outside the car, she opens the driver's-side door and steps out, reaching for her things.

The baby kicks.

Malorie gasps, fumbling with her luggage. She almost opens her eyes to look down at her belly. Instead, she brings her hands there and rubs.

"We're here," she whispers.

She takes hold of the suitcase and, blindly, carefully, walks to the front lawn. Once she feels the grass beneath her shoes, she moves quicker, walking fast into a low bush. The needles prick her wrists and hip. She steps back, listening, and feels concrete beneath her shoes, stepping cautiously to where she thinks the front door is.

She is right. Clattering her suitcase on the porch, she feels along the brick, finding a doorbell. She rings it.

At first, there is no response. There is a sinking feeling that she has reached her end. Has she driven this far, braved this world, for nothing? She rings the bell again. Then again. Again. There is no response. She knocks, frantically beating the door.

Nobody calls to her.

Then . . . she hears muffled voices from within.

Oh my God! Someone's here! Someone's home!

"Hello?" she calls quietly. The sound of her own voice on the empty street scares her. "Hello! I read the ad in the paper!"

Silence. Malorie waits, listening. Then, someone calls to her.

"Who are you?" a man says. "Where are you from?"

Malorie feels relief, hope. She feels like crying.

"My name is Malorie! I've driven from Westcourt!"

There is a pause. Then, "Are your eyes closed?"

It's a different man's voice.

"Yes! My eyes are closed."

"Have they been closed for a long time?"

Just let me in! she thinks. LET ME IN!

"No," she answers. "Or yes. I've driven from Westcourt. I closed them as much as I could."

She hears low voices. Some are angry. The people are debating whether or not to let her in.

"I haven't seen anything!" she calls. "I swear. I'm safe. My eyes are closed. Please. I read the ad in the paper."

"Keep them closed," a man finally says. "We're opening the door. When we do, come inside as quickly as you can. Okay?"

"Okay. Yes. Okay."

She waits. The air is still, calm. Nothing happens. Then she hears the click of the door. She steps forward quickly. Hands reach out and pull her in. The door slams shut behind her.

"Now wait," a woman says. "We need to feel around. We need to know you've come in alone."

Malorie stands with her eyes closed and listens. It sounds like they are feeling along the walls with broomsticks. More than one pair of hands touch her shoulders, her neck, her legs. Someone is behind her now. She hears fingers upon the closed door.

"All right," a man says. "We're okay."

When Malorie opens her eyes, she sees five people standing in a line before her. Shoulder to shoulder, they fill the foyer. She stares at them. They stare at her. One of them wears a helmet of some kind. His arms are covered in what looks like cotton balls and tape. Pens, pencils, and more sharp objects project from the tape like a child's version of medieval weaponry. Two of them hold broomsticks.

"Hello," this man says. "My name is Tom. You understand of course why we answer the door like this. Anything could slip in with you."

Despite the helmet, Malorie sees Tom has blondish brown hair. His features are strong. His blue eyes flare with intelligence. He's not much taller than Malorie. Unshaven, his stubble is almost red.

"I understand," Malorie says.

"Westcourt," Tom says, stepping toward her. "That's a real drive. What you did was extremely brave. Why don't you sit down, so we can talk about what you saw along the way?"

Malorie nods but she does not move. She is clutching her suitcase so tight that her knuckles are white and hurt. A taller, bigger man approaches her.

"Here," he says, "let me take that for you."

"Thank you."

"My name is Jules. I've been here for two months. Most of us have. Tom and Don arrived a little earlier."

Jules's short dark hair looks dirty. Like he's been working outside. He appears kind.

Malorie looks at the housemates from face to face. There is one woman and four men.

"I'm Don," Don says. He, too, has dark hair. A little longer. He wears black pants, a purple button-down shirt rolled up to the elbows. He looks older than Malorie, twenty-seven, twenty-eight. "You scared the hell out of us. Nobody's knocked on that door for weeks now."

"I'm so sorry."

"It's no worry," the fourth man says. "We all did what you did. I'm Felix."

Felix looks tired. Malorie thinks he looks young. Twenty-one, twenty-two. His long nose and bushy brown hair make him look almost cartoonish. He is tall, like Jules, but thinner.

"And I'm Cheryl," the woman says, extending her hand. Malorie shakes it.

Cheryl's expression is less welcoming than Tom's and Felix's. Her brown hair hides some of her face. She is wearing a tank top. She, too, looks like she's been working.

"Jules, will you help me get this thing off?" Tom says. He is trying to remove his helmet, but the makeshift body armor is getting in the way. Jules helps him.

With the helmet off, Malorie gets a better look at him. His sandy blond hair is messy above his fair face. The suggestion of freckles gives him color. His beard is barely more than stubble, but his mustache is more pronounced. His plaid button-down shirt and brown slacks remind Malorie of a teacher she once had.

Seeing him for the first time, she hardly realizes he is looking at her belly.

"I don't mean any offense, but are you pregnant?"

"Yes," she says weakly, frightened that this will be a burden.

"Oh fuck," Cheryl says. "You *have* to be kidding me."

"Cheryl," Tom says, "you're gonna scare her."

"Look, Malorie, was it?" Cheryl says. "I'm not trying to come off as mean when I say this, but bringing a pregnant woman into this house is a real responsibility."

Malorie is quiet. She looks from face to face, noting the expressions they make. They seem to be studying her. Deciding whether or not they are up to the task of housing someone who will eventually give birth. It suddenly strikes Malorie that she hadn't thought of it in these terms. On the drive over, she didn't think that this was where she might deliver her baby.

The tears are coming.

Cheryl shakes her head and, relenting, steps to her.

"My God," she says. "Come here."

"I wasn't always alone," Malorie says. "My sister, Shannon, was with me. She's dead now. I left her."

She is crying now. Through her blurred vision she sees the four men are watching her. They look compassionate. Instantly, Malorie recognizes they're all grieving in their own ways.

"Come on," Tom says. "Let's show you the house. You can use the bedroom at the top of the stairs. I'll sleep down here."

"No," Malorie says. "I couldn't take a room from any of you."

"I insist," Tom says. "Cheryl sleeps at the end of the hall up there. Felix is in the room next to the one that will be yours. You're pregnant, after all. We'll help you with it the best we can."

They are walking through a hall. They pass a bedroom on the left. Then a bathroom. Malorie catches her reflection in the mirror and quickly looks away. On the left, she sees a kitchen. On the counter are large buckets.

"This," Tom says, "is the living room. We hang out a lot in here."

Malorie turns to see his hand is gesturing toward the larger room. There is a couch. An end table with a telephone on it. Lamps. An easy chair. Carpet. A calendar is drawn in what looks like marker on the wall between framed paintings. The windows are covered by hanging black blankets.

Malorie looks up as a dog suddenly trots into the room. It's a border collie. The dog looks at her curiously before stepping to her feet and waiting for her to pet him.

"This is Victor," Jules says. "He's six years old now. I got him as a puppy."

Malorie pets the dog. She thinks Shannon would have liked him. Then Jules leaves the room, carrying her suitcase up a flight of carpeted stairs. Along the walls, pictures hang. Some are photos, some are art.

At the top, she sees him enter a bedroom. Even from down here she can see a blanket covers the window.

Cheryl walks her to the couch. There, Malorie sits, exhausted from sadness and shock. Cheryl and Don say they will prepare some food.

"Canned goods," Felix says. "We went on a run the day I arrived. This was just before the first incident was reported in the Upper Peninsula. The man at the store thought we were crazy. We've got enough to last us about three months still."

"A little less than that now," Don says, vanishing into the kitchen. Malorie wonders if he meant there were more mouths to feed because of her arrival.

Then, sitting beside her on the couch, Tom asks what things she saw on the drive over. He is curious about everything. Tom is the kind of man who would use any information she gives him, and she feels like the insignificant details she remembers are no help at all. She tells him about the dead dog. The mail truck. The empty storefronts and streets, and the abandoned car with the jacket.

"There are some things I'll need to tell you," Tom says. "First off, this house doesn't belong to anybody here. The owner died. I'll explain that to you later. There's no Internet. It's been down since we got here. We're pretty sure the people who run the cell towers have stopped going to work. Or they're dead. No mail comes anymore, and no newspapers. Have you checked your cell phone lately? Ours quit working about three weeks ago. But there is a landline, if you can believe the luck of that, although I don't know who we'll call."

Cheryl enters the room, carrying a plate with carrots and peas. A small glass of water, too.

"The landline still works," Tom says, "for the same reason the lights are still on. The local power plant runs on hydroelectricity. I can't tell you if it will stop working, too, one day, but if the men working the power left the gates open in just the right way, the power could go on indefinitely. That means the river powers this house. Did you know there's a river behind us? Barring disaster, as long as it flows, we may be in luck. We might survive. Is that asking for too much? Probably. But when you go to the well out back to get some water, and it's the water we use for everything, you'll be able to hear the river flowing about eighty yards behind us. There's no running water here. It gave out shortly after I arrived. To go to the bathroom, we use buckets and take turns carrying the slop buckets to the latrines. Those are just ditches we've dug in the woods. Of course, all of this has to be done blindfolded."

Jules comes downstairs. Victor, the dog, follows behind him.

"You're all set," he says, nodding at Malorie.

"Thank you," she says quietly.

Tom points to a cardboard box on a small table against the wall.

"The blindfolds are in there. You can use any of them, whenever you want to."

They are all looking at her. Cheryl is sitting on the arm of the easy chair. Don is standing in the entrance to the kitchen. Jules kneels by Victor at the stairs. Felix is standing by one of the blanketed windows.

They've each grieved, Malorie thinks. *These people have experienced terrible things, like me.*

Malorie, drinking from the glass Cheryl has given her, turns to Tom. She cannot rid her mind of Shannon. But she tries, speaking to Tom wearily.

"What was the stuff I saw you wearing when I arrived?"

"The armor?"

"Yes."

"I'm not sure yet," Tom says, smiling. "I'm trying to build a suit. Something to protect more than just our eyes. We don't know what'll happen if one of those things touches us."

Malorie looks to the other housemates. Then back at Tom.

"You guys believe that there are creatures out there?"

"Yes," Tom says. "George, the man who owned this house, he saw one. Just before he died."

Malorie doesn't know what to say. She instinctively brings a hand to her belly.

"I'm not trying to scare you," Tom says. "And I'll tell you George's story soon. But the radio has been saying the same thing. I think it's a consensus now. Something *living* is doing this to us. And it only takes seeing one for a second, maybe less."

Everything in the room seems to get darker for Malorie. She feels dizzy, light-headed.

"Whatever they are," Tom says, "our minds can't understand them. They're like infinity, it seems. Something too complex for us to comprehend. Do you see?"

Tom's words are getting lost somehow for Malorie. Victor pants heavily at Jules's feet. Cheryl is asking if she is okay. Tom is still speaking.

Creatures . . . infinity . . . our minds have ceilings, Malorie . . . these things . . . they are beyond it . . . higher than it . . . out of reach . . . out of—

But here, Malorie faints.

eight

Malorie wakes in her new bedroom. It is dark. For one blessed moment, the last one she experiences, Malorie wakes with the idea that all of this news about creatures and madness was only some nightmare. Foggily, she remembers Riverbridge, Tom, Victor, the drive, but none of it becomes clear until, staring at the ceiling, she realizes that she's never woken in this room before.

And Shannon is still dead.

Sitting up in bed slowly, she looks to the room's one window. A black blanket is nailed into the wall, keeping her safe from the outside world. Beyond her feet, there is an old vanity. Its pink color is faded but the mirror looks clean. In it, she is paler than usual. Because of this, her black hair looks even blacker. At the base of the mirror are extra nails, screws, a hammer, and a wrench. Except for her bed, this is the extent of the furnishings.

Rising, she swings her feet over the mattress's edge and sees, on the gray-carpeted floor, a second black blanket, folded neatly. It's a spare, she thinks. Beside it is a small stack of books.

Facing the bedroom's door, Malorie hears voices coming from downstairs. She does not know these people yet, and she can't place who is speaking unless it's Cheryl, the only woman, or Tom, whose voice will guide her for years.

When she stands up, the carpet is coarse and old beneath her feet. She crosses the bedroom and peers into the hall. She feels okay. Rested. She's not dizzy anymore. Wearing the same clothes she passed out in the night before, Malorie makes her way down the stairs to the living room.

Just before she reaches the wooden floor, Jules passes, carrying a pile of clothes.

"Hi," he says, nodding. Malorie watches as he walks to the bathroom down the hall. There, she hears him dunking the clothes in a bucket of water.

When she turns toward the kitchen, she sees Cheryl and Don at the sink. Malorie enters the kitchen as Don pulls a glass from a bucket. Cheryl hears her and turns around.

"You worried us last night," she says. "Are you feeling better?"

Malorie, realizing now that she fainted the night before, turns a little red.

"Yes, I'm okay. Just a lot to take in."

"It was like that for all of us," Don says. "But you'll get used to it. Soon, you'll be saying we live a life of luxury."

"Don's a cynic," Cheryl says good-naturedly.

"I'm really not," Don says. "I love it here."

Malorie jumps as Victor licks her hand. As she kneels to pet him, she hears music come from the dining room. She crosses the kitchen and peers inside. The room is empty, but the radio is on.

She looks back to Cheryl and Don at the sink. Beyond them is a cellar door. Malorie is about to ask about it when she hears Felix's voice coming from the living room. He is reciting the home's address.

" . . . Two seventy-three Shillingham . . . my name is Felix . . . we're looking for anyone else who is alive . . . surviving . . ."

Malorie peeks her head into the living room. Felix is using the landline.

"He's calling random phone numbers."

Malorie jumps again, this time at the sound of Tom's voice, who is now peering into the living room with her.

"We don't have a phone book?" she asks.

"No. It's a constant source of frustration for me."

Felix is dialing another number. Tom, holding a piece of paper and pencil, asks, "Want to see the cellar with me?"

Malorie follows him through the kitchen.

"Are you going to take stock?" Don asks as Tom opens the cellar door.

"Yeah."

"Let me know what the numbers are."

"Sure."

Tom enters first. Malorie follows him down wooden stairs. The floor of the cellar is made of dirt. In the darkness, she can smell and feel the earth beneath her bare feet.

The room is suddenly lit as Tom pulls the string on a lightbulb. Malorie is frightened by what she sees. It feels more like a warehouse than a cellar. Seemingly infinite wooden shelves are stocked with canned goods. From ceiling to dirt floor, the place resembles a bunker.

"George built all this," Tom says, fanning a hand toward the woodwork. "He really was ahead of things."

To the left, only partially lit by the light, Malorie sees a hanging, transparent tapestry. Behind it rest a washer and a dryer.

"It looks like a lot of food," Tom says, gesturing toward the cans. "But it's not. And nobody worries more about how much we have left than Don."

"How often do you take stock?" Malorie asks.

"Once a week. But sometimes, when I get restless, I'll come down and check things again the day after I already did it."

"It's cool down here."

"Yeah. A classic cold-storage basement. It's ideal."

"What happens if we run out?"

Tom faces her. His features are soft in the light.

"Then we go get more. We raid grocery stores. Other homes. What-ever we can."

"Right," Malorie says, nodding.

While Tom marks the paper, Malorie studies the cellar.

"I guess this would be the safest room in the house then," she says.

Tom pauses. He thinks about it.

"I don't think so. I think the attic is safer."

"Why?"

"Did you notice the lock on the walk in here? The door is really old. It locks, but it's delicate. It's almost as if this cellar was built first, years ago, before they decided to add a house to it. But the attic door . . . *that* bolt is incredible. If we needed to secure ourselves, if one of those things were to get into the house, I'd say the attic is where we'd want to go."

Malorie instinctively looks up. She rubs her shoulders.

If we needed to secure ourselves.

"Judging by how much stock we have left," Tom says, "we could live another three to four months off it. That sounds like a lot of time, but it passes quickly in here. The days begin to mush together. That's why we started keeping the calendar on the wall in the living room. You know, in a way, time doesn't mean a thing anymore. But it's one of the only things we have that resembles the lives we used to live."

"The passing of time?"

"Yeah. And what we do with it."

Malorie steps to a short wooden stool and sits. Tom is still making notes.

"I'll show you all the chores when we get back upstairs," Tom says. Then, pointing to a space between the shelves and the hanging tapestry, he says, "Do you see that there?"

Malorie looks but can't tell what he means.

"Come here."

Tom walks her to the wall, where some of the brick is broken. Earth shows behind it.

"I can't tell if this scares me or if I like it," he says.

"What do you mean?"

"Well, the ground is exposed. Does that mean we could start digging? Build a tunnel? A second cellar? More room? Or is it just another way to get inside?"

Tom's eyes are bright and sharp in the cellar light.

"The thing is," he says, "if the creatures really wanted to get into our house . . . they'd have no problem doing it. And I guess they would have already."

Malorie stares at the open patch of dirt on the wall. She imagines crawling through tunnels, pregnant. She imagines worms.

After a brief silence, she asks, "What did you do before this happened?"

"My job? I was a teacher. Eighth grade."

Malorie nods."I actually thought you looked like one."

"You know what? I've heard that before. Many times! I kind of like that." He feigns fixing the collar of his shirt. "Class," he says, "today we're going to learn all about canned goods. So, everybody, shut the fuck up."

Malorie laughs.

"What did you do?" Tom asks.

"I hadn't gotten that far yet," Malorie says.

"You lost your sister, huh?" Tom says gently.

"Yes."

"I'm sorry." Then he says, "I lost a daughter."

"Oh God, Tom."

Tom pauses, as if considering whether or not to tell Malorie more. Then he does.

"Robin's mother died during childbirth. It feels cruel, telling you that, given your condition. But if we're going to get to know one another, it's a story you'll need to know. Robin was a great kid. Smarter than her father at eight years old. She liked the oddest things. Like the instructions for a toy more than the toy itself. The credits of a movie instead of the movie. The way something was written. An expression on my face. Once she told me I looked like the sun to her, because of my hair. I asked her if I shined like the sun, and she told me, 'No, Daddy, you shine more like the moon, when it's dark outside.'

"When the reports came on the news and people started to take it seriously, I was the kind of father who said I wasn't going to live in fear. I tried very hard to carry on with our daily life. And I especially wanted to convey that idea to Robin. She'd heard things at school. I just didn't want her to be so afraid. But, after a while, I couldn't pretend anymore. Soon, the parents were taking their kids out of school. Then the school itself shut down. Temporarily. Or until they 'had the confidence of the community to continue providing a safe place for their children.' Those were dark days, Malorie. I was a teacher, too, you know, and the school I taught in shut its doors about the same time. So we suddenly had a lot of time together at home. I got to see how much she'd grown. Her mind was getting so big. Still, she was too young to understand how scary the stories were on the news. I did my best not to hide them from her, but the father in me couldn't help but change the station sometimes.

"The radio got to be too much for her. Robin started having nightmares. I spent a lot of time calming her down. I always felt like I was lying to her. We agreed neither of us would look out the windows anymore. We agreed she wouldn't go outside without my permission. Somehow, I had to make her believe things were safe and horribly unsafe at the same time.

"She started spending the night in my bed, but one morning I woke to find she wasn't there. She'd been talking the night before about wanting things to be how they used to be. She talked of wanting her mother, whom she'd never met. It crushed me, hearing her like that, eight years old and telling me life was unfair. When I woke and didn't find her, I told myself she was just getting used to it. This new life. But I think maybe Robin lost something of her youth the night before, as she realized, before I did, how serious it was, what was happening outside our house."

Tom pauses. He looks to the cellar floor.

"I found her in the bathtub, Malorie. Floating. Her little wrists cut with the razor she'd seen me shave with a thousand times. The water was red. The blood dripped over the tub's edge. Blood on the walls. This was a child. Eight years old. Did she look outside? Or did she just decide to do this herself? I'll never know that answer."

Malorie reaches for Tom and holds him.

But he does not cry. Instead, after a moment, he steps to the shelves and begins marking the paper.

Malorie thinks of Shannon. She, too, died in the bathroom. She, too, took her own life.

When Tom is finished, he asks Malorie if she's ready to go back upstairs. As he reaches for the lightbulb's string, he sees she is looking at the patch of open dirt along the wall.

"Freaky, no?" he says.

"Yeah."

"Well, don't let it be. It's just one of the old-world fears, carrying over."

"What's that?"

"The fear of the cellar."

Malorie nods.

Then Tom pulls the string and the light goes out.

nine

*C*reatures," Malorie thinks. *What a cheap word.*

The children are quiet and the banks are still. She can hear the paddles slicing the water. The rhythm of her rowing is in step with her heartbeat, and then it falters. When the cadences oppose, she feels like she could die.

Creatures.

Malorie has never liked this word. It's out of place, somehow. The things that have haunted her for more than four years are not *creatures* to her. A garden slug is a creature. A porcupine. But the things that have lurked beyond draped windows and have kept her blindfolded are not the sort that an exterminator could ever remove.

"Barbarian" isn't right, either. A barbarian is reckless. So is a brute.

In the distance, a bird sings a song from high in the sky. The paddles cut the water, shifting with each row.

"Behemoth" is unproven. They could be as small as a fingernail.

Though they are early in their journey along the river, Malorie's muscles ache from rowing. Her shirt is soaked through with sweat. Her feet are cold. The blindfold continues to irritate.

"Demon." "Devil." "Rogue." Maybe they are all these things.

Her sister died because she saw one. Her parents must have met the same fate.

"Imp" is too kind. "Savage" too human.

Malorie is not only afraid of the things that may wade in the river, she is also fascinated by them.

Do they know what they do? Do they mean to do what they do?

Right now, it feels as if the whole world is dead. It feels like the rowboat is the last remaining place where life can be found. The rest of the world fans out from the tip of the boat, an empty globe, blooming and vacant with each row.

If they don't know what they do, they can't be "villains."

The children have been quiet a long time. A second birdsong comes from above. A fish splashes. Malorie has never seen this river. What does it look like? Do the trees crowd the banks? Are there houses lining its shore?

They are monsters, Malorie thinks. But she knows they are more than this. They are *infinity.*

"Mommy!" the Boy suddenly cries.

A bird of prey caws; its echo breaks across the river.

"What is it, Boy?"

"It sounds like an engine."

"What?"

Malorie stops paddling. She listens closely.

Far off, beyond even the river's flow, comes the sound of an engine.

Malorie recognizes it immediately. It is the sound of another boat approaching.

Rather than feeling excitement at the prospect of encountering another human being on this river, Malorie is afraid.

"Get down, you two," she says.

She rests the paddle handles across her knees. The rowboat floats.

The Boy heard it, she tells herself. *The Boy heard it because you raised him well and now he hears better than he will ever see.*

Breathing deep, Malorie waits. The engine grows louder. The boat is traveling upstream.

"Ouch!" the Boy yelps.

"What is it, Boy?"

"My ear! I got hit by a tree."

Malorie thinks this is good. If a tree touched the Boy, they are likely near one of the banks. Maybe, by some deserved providence, the foliage will provide cover.

The other boat is much closer now. Malorie knows that if she were able to open her eyes, she could see it.

"Do *not* take off your blindfolds," Malorie says.

And then the boat's engine is level with them. It does not pass.

Whoever it is, Malorie thinks, *they can see us.*

The boat's engine cuts abruptly. The air smells of gasoline. Footsteps cross what must be the deck.

"Hello there!" a voice says. Malorie does not respond. "Hey there! It's okay. You can remove your blindfolds! I'm just an ordinary man."

"No you *cannot,*" Malorie says quickly to the children.

"There's nothing out here with us, miss. Take my word for it. We're all alone."

Malorie is still. Finally, feeling there is no alternative, she answers him.

"How do you know?"

"Miss," he says, "I'm looking right now. I've had my eyes open the entire trip today. Yesterday, too."

"You can't just *look,*" she says. "You know that."

The stranger laughs.

"Really," he says, "there's nothing to be afraid of. You can trust me. It's just us two on the river. Just two ordinary people crossing paths."

"No!" Malorie screams to the children.

She lets go of the Girl and grips the paddle handles again. The man sighs.

"There's no need to live like this, miss. Consider these children. Would you rob them the chance to view a brisk, beautiful day like this?"

"Stay away from our boat," Malorie says sternly.

Silence. The man does not answer. Malorie braces herself. She feels trapped. Vulnerable. In the rowboat against the bank. On this river. In this world.

Something splashes in the water. Malorie gasps.

"Miss," he says, "the view is incredible, if you don't mind a little fog. When's the last time you looked outside? Has it been years? Have you *seen* this river? The weather? I bet you don't even remember what weather looks like."

She remembers the outside world very well. She remembers walking home as a schoolgirl through a tunnel of autumn leaves. She recalls neighboring yards, gardens, and homes. She remembers lying on the grass in her backyard with Shannon and deciding which clouds looked like which boys and girls from class.

"We are keeping our blindfolds on," Malorie says.

"I've given that up, miss," he says. "I've moved on. Won't you do the same?"

"Leave us alone now," she commands.

The man sighs again.

"They can't haunt you forever," he says. "They can't force you to live like this forever. You know that, miss?"

Malorie puts the right paddle into a position where she believes she can push off the bank.

"I ought to remove your blindfolds myself," the man says suddenly.

Malorie does not move.

He sounds gruff. He sounds a little angry.

"We're just two people," he continues. "Meeting on a river. Four if you include the little ones. And they can't be blamed for how you're raising them. I'm the only one here with the nerve to look outside. Your worries only keep you safe long enough to worry some more."

His voice is coming from a different place now. Malorie thinks he has stepped to the front of his boat. She only wants to pass him. She just wants to get farther from the house they left this morning.

"And I'll tell you what," the man suddenly says, horribly near, "I've *seen* one."

Malorie grabs for the Boy and pulls him by the back of his shirt. He hits the steel bottom of the rowboat and yelps.

The man laughs.

"They aren't as ugly as you'd think, miss."

She shoves the paddle against the bank. She is floundering. It's hard to find something solid. Feels like twigs and roots. Mud.

He is going to go mad, Malorie thinks. *And he will hurt you.*

"Where are you going to go?" he yells. "Are you going to cry every time you hear a stick crack?"

Malorie can't get the rowboat free.

"Keep your blindfolds on!" she yells at the children.

The man said he's seen one. When? *When?*

"You think I'm mad, don't you?"

At last the paddle is planted hard against the earth. Malorie pushes, grunting. The rowboat moves. She thinks it might be free. Then it bangs against the man's boat and she shrieks.

He's trapped you.

Will he force their eyes open?

"Who's the mad one here? Look at you now. Two people meet on a river . . ."

Malorie rocks back and forth. She senses a gap behind the rowboat, some kind of opening.

" . . . one of them looks to the sky . . ."

Malorie feels the paddle sink into the earth.

" . . . the other tries to steer a boat with a blindfold on."

The rowboat is almost free.

"So, I have to ask myself . . ."

"Move!" she screams.

" . . . who here has gone mad?"

The man cackles. It sounds like his laughter rises toward the sky he speaks of. She thinks to ask, *How far back did you see one?* But she doesn't.

"Leave us!" Malorie yells.

From her struggle, cold river water splashes into the boat. The Girl shrieks. Malorie tells herself, *Ask the man how far back he saw it.* Maybe the madness hasn't set in. Maybe it's slower with him. Maybe he will perform one final act of benevolence before he loses all sense of reality.

The rowboat is free.

Tom once said it had to be different for everybody. He said a crazy man might never go any madder. And the sanest might take a long time to get there.

"Open your eyes, for Christ's sake!" the man shouts.

His voice has changed. He sounds drunk, different.

"Quit running, miss. *Open your eyes!*" he pleads.

"Don't listen to him!" she yells. The Boy is pressed up against her and the Girl whimpers at her back. Malorie shakes.

"Your mother is the mad one, kids. Take off those blindfolds."

The man suddenly howls, gargling. It sounds like something has died in his throat. How much longer before he strangles himself with the rope rail or lowers himself into the spinning propeller of his boat?

Malorie is paddling furiously. Her blindfold doesn't feel tight enough.

What he saw is near. What he saw is here on this river.

"Do not remove your folds!" Malorie screams again. She is paddling past the boat now. "Do you two understand me? *Answer me.*"

"Yes!" the Boy says.

"Yes!" the Girl says.

The man howls again but he is farther behind them now. He sounds as if he's trying to yell but has forgotten how.

When the rowboat has gone another forty yards, and the sound of the engine behind them is almost out of earshot, Malorie reaches forward and touches the Boy's shoulder.

"Don't worry, Mommy," the Boy says.

Then Malorie reaches behind her and finds the Girl's hand. She squeezes. Then, letting go of both of them, she takes the paddles again.

"Are you dry?" she asks the Girl.

"No," the Girl answers.

"Use the blanket to dry yourself off. Now."

The air smells clean again. The trees. The water.

The gasoline fumes are well behind them.

Do you remember how the house smelled? Malorie thinks.

Despite the horror of having encountered the man on the boat, she remembers. The stale, stuffy air of the house. It was there the day she arrived. And it never got any better.

She does not hate the man with the boat. She feels only sorrow.

"You did so well," Malorie says to the children, trembling, paddling deeper down the river.

ten

Malorie has been living in the house for two weeks. The housemates subsist almost entirely off the canned goods from the cellar, plus whatever frozen meats remain in the freezer. Each morning, Malorie is relieved to find the electricity is still on. The radio is the only source of news anymore, but the last remaining DJ, Rodney Barrett, has nothing new to tell them. Instead, he rambles. He gets angry. He swears. The housemates have heard him sleeping on air before. But despite all this, Malorie understands why they continue to listen to him. Whether his voice is on quietly in the background or fills the dining room where the radio sits, he's the very last link they have to the outside world.

Already, Malorie feels like she's inside a vault. The claustrophobia is incredible, weighing in on her and her baby.

Yet, tonight the housemates are throwing something of a party.

The six of them are gathered around the dining room table. Along with the canned goods, toilet paper, batteries, candles, blankets, and tools in the cellar, there are a few bottles of rum—which nicely complement the grass brought by Felix (who sheepishly admitted he expected more of a "hippie" gathering than the clearheaded troupe he met upon arriving). Malorie, out of respect for her condition, is the only one who doesn't partake in the drinking and smoking. Still, some moods are infectious, and, as Rodney Barrett uncharacteristically plays some soft music, Malorie is able to smile, and sometimes even laugh, despite the unfathomable horrors that have become commonplace.

In the dining room there is a piano. Like the stack of humor books beside the dresser in her bedroom, the piano appears as a remnant, almost out of place, from another lifetime.

Right now, Tom is playing it.

"What key is this song in?" Tom, sweating, is yelling across the dining room to Felix, who sits at the table. "Do you know keys?"

Felix smiles and shakes his head. "How the hell would I know? But I'll sing with you from here, Tom."

"Please don't," Don says, sipping rum from a drinking glass, smiling.

"No, no," Felix says, grinning, "I'm really very good!"

Felix stumbles as he stands up. He joins Tom at the piano. Together they sing along to "It's De-Lovely." The radio rests on a mirrored credenza. The music Rodney Barrett plays clashes quietly with the Cole Porter song.

"How are you doing, Malorie?" Don, sitting across the table, asks her. "How do you like the place so far?"

"I'm okay," she says. "I think a lot about the baby."

Don smiles. When he does, Malorie sees sadness in his features. Don, she knows, lost a sister as well. All the housemates have experienced devastating loss. Cheryl's parents, scared, drove south. She hasn't spoken to them since. Felix hopes to hear news of his brothers with every random phone call he makes. Jules often speaks of his fiancée, Sydney, whom he found in the gutter outside their apartment building before answering the same ad Malorie found. Her throat was slit. But Tom's story, Malorie thinks, is the worst. If such a word applies anymore.

Now, watching him behind the piano, Malorie's heart breaks for him.

For a moment, when "It's De-Lovely" comes to an end, the radio is audible again. The song Rodney Barrett is playing ends as well. Then he begins talking.

"Listen, listen," Cheryl is saying. She is crossing the room to where the radio sits. She crouches before it and turns the volume up. "He sounds more depressed than usual."

Tom ignores the radio. Sweating, sipping from his drink, he fumbles through the opening chords of Gershwin's "I Got Rhythm." Don is turning to see what Cheryl is talking about. Jules, stroking Victor, sitting on the floor with his back to the wall, turns his head slowly toward the radio.

"Creatures," Rodney Barrett is saying. His voice drags. "What have you taken from us? What are you doing here? Do you have any purpose at all?"

Don rises from the table and joins Cheryl by the radio. Tom stops playing.

"I've never heard him speak directly to the creatures before," he says from the piano bench.

"We've lost mothers, fathers, sisters, brothers," Rodney Barrett is saying. "We've lost wives and husbands, lovers and friends. But nothing stings as much as the children you've taken from us. How dare you ask a child to look at you?"

Malorie looks to Tom. He is listening. There is distance in his eyes. She rises and walks to him.

"He's been heavy before," Cheryl says about Rodney Barrett. "But never like this."

"No," Don says. "Sounds like he's drunker than we are."

"Tom," Malorie says, sitting beside him on the bench.

"He's going to kill himself," Don suddenly says.

Malorie looks up, wanting to tell Don to shut up, then hears the same thing Don has. The complete desolation in the voice of Rodney Barrett.

"Today I'm gonna cheat you," Barrett says. "I'm gonna take it first, the one thing I've got left that you can take from me."

"Oh *God*," Cheryl says.

The radio is silent.

"Turn it off, Cheryl," Jules says. "Turn it *off*."

As she reaches for the radio, the sound of a gunshot explodes from the speakers.

Cheryl screams. Victor barks.

"What the *fuck* just happened?" Felix says, staring blankly toward the radio.

"He did it," Jules says emptily. "I can't believe this."

Then silence.

Tom gets up from the piano bench and turns the radio off. Felix sips from his drink. Jules is on one knee, calming Victor.

Then, suddenly, as if an echo of the gunshot, there is a knock at the front door.

A second knock quickly follows.

Felix steps toward the door and Don grabs his arm.

"Do *not* just open that door, man," he says. "Come on. What's the matter with you?"

"I wasn't going to, man!" Felix says. He pulls his arm free.

The knocking comes again. A woman's voice calls to them.

"Hello?"

The housemates are quiet and stand still.

"Somebody answer her," Malorie says, getting up from the piano bench to do it herself. But Tom is ahead of her.

"Yes!" he calls. "We're here. Who are you?"

"Olympia! My name is Olympia! Let me in?"

Tom pauses. He looks drunk.

"Are you alone?" he asks.

"Yes!"

"Are your eyes closed?"

"Yes, my eyes are closed. I'm very scared. Please let me in?"

Tom looks to Don.

"Somebody get the broomsticks," Tom says. Jules leaves to get them.

"I don't think we can afford any more mouths to feed," Don says.

"You're crazy," Felix says. "There's a woman out—"

"I understand what's going on, Felix," Don says angrily. "We can't house the whole country."

"But she's out there right now," Felix says.

"And we're drunk," Don says.

"Come on, Don," Tom says.

"Don't turn me into the villain," Don says. "You know as well as I do exactly how many cans we have in the cellar."

"Hello?" the woman calls again.

"Hang on!" Tom responds.

Tom and Don stare at each other. Jules comes into the foyer. He hands one of the broomsticks to Tom.

"Do whatever you want to, people," Don says. "But we're going to starve sooner because of it."

Tom turns to the front door.

"Everybody," he says, "close your eyes."

Malorie listens as his shoes cross the wood floor in the foyer.

"Olympia?" Tom calls.

"Yes!"

"I'm going to open the door now. When I do, when you hear it's open, step inside as quickly as you can. Do you understand?"

"Yes!"

Malorie hears the front door open. There is a commotion. She imagines Tom pulling the woman inside like the housemates pulled her inside two weeks ago. Then the door slams shut.

"Keep your eyes closed!" Tom says. "I'm going to feel around you. Make sure nothing came inside with you."

Malorie can hear the broomstick bristles against the walls, the floor, the ceiling, and the front door.

"Okay," Tom finally says. "Let's open our eyes."

When Malorie does, she sees a very pretty, pale, dark-haired woman standing beside Tom.

"Thank you," she says breathlessly.

Tom starts to ask her something but Malorie interrupts him.

"Are you pregnant?" she asks Olympia.

Olympia looks down at her belly. Shaking, she looks up, nodding yes.

"I'm four months along," she says.

"That's incredible," Malorie says, stepping closer. "I'm about the same."

"Fuck," Don says.

"I'm a neighbor of yours," Olympia says. "I'm so sorry to scare you like this. My husband is in the air force. I haven't heard from him in weeks. He may be dead. I heard you. The piano. It took me a while to get the courage to walk here. Normally, I'd have brought over cupcakes."

Despite the horror everyone in the room just listened to, Olympia's innocence breaks through the darkness.

"We're glad to have you," Tom says, but Malorie can hear exhaustion and the pressure of looking after two pregnant women in his voice. "Come in."

They walk Olympia down the hall toward the living room. At the foot of the stairs, she gasps and points to a photo hanging on the wall.

"Oh!" she says. "Is this man here?"

"No," Tom says. "He's not here anymore. You must know him. George. He used to own this house."

Olympia nods.

"Yes, I've seen him many times."

Then the housemates are gathered in the living room. Tom sits with Olympia on the couch. Malorie listens quietly as Tom somberly asks Olympia about the objects in her house. What she has. What she left behind.

What can they use here.

eleven

alorie has been rowing for what feels like three hours. The muscles in her arms burn. Cold water sloshes in the boat's bottom, water she has splashed, little by little, with each dip of the oars. Moments ago, the Girl told Malorie she had to pee. Malorie told her to do it. Now the Girl's urine mixes with the river water and it feels warm against Malorie's shoes. She is thinking about the man in the boat they passed.

The children, Malorie thinks, *didn't take off their blindfolds. That was the first living human voice they've ever heard other than one another's. Yet, they didn't listen to him.*

Yes, she has trained them well. But it's not a nice thing to think about. *Training* the children means she has scared them so completely that under no circumstances will they disobey her. As a girl, Malorie rebelled against her parents all the time. Sugar wasn't allowed in the house. Malorie snuck it in. Scary movies weren't allowed in the house. Malorie tiptoed downstairs at midnight to watch them on television. When her parents said she wasn't allowed to sleep on the couch in the living room, she moved her bed in there. These were the thrills of childhood. Malorie's children don't know them.

As babies, she trained them to wake with their eyes closed. Standing above their chicken wire beds, flyswatter in hand, she'd wait. As each woke and opened their eyes, she would smack them hard on the arm. They would cry. Malorie would reach down and close their eyes with her fingers. If they kept their eyes closed, she would lift her shirt and feed them. *Reward.*

"Mommy," the Girl says, "was that the same man who sings in the radio?"

The Girl is talking about a cassette tape Felix used to like to listen to.

"No," the Boy says.

"Who was it then?" the Girl asks.

Malorie turns to face the Girl so her voice will be louder.

"I thought we agreed you two wouldn't ask any questions that have nothing to do with the river. Are we breaking this agreement?"

"No," the Girl quietly says.

When they were three years old, she trained them to get water from the well. Tying a rope around her waist, she wrapped the other end around the Boy. Then, telling him to feel for the path with his toes, she sent him out there to do it on his own. Malorie would listen to the sound of the bucket clumsily being raised. She listened to him struggle as he carried it back to her. Many times she heard it fall from his hands. Each time it did, she made him go back out there and do it again.

The Girl hated it. She said the ground was "too bumpy" out there around the well. She said it felt like people lived below the grass. Malorie denied the Girl food until she agreed to do it.

When they were toddlers, the children were set at opposite sides of the living room. Malorie would roam the carpet. When she said, "Where am I?" the Boy and Girl would point. Then she'd go upstairs, come back down, and ask them, "Where was I?" The children would point. When they were wrong, Malorie would yell at them.

But they weren't often wrong. And soon they were never wrong at all.

What would Tom say about that? she thinks. *He'd tell you that you were being the best mother on Earth. And you'd believe him.*

Without Tom, Malorie only has herself to turn to. And many times, sitting alone at the kitchen table, the children asleep in their bedroom, she asked herself the inevitable question:

Are you a good mother? Does such a thing exist anymore?

Now Malorie feels a soft tap on her knee. She gasps. But it is only the Boy. He is asking for the pouch of food. Midrow, Malorie reaches into her jacket pocket and hands it to him. She hears as his little teeth crunch the once-canned nuts that sat on the cellar shelves for four and a half years before Malorie brought them up this morning.

Then Malorie stops rowing. She is hot. Too hot. She is sweating as much as if it were June. She removes her jacket and places it on the row-boat bench beside her. Then she feels a small tap against her back. The Girl is hungry, too.

Are you a good mother? she asks herself again, handing over a second pouch of food.

How can she expect her children to dream as big as the stars if they can't lift their heads to gaze upon them?

Malorie doesn't know the answer.

twelve

Tom is building something out of an old soft guitar case and a couch cushion. Olympia is sleeping upstairs in the bedroom next to Malorie's. Felix gave it to her just like Tom gave his to Malorie. Felix now sleeps on the couch in the living room. The night before, Tom took detailed notes of the items Olympia has in her house when she told him. What began as a hopeful conversation resulted in the housemates' deciding that the few things they could use weren't worth the risk of getting them. Paper. Another bucket. Olympia's husband's toolbox. Still, as Felix pointed out, if and when the need for these objects outweighed the risk, they could fetch them after all. Some things, Don said, might be needed sooner than later. Canned nuts, tuna, pasta, condiments. While discussing foods, Tom explained to the others how much stock they had remaining in the cellar. Because it was finite, it worried Malorie deeply.

Right now, Jules sleeps down the hall in the den. He is on a mattress on the floor at one end of the room. Don's mattress is at the other. Between them is a high wooden table that holds their things. Victor is in there with him. Jules snores. Soft music plays on the small cassette-deck radio. It's coming from the dining room, where Felix and Don are playing euchre with a deck of Pee-wee Herman playing cards. Cheryl is washing clothes in a bucket in the kitchen sink.

Malorie is alone with Tom on the couch in the living room.

"The man who owned the house," Malorie says. "George, that was his name? He placed the ad? He was here when you got here?"

Tom, who is attempting to make a protective, padded cover for the interior windshield of a car, looks Malorie in the eyes. His hair looks extra sandy in the lamplight.

"I was the first one to answer the ad in the paper," Tom says. "George was great. He'd asked strangers into his home when everyone was locking their doors. And he was progressive, too, a big *thinker*. He was constantly presenting ideas. Maybe we could look out the windows through lenses? Refracted glass? Telescopes? Binoculars? That was his big idea. If it's a matter of sight, maybe what we'd need to do is alter our sight line. Or change the physical ways in which we see something. By looking *through* an object, maybe the creatures couldn't hurt us. We were both really looking for a way to solve this. And George, being the kind of man he was, wasn't satisfied with just talking about it. He wanted us to try these theories out."

As Tom talks, Malorie pictures the face in the photos along the staircase.

"The night Don arrived, the three of us were sitting in the kitchen, listening to the radio, when George suggested there might be some variety of 'life' that was causing this to happen. This is before MSNBC proposed that theory. George said he got the idea from an old book, *Possible Impossibilities*. It talked about irreconcilable life-forms. Two worlds whose compounds were entirely foreign might cause damage to one another if they were to cross paths. And if this other life-form were somehow able to get here . . . well, that's what George was saying had happened. That they *did* figure out a way to travel here, intentionally or not. I loved it. But Don didn't. He was online a lot back then, researching chemicals, gamma waves, anything unseen that might cause harm if you looked at it because you wouldn't know you were looking at it. Yeah, Don was pretty hard on us about it. He's passionate. You can already tell he gets angry. But George was the kind of man who, once he had an idea, was going to see it out, no matter how dangerous it was.

"By the time Felix and Jules arrived, George was ready to test his theory about refracted vision. I read everything with him that he pulled up online. So many websites about eyesight and how the eyes work and optical illusions and refracted light, how exactly telescopes work, and more. We talked about it all the time. When Don, Felix, and Jules were asleep, George and I sat at the kitchen table and drew diagrams. He'd pace back and forth, then he'd stop, turn to me, and ask, 'Have any of the victims been known to wear glasses? Maybe a closed window could protect us, if certain angles were applied.' Then we'd talk about that for another hour.

"We all watched the news constantly, hoping for another clue, a piece of information that we'd be able to use to find a way for people to protect themselves. But the reports just started to repeat themselves. And George got impatient. The more he talked about testing his 'altered vision' theory, the more he wanted to try it. I was scared, Malorie. But George was like the captain of a sinking ship, and he wasn't afraid to die. And if it worked? Well, that would mean he'd helped cure the planet of its most terrifying epidemic."

As Tom speaks, the lamplight dances in his blue eyes.

"What did he use?" Malorie asks.

"A video camera," Tom says. "He had one upstairs. One of those old VHS cameras. He did it without telling us. One night he set it up behind one of the blankets hanging in the dining room. I woke first that morning and found him asleep on the floor in there. When he heard me, he got up and hurried to the camera. 'Tom,' he said, 'I did it. I recorded five hours of footage. It's right here, *here,* inside this camera. I could be holding the cure to this thing. Indirect vision. *Film.* We have to watch this.'

"I told him I thought it was a bad idea. I also thought it wasn't likely he'd captured anything in just a five-hour span. But he had a plan that he presented to all of us. He said he needed one of us to tie him to a chair in one of the upstairs bedrooms. He'd watch the footage in there. The way he saw it, tied to the chair, he shouldn't be able to hurt himself if things went badly. Don got really angry. He told George he was a threat to us all. He rightfully said that we had no idea what we were dealing with, and that if something were to happen to George, then something might happen to us all. But Felix and I weren't opposed. We voted. Don was the only one who didn't want him to do it. He talked about leaving. We talked him out of it. And finally, George told us that he didn't need permission in his own house to do what he wanted to do. So, I told him I'd tie him to the chair."

"And you did?"

"I did."

Tom's eyes travel to the carpet.

"It started with George gasping. Like he had something lodged in his throat. He'd been up there two hours and hadn't made a sound. Then he starting calling to us. 'Tom! You piece of shit. Get up here. *Get up here.*' He would giggle, then scream, then howl. He sounded like a dog. We heard the chair bang hard against the floor. He was screaming profanities. Jules rose to go help him and I grabbed his arm to stop him. There was nothing we could do except listen. And we heard the entire thing. All the way until the crashing of the chair and the screaming stopped. Then we waited. We waited for a long time. Eventually, we went upstairs together. Blindfolded, we turned the VCR off, then opened our eyes. We saw what George had done to himself. He'd pressed so hard against the ropes that they had gone *through* his muscles all the way to the bone. His entire body looked like cake frosting, blood and skin folded over the ropes in his chest, his belly, his neck, his wrists, his legs. Felix threw up. Don and I knelt beside George and began cleaning. When we were finished, Don insisted we burn the tape. So we did. And while it was burning I couldn't stop thinking that with it went our first real theory. It seems that no matter what prism you view them through, they'll hurt you."

Malorie is silent.

"You know what, though? He was right. In a way. He hypothesized it was creatures long before the news said as much. He was obviously onto something. Maybe if he had gone about it in a different way, George could have been the kind of guy to change the world."

There are tears in Tom's eyes.

"You know what worries me most about that story, Malorie?"

"What?"

"The camera was only running for five hours and it caught something. How many of them are out there?"

Malorie looks to the blankets covering the windows. Then she looks back to Tom. He's adjusting the windshield protector he's building. The music comes quietly from the dining room.

"Well," Tom says, lifting the thing in his hands, "hopefully something like this helps. You know, we can't stop trying just because George died. Sometimes I think it scarred Don. It did something to him for sure."

Tom rises and holds the big piece before him. Malorie hears something snap, and the thing Tom is building falls to pieces at his feet.

He turns to Malorie.

"We can't stop trying."

thirteen

Felix is taking the path toward the well. One of the housemates' six buckets hangs from his right hand. It's the wood one. The black iron handle makes it look old. It's heavier than the others, but Felix doesn't mind. Rather, he likes it. It keeps him grounded, he says.

The rope is tied around his waist. The other end of it is tied to a steel stake in the dirt, just outside the home's back door. There is a lot of slack. Some of it rubs against his pant leg and his shoes. He worries about tripping over it, so, with his left hand, he lifts it and holds it away from his body. He is blindfolded. The pieces of old picture frames that outline the path let him know if he's walking too far to one side or another.

"It's like Operation!" he calls to Jules, who waits, blindfolded, by the stake. "Do you remember that game? Every time my toe touches the wood I hear a buzzer going off."

Jules has been talking since Felix started walking toward the well. It's the way the housemates do it. One fetches the water, the other lets him know how far he is from the house through his voice. Jules hasn't been saying anything in particular. Reciting grades he got in college. Listing off his first three jobs after he graduated. Felix can hear some words but not others. It doesn't matter. As long as Jules is talking, Felix feels a little less like he's out to sea.

But not much less.

He bumps into the well when he reaches it. The cobblestone lip scratches his thigh. It amazes Felix to think how much it hurts, walking this slow, and how much it could hurt if he was running.

"I'm at the well, Jules! Securing the bucket now."

Jules isn't the only one waiting for Felix. Cheryl is behind the closed back door of the house. She is standing in the kitchen, listening through the door. The housemate who waits inside the kitchen is only there in case something goes wrong outside. She is hoping her role as a "safety net" won't mean anything today.

Above the well's open mouth is a wooden crossbar. At each end is an iron hook. This is why Felix likes bringing the wooden bucket when he goes. It's the only one that fits perfectly on the hooks. He ties the well rope to the bucket. Once it's secure, he rotates the crank, making the rope as taut as it can go. His hands free, he wipes them on his jeans.

Then he hears something move out here.

Turning his head quickly, Felix raises his hands in front of his face. But nothing happens. Nothing comes at him. He can hear Jules talking by the back door. Something about a job as a mechanic. Fixing things.

Felix listens.

Breathing hard, he gives the crank one turn in the opposite direction, his ear toward the rest of the yard. The rope is just slack enough now for him to remove the bucket from the hooks and let it hang, suspended, above the stone mouth of the well. He waits another minute. Jules calls to him.

"Everything okay, Felix?"

Felix listens a little longer before responding. As he answers, he feels as if his voice suddenly betrays his exact location.

"Yes. I thought I heard something."

"What?"

"I thought I heard something! I'm getting the water now."

Turning the crank, Felix lowers the bucket. He hears it strike the stone sides within. They are followed by hollow echoes. Felix knows that it takes about twenty revolutions of the crank for the bucket to reach the water. He is counting them now.

"That's eleven, that's twelve, that's thirteen . . ."

At nineteen he hears a splash from the bottom of the well. When he thinks the bucket is full, he brings it back up. Securing it to the hooks, he unfastens the rope and begins walking toward Jules again.

He will do this three times.

"I'm bringing back the first one!" Felix calls.

Jules is still talking about fixing cars. When Felix gets to him, Jules touches his shoulder. Usually, here, the housemate who is standing by the stake knocks on the back door, alerting the person waiting inside that the first bucket has been retrieved. But Jules hesitates.

"What did you hear out there?" he asks.

Felix, carrying the heavy bucket, thinks.

"It was probably a deer. I'm not sure."

"Did it come from the woods?"

"I don't know where it came from."

Jules is quiet. Then Felix can hear him moving.

"Are you searching to make sure we're alone?"

"Yes."

When he is satisfied, Jules knocks twice on the back door. He takes the bucket from Felix's hands. Cheryl quickly opens the door and Jules hands it to her. The door closes.

"Here's the second one," Jules says, handing Felix another bucket.

Felix is walking toward the well. The bucket he carries now is made of sheet metal. There are three like this in the house. At the bottom of it are two heavy rocks. Tom placed them there after determining the bucket wasn't quite heavy enough to submerge. It's heavy, but not as heavy as the wooden one. Jules is talking again. Now he brings up breeds of dogs. Felix has heard this before. Jules once owned a white Lab, Cherry, who he says was the most skittish dog he's ever known. When his shoe touches the wood in the dirt, Felix almost falls. He's walking too fast. He knows this. He slows down. This time, at the well, he feels for it with an outstretched hand. He sets the bucket on the cobblestone lip and begins fastening the crossbar rope to the handle.

He hears something. Again. It sounds like wood popping in the distance.

When Felix turns he accidentally knocks the bucket off the well's lip. It falls in; the crank turns without him. The bucket crashes to the bottom. The loud echoes of metal against stone. Jules calls to him. Felix, turning around, feels incredibly vulnerable. Again, he does not know where the sound has come from. He listens, breathing hard. Leaning against the cobblestones, he waits.

Wind rustles the leaves of the trees.

Nothing else.

"Felix?"

"I dropped the bucket into the well!"

"Was it tied?"

He pauses.

Felix nervously turns toward the well. He pulls on the crossbar's rope and discovers that, yes, he tied it to the handle before knocking it in. He releases the rope. He turns toward the rest of the yard. He pauses. Then he begins bringing the second bucket back up.

On the walk back toward the house, Jules is asking him questions.

"Are you all right, Felix?"

"Yes."

"You just dropped it in?"

"I knocked it in. Yes. I thought I heard something again."

"What did it sound like? A stick breaking?"

"No. Yes. Maybe. I don't know."

When Felix reaches Jules, Jules takes the bucket.

"Are you sure you're up for this today?"

"Yes. I've already gotten two buckets. It's all right. I'm just fucking hearing things out there, Jules."

"Want me to get the last one?"

"No. I can do it."

Jules knocks on the back door. Cheryl opens it, receives the bucket, then hands Jules the third.

"Are you guys all right?" she asks.

"Yes," Felix says. "We're fine."

Cheryl shuts the door.

"Here you are," Jules says. "If you need me, tell me. Remember, you're connected here."

He tugs on the rope.

"All right."

On the third trip to the well, Felix has to remind himself to slow down again. He understands why he is rushing. He wants to be back inside, where he can look Jules in the face, where the blankets over the windows make him feel safer. Still, he reaches the well sooner than he expects. Slowly, he ties the crossbar rope to the bucket's handle. Then he pauses.

There are no sounds out here except the voice of Jules, coming from the other end of the rope.

The world, it seems, is unnaturally quiet.

Felix turns the crank.

"That's one, that's two . . ."

Jules is talking. His voice sounds far away. Too far.

" . . . that's six, that's seven . . ."

Jules sounds anxious. Why did he sound anxious? Should he?

" . . . that's ten, that's eleven . . ."

Sweat forms behind Felix's blindfold. It slowly travels down the length of his nose.

We'll be inside in no time, Felix thinks. *Just fill the third bucket and get the fuck—*

He hears the sound again. For the third time.

But now, he can tell where it is coming from.

It is coming from inside the well.

He releases the crank and steps back. The bucket falls, crashing against the stone, before splashing below.

Something moved. Something moved in the water.

Did something move in the water?

Suddenly he feels cold, too cold. He is shaking.

Jules calls to him but Felix doesn't want to call back. He doesn't want to make a sound.

He waits. And the longer he waits, the more scared he gets. Like the silence is getting louder. Like he's about to hear something he doesn't want to hear. But when no sound comes, he slowly begins to convince himself that he was wrong. Sure, it could have been something in the well but it could have been something in the river, too. Or the woods. Or the grass.

It could have come from *anywhere* out here.

He steps toward the well again. Before reaching for the rope, he touches the cobblestone lip. He runs his fingers across it. He is determining how wide it is.

Could you fit in there? Could someone fit in there?

He isn't sure. He turns toward the house, ready to leave the bucket where it is. Then he turns back to the well and begins turning the crank, fast.

You're hearing things. You're losing your marbles, man. Get this thing up. Get back inside. Now.

But as he cranks, Felix feels the very beginning of a fear that could grow too big to handle. The bucket, he thinks, feels the littlest bit heavier than it normally does.

It's NOT heavier! Get the bucket UP and get BACK inside NOW!!

When the bucket reaches the lip, Felix stops. Slowly, with one hand, he reaches toward it. His hand is shaking. When his fingers touch the wet, steel rim he swallows once, hard. He locks the crank. Then he sticks his hand into the bucket.

"Felix?"

Jules is calling.

Felix feels nothing but water in the bucket.

You see? You're imagining—

Behind him, he hears wet feet on the grass.

Felix drops the bucket and runs.

He falls.

Get up.

He gets back up and runs.

Jules is calling to him. He is calling back.

He falls again.

Get up. Get up.

He gets up again. He runs.

Jules's hands are upon him.

The back door is opening. Someone else's hands are upon him. He is inside. Everyone is talking at once. Don is yelling. Cheryl is yelling. Tom is telling everyone to calm down. The back door is closed. Olympia is asking what is going on. Cheryl is asking what happened. Tom is telling everyone to close their eyes. Somebody is touching Felix. Jules yells at everyone to be quiet.

They are.

Then Tom is speaking, quietly.

"Don, did you search by the back door?"

"How the fuck should I know if I did it right, man?"

"I'm just asking if you searched."

"I did. Yes. I did."

Tom says, "Felix, what happened?"

Felix tells them. Every detail he remembers. Tom asks him to go over what happened at the end again. He wants to know more about what occurred at the back door. Before he was let in. As he was let in. Felix tells him again.

"All right," Tom says again. "I'm opening my eyes."

Malorie tenses.

"I'm fine," Tom says. "It's okay."

Malorie opens her eyes. On the kitchen counter there are two buckets of well water. Felix is standing blindfolded by the back door. Jules is removing his blindfold.

"Lock that door," Tom says.

"It is," Cheryl says.

"Jules," Tom says, "stack the chairs from the dining room in front of this door. Then block the window in the dining room with the table."

"Tom," Olympia says, "you're scaring me."

"Don, come with me. We're going to block the front door with the credenza. Felix, Cheryl, turn the couch in the living room on its side. Block one of the windows. I'll find something to block the other one with."

The housemates are staring at Tom.

"Come on," he says impatiently. "Let's go!"

As they begin to scatter, Malorie touches Tom's arm.

"What is it?"

"Olympia and I can help. We're pregnant, not crippled. We'll put the mattresses upstairs over the windows."

"Okay. But do it blindfolded. And be as careful as you've ever been in your entire life."

Then Tom leaves the kitchen. When Malorie and Olympia pass the living room, Don is already in there, moving the couch. Upstairs, the two women delicately place Malorie's mattress on its side against the blanket covering the window. They do the same in Olympia and Cheryl's rooms.

Downstairs again, the doors and windows are blockaded.

The housemates are in the living room. They are standing very close together.

"Tom," Olympia says, "is something out there?"

Tom pauses before answering. Malorie sees something deeper than fear in Olympia's eyes. She feels it herself, too.

"Maybe."

Tom is staring at the windows.

"But it could have been . . . a deer, right? Couldn't it have been a deer?"

"Maybe."

One by one the housemates sit upon the living room's carpeted floor. They are shoulder to shoulder, back to back. In the center of the room, the couch against one window, the kitchen chairs stacked against the other, they sit in silence.

They listen.

fourteen

Cold river water splashes across Malorie's pants as she rows. Each time it does she pictures one of the creatures in the river, cupping its hands, tossing it upon her, mocking her attempt at escape. She shivers.

Olympia's baby book, Malorie recalls, taught her many things. But there was one sentence in *At Last . . . a Baby!* that really struck a chord:

Your baby is smarter than you think.

At first, Malorie struggled to accept this. In the new world, babies had to be trained to wake up with their eyes closed. They had to be raised scared. There wasn't room for unknowns. Yet, there *were* times when the Boy and the Girl surprised her.

Once, having cleaned the upstairs hallway of the children's makeshift toys, Malorie stepped into the living room. There, she heard something move in the room at the end of the first-floor hall.

"Boy?" she called. "Girl?"

But she knew the children were in their bedroom. She'd locked them in their cribs less than an hour before.

Malorie closed her eyes and stepped into the hall.

She knew what the sound was. She knew exactly where every object in the house was located. It was a book falling from the table in the room Don and Jules once shared.

At the children's bedroom doorway, Malorie paused. Within, she heard soft snoring.

A second crash from the unused room and Malorie gasped. The bathroom was only a few feet from her. The children were sleeping. If she could just get into the bathroom, she could defend herself.

Blindly, her arms raised in front of her face, she moved quickly, smashing into the wall before finding the bathroom doorway. Inside, she hit her hip hard against the sink. Frantically feeling along the wall, she felt the cloth of a towel hanging. She wrapped it tightly around her eyes. Knotted it twice. Then, behind the open door, she found what she was looking for.

The garden axe.

Armed, blindfolded, she exited the bathroom. Gripping the axe handle with both hands, she inched toward the door she knew was always closed. A door that was now open.

She stepped inside.

She swung the axe, blindly, at eye level. It struck the wood wall and Malorie screamed as splinters exploded. She turned and swung again, this time connecting with the opposite wall.

"Get out! Leave my children alone!"

Heaving, she waited.

For a response. For movement. For whatever it was that knocked the books over in there.

Then she heard the Boy, at her feet, whimpering.

"Boy?"

Stunned, kneeling, Malorie found him fast. She removed the towel and opened her eyes.

In his tiny hands she saw he held a ruler. Beside him were the books.

She picked him up and carried him into his bedroom. There, she saw the wire lid of the crib open. She set him next to it on the floor. Then she closed it again and asked him to open it. The Boy just stared at her. She toyed with the little lock, asking him to show her if he could open it. Then he did.

Malorie slapped him.

At Last . . . a Baby!

She recalled Olympia's baby book. Now her own.

And the one sentence from it she tried hard to ignore came back to her.

Your baby is smarter than you think.

It used to worry her. But today, in the boat, using the children's ears as guides, she clings to it, hoping the children are as prepared as anybody can be for what may come, farther along the river.

Yes, she hopes they are smarter than what may lay ahead.

fifteen

I'm not drinking that water," Malorie says.

The housemates are exhausted. They slept packed together on the living room floor, though nobody slept for very long.

"We can't go days without water, Malorie," Tom says. "Think about the baby."

"That's who I'm thinking about."

In the kitchen, on the counter, the two buckets Felix filled are still untouched. One by one the housemates lick their dry lips. It has been twenty-four hours and the likelihood of its being much longer weighs on all their minds.

They are thirsty.

"Can we drink the river water?" Felix asks.

"Bacteria," Don says.

"That depends," Tom says. "On how cold the water is. How deep. How fast it flows."

"And anyway," Jules says, "if something got into the well, I'm sure it's gotten into the river."

Contamination, Malorie thinks. It's the word of the hour.

In the cellar are three buckets of urine and feces. Nobody wants to take them outside. Nobody wants to go out there at all today. The smell is strong in the kitchen and hangs faintly in the living room.

"I would drink the river water," Cheryl says. "I'd chance it."

"You'd go out there?" Olympia asks. "There could be something standing right on the other side of the door!"

"I don't know what I heard," Felix says. He's repeated this many times. He's said he feels guilty for scaring everybody.

"It was probably a person," Don says. "Probably somebody looking to rob us."

"Do we have to figure this out right now?" Jules asks. "It's been one day. We haven't heard anything. Let's wait. One more day. See if we feel better."

"I'd even drink from the buckets," Cheryl says. "It's a well, for fuck's sake. Animals fall into wells all the time. They die down there. We've probably been drinking dead animal water this whole time."

"The water in this neighborhood has always been good," Olympia says.

Malorie gets up. She walks to the kitchen's entrance. The water glistens at the rim of the wood bucket, shines in the one of metal.

What would it do to us? she thinks.

"Can you imagine drinking a little part of one?" Tom asks.

Malorie turns. He is standing beside her. His shoulder rubs against hers in the doorway.

"I can't do it, Tom."

"I wouldn't ask you to. But I can ask myself."

When Malorie looks him in the eye she knows he is serious.

"Tom."

Tom turns to face the others in the dining room.

"I'll drink it," he says.

"We don't need a champion," Don says.

"I'm not looking to be one, Don. I'm thirsty."

The housemates are quiet. Malorie sees the same thing in their faces that she's feeling herself. For as scared as she is, she *wants* someone to drink it.

"This is insane," Felix says. "Come on, Tom. We can figure something else out."

Tom steps into the dining room. At the table, he looks Felix in the eye.

"Lock me in the cellar. I'll drink it down there."

"You'll go mad from the smell," Cheryl says.

Tom smiles sadly.

"We have a well, right in our backyard," he says. "If we can't use it, we can't use anything. Let me do this."

"You know who you sound like?" Don asks.

Tom waits.

"You sound like George. Except he had a theory."

Tom looks to the dining room table, set against the window.

"We've been here for months," he says. "If something got in the well yesterday, it probably got in there before."

"You're rationalizing," Malorie says.

Tom answers her without turning to face her.

"Is there any option? Sure, the river. But we could get sick. Real sick. We don't have any medicine. All we've had so far is the water from the well. It's the only medicine we've got. What else can we do? Walk to the next well? And then what? Hope nothing got into that one?"

Malorie watches as, one by one, the housemates acquiesce. The natural rebellion in Don's face gives way to concern. The fear in Olympia's eyes turns to guilt. As for herself, Malorie doesn't want him to do it. For the first time since arriving at the house, Tom's role, how integral he is to everything that happens here, is blinding.

But instead of stopping him, he inspires her. And she helps.

"Not the cellar," she says. "What if you went mad down there and destroyed our food stock?"

Tom faces her.

"All right," he says. "Then the attic."

"A leap from that window is a lot higher than one from down here."

Tom stares into Malorie's eyes.

"I'll make a compromise," he says. "The second floor. You gotta lock me somewhere. And there's no place down here."

"You can use my room."

"That room," Don says, "is the very one George used to watch the video."

Malorie looks back to Tom.

"I didn't know that."

"Let's do it," Tom says.

He pauses, just a moment, before passing Malorie and entering the kitchen. Malorie follows. The housemates file in behind them. When he pulls a glass from the cupboard, Malorie gently grabs his arm.

"Drink it through this," she says. She hands him a coffee filter. "I don't know. A filter. Who knows?"

Tom takes it. He looks her in the eye. Then he dunks the glass in the wooden well bucket.

When he pulls it out, he holds it up. The housemates stand in a semi-circle around it. They stare at the contents of the glass.

The details of Felix's story chill Malorie all over again.

Carrying the glass, Tom leaves the kitchen. Jules gathers some rope from the kitchen pantry and follows him.

The other housemates do not speak. Malorie places one hand on her belly and the other on the counter. Then she lifts it quickly, as if she's just put her hand in a deadly substance.

Contamination.

But there was no water where she put her hand.

Upstairs, the door to her bedroom closes. She listens as Jules ties the rope around the doorknob and fastens it to the railing of the staircase.

Now Tom is locked in.

Like George.

Felix paces. Don leans against the wall, arms crossed, staring at the floor. When Jules returns, Victor goes to him.

A sound comes from upstairs. Malorie gasps. The housemates look to the ceiling.

They wait. They listen. Felix moves as if he's going to go up there. Then he stops.

"He must have drunk it already," Don says quietly.

Malorie steps to the entrance of the living room. There, ten feet away, is the foot of the stairs.

There is only silence.

Then there is a knock.

And Tom yells.

Tom yells Tom yells Tom yells Tom

Malorie is already moving to the stairs, but Jules passes her.

"Stay here!" he commands.

She watches him climb the stairs.

"Tom!"

"Jules, I'm okay."

At the sound of Tom's voice, Malorie exhales. She reaches for the railing to steady herself.

"Did you drink it?" Jules says through the door.

"I did. I drank it. I'm fine."

The other housemates are gathered behind her now. They begin talking. Quietly at first. Then excitedly. Upstairs, Jules unties the rope. Tom emerges from the bedroom holding the empty glass before him.

"What was it like?" Olympia asks.

Malorie smiles. So do the others. It's funny, in a dark way, right now, asking what drinking a glass of water was like.

"Well," Tom says, descending, "it was probably the best glass of water I've ever had."

When he reaches the bottom he looks Malorie in the eye.

"I liked the filter idea," he says. When he passes her, he sets the glass on the end table with the telephone. Then he turns to the others. "Let's put the furniture back in order. Let's put this place back together again."

sixteen

O n the river, Malorie feels the heat of the midday sun. Instead of bringing her peace, it reminds her how visible they must be.

"Mommy," the Boy whispers.

Malorie leans forward. Her palm is pierced by a splinter from the oar. This makes three.

"What is it?"

"Shhh," the Boy says.

Malorie stops rowing. She is listening.

The Boy is right. Something moves on land to their left. Sticks break. More than one.

The man in the boat, Malorie's mind screams, *saw something on this river.*

Could it be him? Could *he* be out in the woods? Could he be after her, waiting for her to get stuck, ready to rip off her blindfold? The children's?

More sticks break. It moves slowly. Malorie thinks of the house they've left behind. They were safe there. Why did they leave? Is the place they are heading going to be any safer? How could it be? In a world where you can't open your eyes, isn't a blindfold all you could ever hope for?

We left because some people choose to wait for news and others make their own.

Like Tom used to say. Malorie, she knows, will never stop being inspired by him. The very thought of him, here, on the river, brings her hope.

Tom, she wants to tell him, *your ideas were good.*

"Boy," she whispers, paddling again, fearful that they are too close to the left bank, "what do you hear?"

"It's close, Mommy." Then, "I'm scared."

There is a moment of silence. In it, Malorie imagines a danger only inches away.

She stops paddling again, to listen better. She cranes her neck to the left.

The front of the rowboat connects with something hard. Malorie shrieks. The children scream.

We've run into the bank!

Malorie jabs a paddle at where she thinks the mud is but she does not connect.

"Leave us alone!" she yells, her face contorted. Suddenly, she *longs* for the walls of the house. There are no walls on this river. No cellar beneath them. No attic above.

"Mommy!"

As the Girl screams for her, something breaks through the branches. Something big.

Malorie jabs the paddle again but it only breaks the water. She grabs the Boy and Girl and pulls them close.

She hears a growl.

"Mommy!"

"Quiet!" she yells, pulling the Girl even closer.

Is it the man? Deranged? Do the creatures growl? Do they make any noise at all?

A second growl now and suddenly Malorie understands what it is. It's doglike. Canine.

Wolves.

She doesn't have time to coil before a wolf's claw slashes her shoulder.

She screams. Immediately she feels the warm blood cascading the length of her arm. Cold water sloshes in the rowboat's bottom.

Urine, too.

They smell it on us, Malorie thinks, frantic, turning her head in every direction and aimlessly wielding the paddle. *They know we can't defend ourselves.*

She hears another low growling. It's a pack. The rowboat's tip is snagged on something. Malorie can't find it with her paddle. But the boat swivels, as if the wolves have taken ahold of the bow.

They could jump in! THEY COULD JUMP IN! Crawl to the front of the boat. You have to set it free.

Swinging the paddle above the heads of the children, screaming, Malorie rises. The boat leans to the right. She thinks they're going to tip. She steadies herself. The wolves snarl. Her shoulder is hot with a kind of pain she has never experienced before. Holding it, blindly, wildly, she waves a paddle at the boat's tip. But she cannot reach it. So she steps forward.

"Mommy!"

She drops to her knees. The Boy is beside her now. He is holding on to her shirt.

"I need you to let go!" she yells.

Something jumps into the water.

Malorie turns her head toward the sound.

How shallow is it here? Can they get in the boat? Can the wolves GET IN THE BOAT??

Turning quickly, she crawls to the end of the rowboat and reaches out, into the darkness.

The children scream behind her. Water splashes. The boat rocks. Wolves bark. And in the darkness of her own closed eyes, Malorie's hand feels a stump.

She yells as she reaches with both arms now. Her left shoulder aches. She feels the frigid October air on her shredded skin. With her second hand she feels a second stump.

We're wedged. That's all! We're wedged!

As she pushes hard against the two stumps, something bangs against the boat. She can hear claws, scratching, trying to climb in.

The boat grates against the wood. Water splashes. Malorie hears it from every direction. There's another growl, and heat, too. Something is close to her face.

She screams loudly and pushes.

Then, they are free.

Turning fast, Malorie stumbles and falls into the middle bench.

"Boy!" she screams.

"Mommy!"

Then she reaches for the Girl and finds she is pressed against the middle bench.

"Are you two all right? *Speak to me!*"

"I'm scared!" the Girl says.

"I'm fine, Mommy!" the Boy says.

Malorie is paddling hard. Her left shoulder, already pressed past the point of exhaustion, resists. But she forces it to work.

Malorie paddles. The children are tucked at her knees and feet. The water breaks beneath the wood. She paddles. What else can she do? *What else can she do but paddle?* The wolves could be coming. How shallow is the river here?

Malorie paddles. It feels like her arm is dangling from her body. But she paddles. The place she is taking the children to may no longer exist. The excruciating trip, blindly taking the river, could result in nothing. When they get there, down the river, will they be safe? *What if what she's looking for isn't there?*

seventeen

"They're scared of us," Olympia suddenly says.

"What do you mean?" Malorie asks. The two are sitting together on the third step up the staircase.

"Our housemates. They're scared of our bellies. And I know why. It's because one day they're going to have to deliver these babies."

Malorie looks into the living room. She has been at the house for two months. She is five months pregnant. She too has thought of this. Of course she has.

"Who do you think will do it?" Olympia asks, her wide, innocent eyes trained on Malorie.

"Tom," Malorie says.

"Okay, but I'd feel a lot better if there was a doctor in the house."

This thought is always looming for Malorie. The inevitable day she gives birth. No doctors. No medicine. No friends or family. She tries to imagine it as a quick experience. Something that will happen fast and be over with. She pictures the moment her water breaks, then imagines holding the baby. She doesn't want to think about what'll happen in between.

The others are gathered in the living room. The morning's chores are finished. All day Malorie has had a sense that Tom is working something out. He's been distant. Isolated with his thoughts. Now he stands in the center of the living room, every housemate in earshot, and reveals what's been on his mind. It's exactly what Malorie was hoping it wasn't.

"I've got a plan," he says.

"Oh?" Don asks.

"Yes." Tom pauses, as if making sure of what he's about to say one final time. "We need guides."

"What do you mean?" Felix asks.

"I mean I'm going to go looking for dogs."

Malorie gets up from the stairs and walks to the entrance of the living room. Just like the others, the idea of Tom leaving the house has dramatically gotten her attention.

"Dogs?" Don asks.

"Yes," Tom says. "Strays. Former pets. There must be hundreds out there. Loose. Or stuck inside a home they can't get out of. If we're going to go on stock runs, which we all know we're going to have to do, I'd like us to have help. Dogs could warn us."

"Tom, we don't know the effect they have on animals," Jules says.

"I know. But we can't sit still."

The tension in the room has risen.

"You're crazy," Don says. "You're really thinking of going out there."

"We'll bring weapons," Tom says.

Don leans forward in the easy chair.

"What exactly are you thinking of here?"

"I've been working on helmets," Tom says. "To protect our blind-folds. We'll carry butcher knives. The dogs could lead us. If one goes mad? Let the leash go. If the animal comes after you, kill it with the knife."

"Blind."

"Yes. Blind."

"I don't like the sound of this at all," Don says.

"Why not?"

"There could be maniacs out there. Criminals. The streets aren't what they used to be, Tom. We're not in suburbia anymore. We're in chaos."

"Well, something has to change," Tom says. "We need to make progress. Otherwise we're waiting for news in a world where there is no longer any news."

Don looks to the carpet. Then back to Tom.

"It's too dangerous. There's just no reason for it."

"There's every reason for it."

"I say we wait."

"Wait for what?"

"Help. Something."

Tom looks to the blankets covering the windows.

"There's no help coming, Don."

"That doesn't mean we should run outside looking for it."

"We'll vote," Tom says.

Don looks to the faces of the other housemates. It's clear he's looking for someone to agree with him.

"A vote," Don says. "I don't like that idea at all, either."

"Why not?" Felix says.

"Because, Felix, we're not talking about which buckets we drink from and which ones we piss in. We're talking about one or more of us leaving the house, for no good reason."

"It's not no good reason," Tom says. "Think of the dogs as an alarm system. Felix heard something by the well two weeks ago. Was it an animal? Was it a man? Was it a creature? The right dog might've barked. I'm talking about searching our block. Maybe the next one, too. Give us twelve hours. That's all I'm asking."

Twelve hours, Malorie thinks. *Getting water from the well takes only half of one.*

But the number, finite as it is, calms her.

"I don't see why we need to round up strays at all," Don says. He fans a hand toward Victor at Jules's feet. "We've got one right here. Let's train him."

"No way," Jules says, rising now.

"Why not?"

"I didn't bring him here so he could be a sacrifice. Until we know how dogs are affected, I'm not agreeing to that."

"A sacrifice," Don says. "Good choice of words."

"The answer is no," Jules says.

Don turns to Tom.

"You see? The one dog owner we have in the house is even against it."

"I didn't say I was against Tom's idea," Jules says.

Don looks around the room.

"So, is everyone for this then? Really? All of you think it's a good idea?"

Olympia looks to Malorie, wide eyed. Don, seeing an opportunity for an ally, approaches her.

"What do you think, Olympia?" he demands.

"Oh! I . . . well . . . I . . . don't know!"

"Don," Tom says. "We'll take a legitimate vote."

"I'm for it," Felix says.

Malorie looks around the living room.

"I'm for it, too," Jules says.

"I'm in," Cheryl says.

Tom turns to Don. As he does, Malorie feels something sink inside her.

The house, Malorie realizes, *needs him.*

"I'll go with you," Jules says. "If I'm not going to let you use my dog, I can at least help you round up others."

Don shakes his head.

"You guys are fucking *nuts.*"

"Then let's start making you a helmet, too," Tom says, planting a hand on Jules's shoulder.

By the next morning, Tom and Jules are putting the finishing touches on the second helmet.

They are leaving today. For Malorie, it is all moving too fast. They just voted on them leaving, but do they have to leave *right away?*

Don makes no move to hide his feelings. The others, like Malorie, are hopeful. It is difficult, Malorie knows, not to be swept up in Tom's energy. If it were Don about to leave, she might have less faith in his returning with Seeing Eye dogs. But Tom has an energy about him. When he says he's going to do something, it feels like it's already done.

Malorie watches from the couch. Both *With Child* and *At Last . . . a Baby!* talk about the "stress link" between mother and child. Malorie doesn't want her baby to feel the anxiety she feels now, watching Tom prepare to leave the house.

There are two duffel bags against the wall. Both are half-stocked with canned goods, flashlights, and blankets. Beside them are big knives and the former legs of a kitchen stool, chiseled now into sharp stakes. They will use the broomsticks as walking sticks.

"Maybe," Olympia says, "animals can't go mad because their brains are too small."

By the expression on Don's face, it looks like he might say something. But he holds his tongue.

"It's possible that animals don't have the capacity to *go mad*," Tom says, adjusting a helmet strap. "Maybe a thing has to be smart enough to lose its mind."

"Well, I would like to know something like that before I go out there," Don says.

"Maybe," Tom continues, "there are degrees of insanity. I'm constantly curious to know how the creatures affect people who are already insane."

"Why don't you round up some of them, too?" Don huffs. "Are you sure you want to risk your life on the hope that animals aren't as smart as us?"

Tom looks him in the eye.

"I'd like to tell you I have more respect for animals than that, Don. But right now, all I care about is surviving."

At last, Jules straps his helmet on. He turns his head to see how it fits. The back of it snaps apart and the whole thing falls to his feet.

Don slowly shakes his head.

"Damn it," Tom says, picking up the pieces. "I had that worked out. Don't worry, Jules."

Lifting the pieces, Tom reassembles them, then fortifies the strap with a second one. He places it upon Jules's head.

"There. All better."

With these words, Malorie feels ill. She has known all morning that Tom and Jules would be leaving, but the moment seems to come too quickly.

Don't go, she wants to say to Tom. *We need you. I need you.*

But she understands that the reason the house needs Tom is because he's the kind of man who would do what he is doing today.

By the wall, Felix and Cheryl help Tom and Jules strap the duffel bags to their backs.

Tom is jabbing at the air with one of the stakes.

Malorie feels a second wave of nausea. There is no greater reminder of the horror of this new world than seeing Tom and Jules prepared the way they are, for a walk around the block. Blindfolded, armed, they look like soldiers of a makeshift war.

"Okay," Tom says. "Let us out."

Felix steps to the front door. The housemates gather behind him in the foyer. Malorie watches them close their eyes, then she does the same. In her private darkness, her heart beats louder.

"Good luck," she suddenly says, knowing that she would regret it if she didn't.

"Thank you," Tom says. "Remember what I said. In twelve hours we'll be back. Are everybody's eyes closed?"

The housemates tell him they are.

Then the front door opens. Malorie can hear their shoes upon the front porch. Then the door is shut.

To Malorie, it feels like something imperative has been locked outside.

Twelve hours.

eighteen

As the rowboat glides, taken by the water slowly on its own, Malorie cups a handful of river water and washes the wound on her shoulder.

It's not an easy task and the pain is severe.

"Are you okay, Mommy?" the Boy asks.

"No questions," she answers. "*Listen.*"

When the wolf struck her, Malorie saw red as the dark world behind her blindfold erupted into bright pain. Now, as she cleans, she sees purples, grays, and worries that this means she is close to passing out. Fainting. Leaving the children to fend for themselves.

Her jacket is off. Her tank top is bloodied and she shivers, wondering how much of that is the cold air and how much is the loss of blood. From the right pocket of the jacket, she removes a steak knife. Then she cuts a sleeve off the jacket and ties it tightly around her shoulder.

Wolves.

By the time the children turned three, Malorie had gotten complex with her lessons. The pair was instructed to remember ten, twenty sounds in a row before revealing what they thought they were. Malorie would walk through the house, then outside, then upstairs. Along the way she made noises. Upon returning, the children told her what she had done. Soon, the Girl got all twenty right. But the Boy was reciting forty, fifty sounds, adding the unintentional noises she made on her way to the ones she meant.

You started in our bedroom, Mommy. You sighed before leaving. Then you walked to the kitchen and on the way your ankle cracked. You sat in the middle chair at the kitchen table. You put your elbows on the table. You cleared your throat and then went into the cellar. You took the first four steps slower than the last six. You tapped your finger on your teeth.

But no matter how much she's taught them, the children could not be prepared to name the beasts who roam the woods on the river. The wolves, Malorie knows, have every advantage. So will anything else they encounter.

She tightens the tourniquet even more. Her shoulder throbs. Her thighs ache. Her neck aches. This morning she felt strong enough to row the twenty-mile trip. Now, wounded, she needs rest. She debates this with herself. She knows that in the old world, a break would have been advised. But stopping out here could mean death.

A loud screech from above makes Malorie jump. It sounded like a bird of prey. Like it was a hundred feet long. Ahead, something splashes. It's brief but the sound is unnerving. Something moves in the woods to the left. More birds call out. The river is coming to life and with each piece of evidence of this, Malorie grows more afraid.

As the life grows around her, it seems to diminish within.

"I'm okay," she lies to the kids. "I want us to listen now. That's all. Nothing more."

Rowing again, Malorie tries not to think about the pain. She doesn't have a clear idea of how much farther she has to go. But she knows it's a lot. At least as far as she's already gone.

Years ago, the housemates were unsure if animals went insane. They talked about it all the time. Tom and Jules took a walk, looking for dogs to guide them. As Malorie and the others waited for them to return, she was overwhelmed with terrible images of rabid animals gone mad. She experiences the same thoughts today. As the river comes alive with nature, she imagines the worst. Just like she did those years ago, before the children were born, when the inertia of the front door reminded you that things like insanity were lurking whether or not someone you cared about was out there with it.

nineteen

Five months along now, Malorie's pregnancy is developing. It's the end of the "nauseous months," but some queasiness lingers. She experiences heartburn. Her legs ache. Her gums bleed. Her dark hair is fuller, as is all the other hair on her body. She feels monstrous, distorted, changed. But as she walks through the house, carrying a bucket of urine, none of these things occupy her thoughts like the whereabouts and safety of Tom and Jules.

It's astonishing, she thinks, how much she already feels for each of her housemates. Prior to arriving, she heard so many stories of people hurting one another on the way to hurting themselves. Back then, the horrors worried Malorie because of what they meant for herself and her child. Now the safety of the entire house consumes her.

It has been five hours since the men left. And with each minute passing, the tension has grown, so that now Malorie can't remember if the housemates are repeating their chores or carrying them out for the first time.

Malorie sets the bucket by the back door. In a few minutes, Felix will dump it outside. Right now, he's at the dining room table, repairing a chair. Passing through the kitchen, Malorie enters the living room. Cheryl is cleaning the surfaces. The picture frames. The telephone. Malorie notes that Cheryl's arms look pale and thin. In the two months she's been living here, their bodies have gotten much worse. They do not eat well. They do not exercise enough. Nobody gets any sun. Tom is outside, chasing a better life for them all. But how much better can he make it?

And who would let the housemates know if they vanished out there, forever?

Anxious, Malorie asks Cheryl if she needs any help. Cheryl says no before leaving the room, but Malorie is not alone. Victor sits behind the easy chair, facing the blankets that cover the windows. His head is up. His tongue hangs and he pants heavily. Malorie thinks he's waiting, like she is, for his master to return.

As if aware that he is being watched, Victor slowly turns toward Malorie. Then he looks back to the blankets.

Don enters the room. He sits in the easy chair, then gets up and leaves. Olympia comes downstairs. She looks for something under the sink in the kitchen. Malorie watches her as she realizes she's already holding what she seeks. She heads back upstairs. Cheryl is back, checking the picture frames. She just did this. She's doing it again. They're all *doing it again*. Nervously passing through the house, trying to occupy their minds. They hardly speak to one another. They hardly look up. Getting water from the well is one thing, and the housemates worry about one another when they do. But what Tom and Jules are doing is almost impossible to suffer.

Malorie stands up and heads for the kitchen. But there is only one place in the house that feels less like the house. Malorie wants to go there. She needs to. To get away.

The cellar.

Felix is in the kitchen but he does not acknowledge her as she passes. He doesn't say a word as she opens the cellar door and takes the stairs down to the dirt floor beneath.

She pulls the string and the light comes on, illuminating the space as it did when Tom showed it to her two months ago. But it looks different now. There are fewer cans. Fewer colors. And Tom is not here, making notes, counting in rations the amount of time the housemates have before starvation and desperation arrive.

Malorie steps to the shelves and distractedly reads the labels.

Corn. Beets. Tuna. Peas. Mushrooms. Mixed fruit. Green beans. Sour cherries. Lingonberries. Grapefruit. Pineapple. Refried beans. Vegetable blend. Chili peppers. Water chestnuts. Diced tomatoes. Plum tomatoes. Tomato sauce. Sauerkraut. Baked beans. Carrots. Spinach. Varieties of chicken broth.

She remembers it feeling crowded down here. The cans once looked like a wall of their own. Now there are holes. Big ones. As if a battle occurred, and their supply was targeted first. Is there enough food to last until the baby comes? If Tom and Jules do not return, will the remaining stock carry her to that dreaded day? What exactly will they do when they run out of canned goods? Hunt?

The baby can drink her mother's milk. But only if her mother has eaten.

Caressing her belly, Malorie walks to the stool and sits.

Despite the cool air down here, she is sweating. The restless footsteps of the housemates are loud. The ceiling creaks.

Wiping her hair from her forehead, Malorie leans back against the shelves. She counts cans. Her eyelids feel heavy. It feels good to rest.

Then . . . she drifts.

When she comes to, Victor is barking upstairs.

She sits up quickly.

Victor is barking. What is he barking at?!

Crossing the cellar quickly, Malorie climbs the stairs and rushes into the living room. The others are already here.

"Cut it out!" Don yells.

Victor is facing the windows, barking.

"What's happening?" Malorie demands, surprised at the panic in her own voice.

Don yells at Victor again.

"He's just edgy without Jules," Felix nervously says.

"No," Cheryl says. "He *heard* something."

"We don't know that, Cheryl," Don snaps.

Victor barks again. It's loud. Sharp. Angry.

"Victor!" Don says. "Come on!"

The housemates are gathered close to one another in the center of the living room. They are unarmed. If Cheryl is right, if Victor thinks something is outside the house, what can they do?

"*Victor!*" Don yells again. "*I'm gonna fucking kill you!*"

But Victor won't stop.

And Don, yell as he might, is as afraid as Malorie is.

"Felix," Malorie says slowly, staring at the front window. "You told me there was a garden outside. Are there any tools?"

"Yes." Felix is staring at the black blankets, too.

"Are they in the house?"

"Yes."

"Why don't you get them?"

Felix turns toward her and pauses. Then he leaves the room.

Malorie goes through the items of the house in her mind. Every furniture leg is a potential weapon. Every solid object ammunition.

Victor keeps barking and it's getting worse. And in the brief spaces between his barks, Malorie hears Felix's anxious footsteps, searching for the paltry garden tools that might protect them from whatever it is that's out there.

twenty

It is noon the next day. Tom and Jules have not returned.

Tom's twelve hours have been more than doubled. And with each one, the emotions within the house grow darker.

Victor still sits by the blanketed window.

The housemates were up late, gathered together, waiting for the dog to stop barking.

They'll eventually get us, Don said. *There's no reason to think otherwise. It's end times, people. And if it's a matter of a creature our brains are incapable of comprehending, then we deserve it. I always assumed the end would come because of our own stupidity.*

Eventually, Victor did stop barking.

Now, in the kitchen, Malorie dunks her hands in a bucket of water. Don and Cheryl went to the well this morning. Each time they knocked to present Felix with a new bucketful, Malorie's heart leapt, hoping, *believing* it was Tom.

She brings the water to her face and runs her wet fingers through her matted, sweaty hair.

"God*damn* it," she says.

She is alone in the kitchen. She is staring at the drapes that cover the room's one window. She is thinking of all the infinite terrible things that could've happened.

Jules killed Tom. He saw a creature and dragged Tom to the river by his hair. He held him underwater till he drowned. Or they both saw something. In a house. They destroyed each other. Their ruined bodies lie on the floor in a stranger's den. Or only Tom saw something. Jules tried to stop him, but Tom got away. He's in the woods somewhere. Eating bugs. Eating bark. Eating his own tongue.

"Malorie?"

Malorie jumps as Olympia enters the kitchen.

"What?"

"I'm really worried, Malorie. He said twelve hours."

"I know," Malorie says. "We all are."

Malorie reaches out to put her hand on Olympia's shoulder and hears Don's voice from the dining room.

"I'm not convinced we should let them back in."

Malorie quickly goes to the dining room.

"Come on, Don," Felix, already in there, says. "How can you mean that?"

"What do you think is going on out there, Felix? You think it's a nice neighborhood we're living in? If anybody's alive out there, they're not surviving on manners, man. Who's to say Tom and Jules weren't kidnapped? They could be hostages right now. And their fucking captors could be asking about our food. *Our food.*"

"Fuck you, Don," Felix says. "If they come back, I'm letting them in."

"*If* it's them," Don says. "And if we're sure there's not a gun to Tom's head on the other side of the door."

"Will you two *shut up*!" Cheryl says, passing Malorie and entering the dining room.

"You can't be serious, Don," Malorie says.

Don turns toward her.

"You're damn right I'm serious."

"You don't want to let them back *in*?" Olympia asks, standing beside Malorie now.

"I didn't *say* that," Don snaps. "I'm saying there could be bad people out there. Do you understand that, Olympia? Or is that too complicated for you?"

"You're a fucking asshole," Malorie says.

For a second, it looks like Don might come at her.

"I don't want to have this discussion," Cheryl says.

"It's been over twenty-four hours," Don says chidingly.

"Just . . . go do something else for a minute, will you?" Felix says. "You're making this worse for everybody."

"We need to start considering a future without them."

"It's been a *day*," Felix says.

"Yeah, a day out *there*."

Don sits at the piano. He looks like he might relent, for a moment. Then he continues.

"The good news is that our stock will last longer."

"*Don!*" Malorie snaps.

"You have a *baby* coming, Malorie. Don't you hope to survive?"

"Don, I could kill you," Cheryl says.

Don gets up from the piano bench. His face is red with anger.

"Tom and Jules aren't coming back, Cheryl. Accept it. And when you live an extra week because you were able to eat *their* share of the food and then you were able to eat Victor, too, *then* maybe you'll understand that there's no such thing anymore as hope."

Cheryl steps toward him. Her hands are in fists. Her face is inches from Don's.

Victor barks from the living room.

Felix gets between Don and Cheryl. Don shoves him away. As Malorie steps toward them, Felix's hand is raised.

He is going to strike Don.

He brings his fist back.

There is a knock at the front door.

twenty-one

Malorie is thinking of Don specifically.

"Mommy," the Boy says, "the blindfold is hurting me."

"Scoop some water out of the river, carefully," Malorie says, "and rub it where it hurts. Do *not* take off your fold."

Once, after the housemates had finished dinner, Malorie sat alone with Olympia at the dining room table. They were talking about Olympia's husband. What he was like. His desire to have a child. Don entered the room alone. He didn't care what Olympia was saying.

"You oughta blind those babies," he said. "The second they come out."

It was as if he'd been thinking about it for a long time, then decided to tell them his decision.

He sat down with them at the table and explained himself. As he did, Olympia grew more withdrawn. She thought it was insane. And worse, she thought it was *cruel*.

But Malorie didn't think so. A deep part of her understood what Don was saying. Every moment of her pending motherhood would be centered on protecting the eyes of her child. How much more could be done if this worry were taken away? The seriousness Don wore when he said it conveyed more than cruelty to Malorie. It opened the door to a realm of harrowing possibilities, things that might need to be done, actions she might have to take that nobody from the old world could ever be fully prepared to endure. And the suggestion, dark as it was, never entirely vanished from her mind's eye.

"It's better, Mommy," the Boy says.

"Shhh," Malorie says. "*Listen.*"

When the children were six months old, she already had them sleeping in their chicken wire cribs. It was night. The world outside the windows and walls was quiet. The house was dark.

In the early days with the babies, Malorie would often listen to them breathe as they slept. What may have been a touching observation for some mothers was a study for Malorie. Did they sound healthy? Were they getting enough nutrients from well water and the breast milk of a mother who hadn't had a decent meal in a year? Always, their health was on her mind. Their diet. Their hygiene. And their eyes.

You oughta blind those babies the second they come out.

Sitting at the kitchen table in the dark, Malorie understood clearly that the idea did not pose a moral dilemma as much as it presented her with something she wasn't sure she was physically capable of doing. Looking toward the hall, listening to their tiny exhales, she believed Don's idea wasn't a bad one.

Every waking moment is spent protecting them from looking outside. You check the blankets. You check their cribs. They won't remember these days when they're older. They won't remember sight.

The children, she knew, would not be robbed of anything in the new world if they weren't able to see it to begin with.

Rising, she stepped to the cellar door. Downstairs, on the cellar's dirt floor, was a can of paint thinner. Long ago she'd read the side label and knew the danger the substance posed if it made contact with the eyes. A person could go blind, it said, if they didn't wash it out in thirty seconds.

Malorie went to it. She took its handle and brought it upstairs.

Do it quick. And do not rinse.

They were just babies. Could they possibly remember this? Would they forever fear her, or would it one day be buried beneath a mountain of blind memories?

Malorie crossed the kitchen and entered the dark hall leading to their bedroom.

She could hear them breathing within.

At their door, she paused and looked into the blackness in which they slept.

In this moment, she believed she could do it.

Quietly, Malorie entered the bedroom. She set the can on the floor and removed the cloth lids covering their protected cribs. Neither child stirred. Both continued to breathe steadily, as if experiencing pleasant dreams, far away as possible from the nightmares coming to them.

Quickly, Malorie unhooked the wire lid to the Girl's crib. She bent and lifted the can.

The Girl breathed, steadily.

Malorie reached into the crib and lifted the baby's head. She removed the Girl's blindfold. The Girl started to cry.

Her eyes are open, Malorie thought. *Pour it.*

She forced the Girl's head closer to the crib's edge and then brought the open can of paint thinner inches from her reddening, crying face. The Boy woke behind her and began crying, too.

"Stop it!" Malorie said, fending off tears of her own. "You don't want to see this world."

She tilted the can a little farther and felt the contents slide over her hand before splashing on the floor at her feet.

Feeling it on her skin made it real.

She couldn't do it.

She let go of the baby's head and the Girl continued to cry.

Setting the can on the ground, Malorie slowly backed out of the bedroom. The children wailed in the darkness.

In the hall, Malorie pressed herself against the wall for support and brought a hand to her mouth. Then she threw up.

"Mommy," the Boy says now, on the river, "it worked!"

"*What worked?*" Malorie says, torn from her memories.

"The blindfold doesn't hurt anymore."

"Boy," she says. "No more talking. Unless you hear something."

Malorie breathes deep and feels something akin to shame. The pain in her shoulder is worse. She is dizzy with fatigue. A deeper sense of disorientation sets in. It feels like something is very wrong within her. Yet, she can hear the children: the Boy breathing in front of her, the Girl fingering puzzle pieces in the back of the rowboat. They are not blind beneath their folds. And today could end with the possibility of an ever newer world, one in which the children would see things they've never seen before.

If she can get them there.

twenty-two

Malorie hears something moving on the other side of the door. She hears panting, too. Something is scratching the wood. She and the others are in the foyer. Felix just called out, asked who it was. In the moment between his asking and getting a response, it sounds like the scratching could be made by anything.

Creatures, she thinks.

But it is not creatures at the door. It is Tom and Jules.

"Felix! It's Tom!"

"Tom!"

"We're still wearing our helmets. But we're not alone. We found dogs."

Felix, sweating, exhales in a big way. For Malorie, the relief is so rich it hurts.

Victor is barking. His tail is wagging. Jules calls to him.

"Victor, buddy! I'm back!"

"All right," Felix says to the housemates inside. "Close your eyes."

"Wait," Don says.

"For what?" Felix says.

"How do we know they're alone? How do we know they're not being followed? Who knows *what* could follow them in?"

Felix pauses. Then he calls to Tom.

"Tom! Are you two alone? Just you two and the dogs?"

"Yes."

"It doesn't mean it's true," Don says.

"Don," Malorie says impatiently, "if someone wanted to break in to this house, they could at any time."

"I'm trying to be safe, Malorie."

"I know."

"I live here, too."

"I know. But Tom and Jules are on the other side of the door. They made it back. We have to let them in now."

Don holds her gaze. Then he looks to the foyer floor.

"You guys are going to get us killed one day," he says.

"Don," Malorie says, seeing that he is, at last, relenting, "we're going to open the door now."

"Yes. I know. No matter what I fucking say."

Don closes his eyes.

Malorie does the same.

"Are you ready, Tom?" Felix calls.

"Yes."

Malorie hears the front door open. The sounds of paws on the foyer tile make it sound like many people have entered at once.

The front door closes quickly.

"Hand me a broomstick," Felix says.

Malorie hears the bristles against the walls, the floor, and the ceiling.

"All right," Felix says. "We're ready."

The moment between deciding to open your eyes and then actually doing it is as scary a thing as there is in the new world.

Malorie opens her eyes.

The foyer erupts into color. Two huskies move quickly, smelling the floor, checking out the new people, checking out Victor.

The excitement Malorie feels at seeing Tom's face is all-encompassing. Yet, he doesn't look good. He looks exhausted. Dirty. And like he's been through something Malorie can only imagine.

He holds something in his hand. It's white. A box. Big enough to carry a small TV. Sounds come from within it. Clucking.

Olympia lunges forward and hugs Tom, who laughs as he's trying to remove his helmet. Jules has his off and kneels to embrace Victor. Cheryl is crying.

Don's expression is a mixture of astonishment and shame.

We almost came to blows, Malorie thinks. *Tom was gone a day and a half and we almost came to blows.*

"Well, oh my *God,*" Felix says, looking wide-eyed at the new animals. "It worked!"

Tom and Malorie's eyes meet. He doesn't have the sparkle he left with.

What did they experience out there?

"These are the huskies," Jules says, fanning a hand toward the dogs. "They're friendly. But they take a minute to warm up."

Then Jules suddenly howls with relief.

Like war veterans coming home, Malorie thinks. *From a trip around the block.*

"What's in the box?" Cheryl asks.

Tom raises it higher. His eyes are glassy. Distant.

"In the *box,* Cheryl," he says, holding it out with one hand and lifting the lid a little with the other, "are birds."

The housemates gather around the box in a circle.

"What kind are they?" Olympia asks.

Tom slowly shakes his head.

"We don't know. Found them in a hunter's garage. We have no idea how they survived. We think the owners left them a lot of feed. As you can tell, they're loud. But only when we're near. We tested it. Whenever we got close to the box, they got louder."

"So that's dinner?" Felix asks.

Tom smiles a tired smile.

"An alarm system."

"Alarm system?" Felix asks.

Jules says, "We're going to hang the box outside. By the front door. We'll be able to hear them in here."

Only a box of birds, Malorie thinks. Yet, it *does* feel like progress.

Tom closes the lid slowly.

"You've got to tell us everything that happened," Cheryl says.

"We will," Tom says. "But let's go in the dining room. The two of us would love to sit down for a minute."

The housemates smile.

Except Don.

Don who declared them dead. Don who was already counting their rations as his own.

In the hall, Tom sets the box of birds on the floor, against the wall. Then the housemates gather in the dining room. Felix gets some water for Tom and Jules. Once they have their glasses in front of them, they tell the story of what they experienced out there.

twenty-three

The moment the door closes behind them, Tom is more afraid than he thought he'd be.

Out here, the creatures are closer.

When we get to the street, Tom thinks, *far enough from the house, will they attack us?*

He imagines cold hands closing over his own. His throat slit. His neck broken. His mind destroyed.

But Tom is very aware that no report described a man being attacked.

This is the way to think, he decides, still standing on the front porch. Forcing this philosophy deeper into his mind, searching for the soil of its roots, he allows himself to breathe, slowly. As he does, other feelings emerge.

For one, there is the unbridled, slightly reckless, sense of freedom.

Tom *has* been outside since arriving at the house. He's retrieved water from the well as often as anyone. He's carried shit and piss to the trenches. But this time it's different. The *air* feels different. Just before he and Jules agree to start walking, a breeze passes over them. It moves across his neck. His elbows. His lips. It's one of the strangest feelings he's ever known. It calms him. As the creatures lurk behind every tree and street sign in his piqued imagination, the clean, open air brings him giddiness.

If only for a moment.

"Are you ready, Jules?" he says.

"Yes."

Like truly blind men, they tap the ground before them with broomsticks. They step from the porch. Within three feet, Tom senses he's no longer walking on concrete. With the lawn beneath him, it's as if the house has vanished. He is *out to sea*. Vulnerable. For a second, he's not sure he can do this.

So he thinks of his daughter.

Robin. I'm just going to get us some dogs.

This is good. This helps him.

The broomstick passes over what must be the curb and Tom steps onto the concrete of the street. Here he stops and kneels. On his knees, he searches for a corner of the front lawn. He finds it. Then he removes a small wood stake from his duffel bag and jams it into the earth.

"Jules," he says, "I've marked our lawn. We may need the help finding our way back."

When he rises and turns, Tom bumps hard into the hood of a car.

"Tom," Jules says, "are you okay?"

Tom steadies himself.

"Yes," he says, "I think I just walked into Cheryl's Wagoneer. I feel wood paneling."

The sounds of Jules's boots and broomstick guide Tom away from the car.

Under different circumstances, with the sun shining against only his eyelids, with no blindfold and helmet to obscure it, Tom knows he'd be passing through a peach and orange world. His closed eyes would see colors change with the clouds, shift with the shadows of the treetops and roofs. But today he sees only black. And somewhere in the blackness he imagines Robin, his daughter. Small, innocent, brilliant. She is encouraging him to walk, *walk, Daddy,* farther from the house, toward things that could help those still inside.

"Fuck!" Jules says. Tom hears him fall to the street.

"*Jules!*"

Tom freezes.

"Jules, what happened?"

"I tripped over something. Do you feel it? It felt like a suitcase."

Using his broom, Tom traces a wide arc. The bristles come to an object. Tom crawls to it. Setting the broom beside him on the hot pavement, he uses both hands to feel for what is lying here in the middle of the street. It doesn't take long before he knows what it is.

"It's a body, Jules."

Tom can hear Jules standing up.

"It's a woman, I think," Tom says. Then he quickly removes his hands from her face.

He rises and the two continue.

It all feels too fast. Things are moving too quickly already. In the old world, discovering a dead body in the street would have taken hours to assimilate.

Yet, they continue.

They cross a lawn until they reach some bushes. Behind the bushes is a house.

"Here," Jules says. "It's a window. I'm touching the glass of a window."

Following his voice, Tom joins Jules at the window. They feel along the bricks of the house until they reach the front door. Jules knocks. He calls hello. He knocks again. They wait. Tom speaks. He worries that in this silent world, his voice might attract something. But he doesn't see a choice. He explains to any possible inhabitants that they mean no harm, that they're here to look for more supplies, anything that might help. Jules knocks again. They wait again. There is no movement from within.

"Let's go in," Jules says.

"Okay."

They walk back to the window. From his duffel bag, Tom removes a small towel. He wraps it around his fist. Then he punches through the glass. It meets no blanket. No cardboard. No wood. This, he knows, means that whoever lived here did so without protection.

Maybe they left town before things went really bad. Maybe they're safe somewhere else.

Tom calls into the house through the broken window.

"Is anybody in here?"

Getting no response, Jules clears the glass. Then he helps Tom crawl through. Inside, Tom knocks something over. It lands with a heavy thud. Jules climbs in through the window behind him.

Then they hear music, a piano, in the room with them.

Tom raises his broomstick to defend himself. But Jules is talking to him.

"I did that, Tom!" he says. "I'm sorry, my broom hit the piano."

Tom is breathing heavily. As he calms himself, the two are silent.

"We can't open our eyes in here," Jules quietly says.

"I know," Tom says. "There's a cross breeze. There's another window open."

He wants so badly to be able to open his eyes. But the house is not safe.

"Still, we're here," Tom says. "Let's take what we can."

But most of the first floor is empty of anything useful. In the kitchen, they search the cupboards. Tom slaps his hands around a shelf until he finds some batteries. Small candles. Pens. As he puts each item into his duffel bag, he announces it to Jules.

"Let's move on," Tom says.

"What about the upstairs?"

"I don't like it here. And if there was any food, it'd be down here."

Using the broomsticks, they find their way to the front door, unlock it, and step outside again. They do not walk back to the street. Instead, they cross the lawn to the neighbor's house, one farther yet from their own.

On a second front porch, they carry out the same ritual. They knock. They announce themselves. They wait. When they hear no movement inside, they break a window. Jules does it this time.

His fist comes in contact with some kind of weak protection. He thinks it's cardboard.

"There could be somebody in here," he whispers.

They wait for a response to the noise they've made. There is none. Tom calls out. He tells the house that they are neighbors. That they are looking for animals and can offer shelter in exchange. There is no response. Jules clears the glass and helps Tom through the window.

Inside, they repair the cardboard.

Using their brooms, they check the place. This takes hours to do. Moving with their backs against each other, they swing their brooms in arcs. Tom leads, telling Jules where to go. When they are done, when they're convinced the house is empty, the windows are covered, and the doors are all locked, Tom declares the house safe.

Both men understand what must come next.

They're going to remove their helmets and blindfolds and open their eyes. Neither has seen anything but the inside of their house for many months now.

Jules moves first. Tom hears him unfastening his helmet. Then he does the same. After sliding his blindfold up to his hairline, Tom turns, eyes closed, to face Jules.

"Ready?"

"Ready."

The two men open their eyes.

Once, as a child, Tom and a friend snuck into a neighbor's house through an unlocked back door. There was no plan, no agenda. They just wanted to see if they could do it. But they got more than they hoped for when, hiding in a pantry, they were forced to wait the entire duration of the family's dinner. When they were finally outside again, his friend asked him how he felt about it.

"Dirty," he said then.

His eyes open now, inside a stranger's home, he feels the same way.

This is not their house. But they're in it. These are not their things. But they could be. A family lived here. They had a child. Tom recognizes a toy or two. A photo tells him that it was a boy. His fair hair and young smile remind Tom of Robin. In a way, every single thing Tom has encountered since Robin's death has reminded him of her. And being here, in a stranger's home, he imagines the way they once lived. The child telling Mom and Dad what he heard about at school. Dad reading the earliest reports in the newspaper. Mom calling the child inside. All of them, together on the couch, watching the news, frightened, as Dad reaches across their son and takes Mom's hand.

Robin.

There is no evidence of a pet. No forgotten chew toy. No cat's bed. And no smell of a dog. But it is the absence of people Tom thinks about.

"Tom," Jules says. "You check upstairs. I'll continue down here."

"Okay."

At the foot of the stairs, Tom looks up. He pulls his blindfold from his pocket and ties it around his eyes again. Despite their having checked the house, Tom can't bring himself to climb the stairs with his eyes open.

Did they check well enough?

Climbing, he uses the broom to guide him. His shoulder brushes against hanging photos. He thinks of George's photo, hanging on the wall at home. His boot tip catches a stair and he stumbles forward. There is carpet beneath his hands. He gets back up. More stairs. So many that it feels impossible, like he's walked through the roof of the house already.

At last, the bristles tell him he's reached the top. But his mind is behind the broom and he stumbles again, this time into a wall. It is silent up here. He kneels and sets the broomstick beside him. Then he takes the duffel bag and unzips it, searching for the flashlight. He's got it.

Rising again, he uses the broom to guide him. Turning right, his wrist knocks into something cold and hard. He pauses and feels it. It's glass, he thinks. A vase. There's a bad smell. He didn't smell it before. His hand comes to a gathering of crinkly, dead leaves. Slowly feeling along the stalks, he understands they are flowers. Roses perhaps. Long dead. He turns left again. The smell of the dead roses fades as he's confronted with something much stronger.

He stops in the hall. How could he and Jules have missed this smell? "Hello?"

There is no response. Tom covers his nose and mouth with his free hand. The stench is awful. He continues down the hall. Coming to a door on his right, Tom enters a room. It's a bathroom. The bristles echo on the tile. There is a damp, moldy smell of unused plumbing. He pokes at the shower curtain and checks the tub with the broom. Then he finds the medicine cabinet. There are pill bottles. Tom pockets them. He kneels and rifles through the cabinets beneath the sink. He hears something behind him and he turns.

He is facing the bathtub.

You just checked it. There was nothing in there.

One hand is on the counter behind him. The other slowly raises the broom. He holds it out before him, blindfolded.

"Is someone in here with me?"

He inches forward, toward the tub.

He swings the broom once. Then twice.

His stomach is turning. Hot. The smell.

Tom lunges forward and swings the broom wildly about the bathtub. He checks the ceiling above it. Then, stepping back again, he lets the broom fall to the bathroom floor, where it connects with something and makes the same sound he heard while kneeling before the cabinets.

He quickly locates a plastic bottle. It's empty.

Tom sighs.

He exits the room and continues down the hall. Quickly, he comes to another door. This one is closed. He can hear Jules moving faintly downstairs. Tom breathes deep and opens the door. It is cold in here. The broom tells him there is something in front of him. He feels for it and discovers a mattress. It's a little bed. Without opening his eyes, he knows this is the boy's bedroom. He closes the door, searches the room entirely with the broom, then turns on the light.

Then he takes off his blindfold and opens his eyes.

Pennants hang from the wall. Local sports teams. One for the zoo. The bedcover is Formula 1 racing cars. It is stuffy in here. Unused. Because the electricity works, he puts the flashlight back into his pack. A brief search tells him there is nothing of real use in here. He thinks of Robin's bedroom.

He closes his eyes again and leaves.

Farther down the hall the smell grows more terrible. He can't leave his mouth uncovered. At the end of the hall, he comes to a wall. As he turns, the broomstick connects with a door behind him. Tom freezes as the door slowly opens.

Did you and Jules check this room? DID YOU?!

"Hello?"

There is no response. Tom enters slowly. He turns on the lights and searches the walls for windows. He finds two. Both heavily fortified with wood. The room is big.

It's the master bedroom.

He crosses the room. The smell is so strong in here it feels physical, like he can touch it. The broomstick guides him to what feels like a walk-in closet. Clothes. Coats. He thinks of taking them with him. He thinks of the winter they will soon face.

Turning, he discovers another, smaller door. A second bathroom. Again he checks the medicine cabinet and the drawers. More pill bottles. Toothpaste. Toothbrushes. He searches for a window. He finds one. Covered in wood. He uses the broom to guide him out of the bathroom. He closes the door behind him.

Believing he's checked the windows, believing he is safe, Tom, standing by the closet, opens his eyes.

A child is sitting on the bed, looking at him.

Tom closes his eyes.

Is this what the creatures look like?

You weren't safe! YOU WEREN'T SAFE!

His heart is thundering. What did he see? It was a face. An old face? No, it was young. Young? But decayed. He wants to call to Jules. But the longer his eyes are closed, the clearer the image becomes.

It was the boy. From the photos downstairs.

He opens his eyes again.

The boy is wearing a suit. Propped against a dark headboard, his face is unnaturally turned toward Tom. His eyes are open. His mouth hangs. His hands are folded across his lap.

You starved here, Tom thinks. *In your parents' bedroom.*

Stepping toward him, his mouth and nose covered, Tom compares him to the photos. The boy looks mummified. Shrunken.

How long ago did you die? How close was I to getting you out of here?

He stares into the boy's dead eyes.

Robin, he thinks. *I'm so sorry.*

"Tom!" Jules yells from below.

Tom turns.

He crosses the room and enters the hall.

"Jules! Are you okay?"

"Yes! Yes! Come quick! I've found a dog."

Tom is torn. The father in him doesn't want to leave this boy. Robin lies in a grave behind the house he left a long time ago.

"If I would have known you were here," Tom says, turning toward the master bedroom, "I would have come sooner."

Then he turns and rushes to the stairs.

Jules found a dog.

He meets Jules at the bottom. Before Tom has a chance to tell him about the boy, Jules is walking through the kitchen, talking about what he's found. At the head of the basement stairs, Jules points and tells Tom to look. Closely.

At the foot of the stairs, lying on their backs, are the parents. They are dressed as if for church. Their clothes are torn at the shoulders. On the mother's chest is a piece of notebook paper. In marker, someone has written: ReStiNg pEaCe

"I just found the boy who wrote that," Tom says. "The boy who laid them here."

"They must have starved," Jules says. "There's no food in here. I have no idea what *he* survived on."

Jules is pointing past the parents. Tom crouches and sees a husky hunched between fur coats on a dress rack.

He is close to emaciated. Tom imagines he's been feeding on the dead parents.

Jules removes some meat from his duffel bag, rips off a piece, and tosses it down to the dog. At first, the dog slowly comes out. Then he devours it.

"Is he friendly?" Tom says quietly.

"I've discovered," Jules says, "that a dog will become fast friends with the people who feed him."

Jules carefully tosses more meat down the stairs. He speaks encouragingly.

But the dog takes work. And *time*.

The two men spend the rest of the day in the house. With the meat, Jules is forging a bond. As he does, Tom searches the same places Jules already has. There is very little that they don't have at the house already. He finds no phone book. No food.

Jules, knowing dogs much better than Tom, tells him that they aren't ready to leave. That the dog is too erratic, doesn't trust him yet.

Tom thinks of the twelve hours he gave the housemates for their return. A clock, it seems, is ticking.

Finally, Jules tells Tom he thinks the dog is ready to leave the house.

"Then let's get going," Tom says. "We'll have to keep working with him as we go. We can't sleep here, with this smell of death."

Jules agrees. But it takes a few attempts to leash the dog. More time passes. When Jules finally does it, Tom has decided that twelve hours be damned; one afternoon has delivered them a dog, who knows what tomorrow morning might bring.

Still, the clock *is* ticking.

In the home's foyer, they fasten their blindfolds and put their helmets back on. Then Tom unlocks the front door and they exit the house. Now Tom uses his broomstick, but Jules uses the dog. The husky pants.

Crossing the lawn again, going farther yet from Malorie, Don, Cheryl, Felix, and Olympia, they come to another house.

This one, Tom hopes, is where they'll spend the night. If the windows are protected, if a search brings them confidence, and if they aren't greeted with the smell of death.

twenty-four

The pain in Malorie's shoulder is so exact, so detailed, that she can see its outline in her mind. She can see it move as her shoulder moves. It's not a bright pain like it was when it happened. Now it's deep and dull and throbbing. Muted colors of decay rather than the explosive hues of impact. She imagines what the floor of the rowboat must look like right now. Piss. Water. Blood. The children asked her if she was okay. She told them she was. But they know when they're lied to. Malorie has trained them beyond words.

She is not crying right now, but she was. Silent tears behind her blindfold. Silent to her. But the children can pluck sounds from the silence.

Okay, guys, she used to say, sitting around the kitchen table. *Close your eyes.*

They did.

What am I doing?

You are smiling.

That's right, Girl. How did you know?

You breathe different when you smile, Mommy.

And the next day they would do it again.

You're crying, Mommy!

That's right. And why would I cry?

You're sad.

That's not the only reason.

You're scared!

That's right. Let's try another one.

Now the water is getting colder. Malorie feels its spray with each grueling row.

"Mommy," the Boy says.

"What?"

She is immediately alert at the sound of his voice.

"Are you okay?"

"You already asked me that."

"But you don't sound okay."

"I said I am. That means I am. Don't question me."

"But," the Girl says, "you're breathing differently!"

She is. She knows she is. *Laboring,* she thinks.

"It's only because of the rowing," she lies.

How many times did she question her duty as a mother as she trained the children into becoming listening machines? For Malorie, watching them develop was sometimes horrific. Like she was left to care for two mutant children. Small monsters. Creatures in their own right capable of learning how to hear a smile. Able to tell her if she was scared before she knew it herself.

The shoulder wound is bad. And for years now Malorie has feared sustaining an injury of this magnitude. There were other instances. Close calls. Falling down the cellar stairs when the children were two. Tripping while carrying a bucket back from the well, banging her head on a rock. She thought she broke her wrist once. A chipped tooth. It's difficult to remember what her legs once looked like without bruises. And now the flesh of her shoulder feels peeled from her body. She wants to stop the boat. She wants to find a hospital. Run through the streets, screaming, *I need a doctor, I need a doctor, I NEED A DOCTOR OR I'M GOING TO DIE AND THE CHILDREN WILL DIE WITHOUT ME!!*

"Mommy," the Girl says.

"What is it?"

"We're facing the wrong way."

"*What?*"

As she's grown more exhausted, she's overused her stronger arm. Now she rows against the current and didn't even know it.

Suddenly, the Boy's hand is upon hers. Malorie recoils at first, then understands. His fingers over hers, he moves, with her, as if turning the crank of the well.

In all this cold, painful world, the Boy, hearing her struggle, is helping her row.

twenty-five

The husky is licking Tom's hand. Jules snores to his left on the carpeted floor of the home's family room. Behind him, a giant silent television rests on an oak stand. Boxes of records are set against the wall. Lamps. A plaid couch. A stone fireplace. A big painting of a beach fills the space above the mantel. Tom thinks it's of northern Michigan. Above him, a dusty ceiling fan rests.

The dog is licking his hand because he and Jules feasted the night before on stale potato chips.

This house proved to be a little more fruitful than the last. The men packed a few canned goods, paper, two pairs of children's boots, two small jackets, and a sturdy plastic bucket before falling asleep. Still, no phone book. In the modern age, with cell phones in everybody's pocket, the phone book, it seems, has passed on.

There is evidence of the original homeowners deliberately leaving town. Directions to a small city in Texas at the Mexican border. A crisis survivor manual marked up in pen. Long lists of supplies that include gasoline and car parts. Receipts told Tom they'd purchased ten flashlights, three fishing poles, six knives, boxed water, propane, canned nuts, three sleeping bags, a generator, a crossbow, cooking oil, gasoline, and firewood. As the dog licks his hand, Tom thinks of Texas.

"Bad dreams," Jules says.

Tom looks over to see his friend is awake.

"Dreamed we never found our way back to the house," Jules continues. "I never saw Victor again."

"Remember the stake we stuck in the lawn," Tom says.

"I haven't forgotten it," Jules says. "Dreamed somebody took it."

Jules gets up and the men eat a breakfast of nuts. The husky gets a can of tuna.

"Let's cross the street," Tom says.

Jules agrees. The men pack up. Soon, they leave.

Outside, the grass gives way to concrete. They are in the street again. The sun is hot. The fresh air feels good. Tom is about to say as much, but Jules suddenly calls out.

"What is *this*?"

Tom, blind, turns.

"What?"

"It's a post, Tom. Like . . . I think this is a *tent*."

"In the middle of the street?"

"Yes. In the middle of *our* street."

Tom approaches Jules. The bristles of his broomstick connect with something that sounds like it's made of metal. Cautiously, he reaches into the darkness and touches what Jules found.

"I don't understand," Tom says.

Setting the broomstick down, Tom uses both hands to feel above his head, along the base of the canvas tarp. It reminds him of a street fair he once took his daughter to. The roads were blocked off by orange cones. Hundreds of artists sold paintings, sculptures, drawings. They were set up side by side, too many to count. Each of them sold their goods under a floppy canvas tent.

Tom steps under it. He uses his broom to sweep a wide arc in the air above him. There is nothing here but the four poles that support the tarp.

Military, Tom thinks. The image is a far cry from a street fair.

As a boy, Tom's mother used to brag to her friends that her son "refused to let a problem sit." *He tries to figure it out,* she'd say. *There isn't a thing in this house that doesn't interest him.* Tom remembers watching the faces of his mother's friends, how they smiled when she said these things. *Toys?* his mother would say. *Tom doesn't need toys. A tree branch is a toy. The wires behind the VCR are toys. The way the windows work.* His whole life he'd been described this way. *The kind of guy who wants to know how something works. Ask Tom. If he doesn't know, he'll learn it. He fixes things. Everything.* But to Tom, this behavior wasn't remarkable. Until he had Robin. Then a child's fascination with the machinations of things overcame him. Now, standing beneath this tent, Tom can't tell if he's like the child who wants to figure out the tent or like the father who advises him to walk away from this one.

The men examine the thing, blindly, for many minutes.

"Maybe we could use this," Tom says to Jules, but Jules is already calling him from a distance.

Tom crosses the street. He follows Jules's voice until they meet up on another lawn.

The very first house they go to is unlocked. They agree they will not open their eyes in this house. They enter.

Inside is drafty. The men know that the windows are open before they check them. Tom's broomstick tells him the first room they enter is full of boxes. These people, he thinks, were getting ready to leave.

"Jules," Tom says, "check these. I'm going to search farther into the house."

It's already been twenty-four hours since they left their own house.

Now, with carpeting beneath him, he walks slowly through a stranger's home. He comes to a couch. A chair. A television. Jules and the husky are barely audible now. Wind blows through the open windows. Tom comes to a table. He feels along its surface until his fingers stop at something.

A bowl, he thinks.

Lifting it, he hears something fall to the tabletop. He feels for it, finds it, and discovers it's a utensil he didn't expect.

It's like an ice-cream scooper, but smaller.

Tom runs a finger into the scooper. There's a thick substance in there.

He shivers. It's not ice cream. And once, Tom touched something just like it.

On the bathtub's edge. By her little wrist. The blood there was like this. Thick. Dead. Robin's blood.

Shaking, he brings the bowl closer to his chest as he sets down the scooper. He slides his fingers slowly down the smooth ceramic curve of the bowl until he touches something resting in the basin. He gasps and drops the bowl onto the carpeted floor.

"Tom?"

Tom doesn't answer at first. The thing he just touched, he once touched something like *that,* too.

Robin had brought it home from school. From science class. She kept it in an open coffee can full of pennies. Tom found it when Robin was at school. When he was searching the house for that *smell.*

He knew he'd found it when, just inside the rim of the can, atop the pile of coins, he saw a small discolored ball. Instinctively, he reached for it. It squished between his fingers.

It was a pig's eye. Dissected. Robin had mentioned doing that in class.

"Tom? What happened in there?"

Jules is calling you. Answer him.

"Tom?"

"I'm all right, Jules! I just dropped something."

Backing up, wanting to leave this room, his hand nudges something.

He knows this feeling, too.

That was a shoulder, he thinks. *There's a body sitting in a chair at this table.*

Tom imagines it. Seated. Eyeless.

At first he cannot move. He's facing where the body must be.

He hurries out of the room.

"Jules," he says, "let's get out of here."

"What happened?"

Tom tells him. Within minutes they are out of the house. They've decided to work their way back home. A dog is enough. Between the tent and what Tom found in the bowl, neither of them want to be out here anymore.

They cross one lawn. Then a driveway. Then two. The dog is pulling Jules. Tom struggles to keep up. He feels like he's getting lost out here in the darkness of his blindfold. He calls to Jules.

"I'm over here!" Jules calls.

Tom follows his voice. He catches up to him.

"Tom," Jules says. "The dog is making a big deal about this garage."

Still trembling from his discovery in the house, and still frightened, deeper, by the senselessness of the tent in the street, Tom says they should continue home. But Jules wants to know what the dog is so interested in.

"It's a freestanding garage," Jules says. "He's acting like something's alive in there."

A side door is locked. Finding only one window, Jules breaks it. He tells Tom that it's protected. Cardboard. It's a small fit, but one of them should go inside. Jules says he'll do it. Tom says he'll do it, too. They tie the dog to a gutter and both men crawl in through the window.

Once inside, something growls at them.

Tom turns back toward the window. Jules calls out.

"It sounds like another dog!"

Tom thinks it does, too. His heart is beating fast, too fast he thinks, and he stands with one hand on the window ledge, ready to pull himself back out.

"I can't believe this," Jules says.

"What?"

"It's another husky."

"*What?* How do you know?"

"Because I'm touching his face."

Tom eases from the window. He can hear the dog eating. Jules is feeding it.

Then, by Tom's elbow, there is another sound.

At first, it sounds like children laughing. Then like a song.

Then the unmistakable sound of chirping.

Birds.

Gently, Tom backs away. The chirping quiets. He steps forward again. It gets louder.

Of course, Tom thinks, feeling the excitement he'd hoped for when they left the house the day before.

As Jules talks quietly to the dog, Tom approaches the birds until their squawking is unbearable. He feels along a shelf.

"Tom," Jules says in the darkness, "be careful—"

"They're in a box," Tom says.

"What?"

"I grew up with a guy whose father was a hunter. His birds made the same sound. They get louder the closer you get to them."

Tom's hands are on the box.

He is thinking.

"Jules," he says, "let's go home."

"I'd like more time with the dog."

"You'll have to do it at home. We can lock them in a room if there's a problem. But we found what we set out to find. Let's go home."

Jules leashes the second husky. This one is less difficult. As they exit the garage by the side door, Jules asks Tom, "You're bringing the birds?"

"Yeah. I've got an idea."

Outside, they retrieve the first husky and head toward home. Jules walks with the second dog, Tom with the first. Slowly, they cross lawns, then driveways, until they reach the marker they set the day before.

On the front porch, before knocking on the door, Tom hears the housemates arguing inside. Then he thinks he hears a sound coming from the street behind him.

He turns.

He waits.

He wonders how close the tent is to where he stands.

Then he knocks.

Inside, the argument ceases. Felix calls out to him. Tom responds.

"Felix! It's Tom!"

twenty-six

*Y*ou're going to have to open your eyes . . .

"You need to eat, Girl," Malorie manages to say. Her voice is weak.

The Boy has eaten nuts from the pouch. The Girl refuses.

"If you don't eat," Malorie says between grimaces, "I'm going to stop this boat and leave you here."

Malorie feels the Girl's hand upon her back. She stops rowing and shakes some nuts out of the pouch for her. Even this hurts her shoulder.

But above the pain, a thought hovers. A truth that Malorie does not want to face.

Yes, the world behind her blindfold is an ill gray. Yes, she is worried she might be losing consciousness. But a much darker reality weaves through her myriad fears and problems, serpentine, clever. It floats, then hovers, then lands at the front lines of her imagination.

It's a thing she's been protecting, hiding, from the rest of herself all morning.

But it's been the focus of her decision making for years.

You tell yourself you've waited four years because you were afraid to lose the house forever. You tell yourself you waited four years because you wanted to train the children first. But neither of these are true. You waited four years because here, on this trip, on this river, where madmen and wolves lurk, where creatures must be near, on THIS DAY you will have to do something you haven't done outside in even longer than four years.

Today you're going to have to open your eyes.

Outside.

It's true. She knows this. She's known this forever, it seems. And what is she more frightened by—the possibility of a creature standing in her line of sight? Or the unfathomable palette of colors that will explode before her when she opens her eyes.

What does the world look like now? Will you recognize it?

Is it gray? Have the trees gone mad? The flowers, the reeds, the *sky*? Is the entire world insane? Does it battle itself? Does the Earth refute its own oceans? The wind has picked up. Has it seen something? Is it mad, too?

Think, Tom would say. *You're doing it. You're rowing. Just keep rowing. This all means that you're going to make it. You'll have to open your eyes. You can do it. Because you have to.*

Tom. Tom. Tom. Tom. Tom.

She yearns for him more now than she ever has.

Even in this newer world, here on the river, as the wind starts to howl, cold water splashes across her jeans, wild animals stalk the banks, where her body is broken, her mind is a prisoner of the grays, even here Tom comes to her as something bright, something right, something *good*.

"I'm eating," the Girl says.

This is good, too. Malorie finds the strength to encourage her.

"Well done," she says between heavy breaths.

More movement from the woods to the left. Sounds like an animal. Could be the man with the boat. Could be a creature. Could be a dozen of them. Will the rowboat interrupt a pack of hungry bears, searching for fish?

Malorie is *wounded*. The word keeps recurring. It's on a swivel, too.

Just like Tom. Just like the gray colors behind her blindfold. Just like the noises of the river and the new world. Her shoulder. Her *wound*. It's happened. The very thing people would have warned her about had there been anyone around to warn her.

Take the river if you have to, but just know you might get hurt.

Oh, I don't know if I'd do that. You might get hurt.

That's too dangerous. What would become of the children if you were to get hurt out there?

It's an animal's world now, Malorie. Don't go out there. Don't take that river.

You might get hurt.

Hurt.

HURT.

HURT!

Shannon. Think of Shannon. Hold on to her.

She tries. A memory elbows its way into the crowd of black thoughts already upon her. She remembers herself and Shannon on a hillside. It was sunny then. She shielded her eyes with her little forearm. She pointed to the sky.

It's Allan Harrison! she said, meaning a boy from class. *That cloud there looks like Allan Harrison!*

She was laughing.

Which one?

That one! Do you see it?

Shannon inched toward her on the grass. She laid her head beside Malorie's.

Yes! Haha! I see him, too! And look at that one! That one is Susan Ruth!

The sisters lay there for hours, picking out faces in the clouds. A nose was enough. An ear. Maybe the top of one had curls, like Emily Holt.

Do you remember the sky? she asks herself, still, incredibly, rowing. *It was so blue. And the sun was as yellow as it would be in a child's drawing. The grass was green. Shannon's face was pale, smooth, white. So were your hands, gesturing toward the clouds. Everywhere you looked, that day, there were colors.*

"Mommy?" the Boy says. "Mommy, are you crying?"

When you open your eyes, Malorie, you're going to see them again. Your entire world will come to light. You've seen walls and blankets. Stairs and carpet. Stains and buckets of well water. Rope, knives, an axe, chicken wire, speaker wire, and spoons. Canned goods, candles, and chairs. Tape, batteries, wood, and plaster. For years now the only thing you've been allowed to see is the faces of your housemates and the faces of your children. The same colors. The same colors. The same colors for years. YEARS. Are you prepared? And what scares you more? The creatures or yourself, as the memories of a million sights and colors come flooding toward you? What scares you more?

Malorie is rowing very slowly now. Less than half the speed she was going ten minutes ago. The water, piss, and blood slosh at her ankles. Animals or madmen or creatures move on the banks. The wind is cold. Tom is not here. Shannon is not here. The gray world behind her blindfold begins to spin, like thick sludge inching toward the drain.

She throws up.

At the last moment she worries if it's a terrible thing, what is happening to her. Passing out. What will happen to the children? Are they going to be okay if Mommy just passes out?

And that's it.

Malorie's hands fall from the oars. In her mind, Tom is watching her. The creatures are watching her, too.

Then, as the Boy is asking her something, Malorie, the captain of this little ship, passes out completely.

twenty-seven

Malorie wakes from dreams about babies. It is either early morning or very late at night, she guesses. The house is silent. The farther along in her pregnancy she gets, the more vivid her reality becomes. Both *With Child* and *At Last . . . a Baby!* briefly discuss home deliveries. It's possible, of course, to do it without help from a professional, but the books are wary of this. Cleanliness, they say. *Unforeseen circumstances.* Olympia hates reading those parts, but Malorie knows they must.

One day, the pain your mother and the pain every mother speaks of will come to you in the same form: childbirth. Only a woman can experience it and because of this all women are bonded.

Now that moment is coming. *Now.* And who will be there when it does? In the old world, the answer was easy. Shannon, of course. Mom and Dad. Friends. A nurse who would assure her she was doing fine. There would be flowers on a table. The sheets would smell fresh. She'd be doted on by people who had delivered babies before; they'd act like it was like removing a pistachio from its shell. And the ease they'd express would be exactly what calmed her impossible nerves.

But this isn't the answer anymore. Now the labor Malorie expects sounds like that of a mother wolf: brute, mean, inhuman. There will be no doctor. No nurse.

No medicine.

Oh how she imagined she'd know what to do! How prepared she thought she'd be! Magazines, websites, videos, advice from her ob-gyn, stories from other mothers. But none of this is available to her now. *None!* She's not going to give birth in a hospital, it's going to happen right here in this house. In one of the rooms of *this house*! And the most she can expect is Tom assisting while Olympia holds her hand and looks on in horror. Blankets will be covering the windows. Maybe a T-shirt will be under her ass. She'll drink from a glass of murky well water.

And that's it. That's how it's going to happen.

She shifts onto her back again. Breathing hard and slow, she stares at the ceiling. She closes her eyes, then opens them again. Can she do this? *Can she?*

She has to. And so she repeats mantras, words to get her ready.

In the end, it doesn't matter if it happens in a hospital or on the kitchen floor. Your body knows what to do. Your body knows what to do. Your body knows what to do.

The baby-to-be is all and everything that matters.

Abruptly, as if they're imitating the sound of the baby Malorie prepares for, she hears the birds cooing outside the front door. She withdraws from her thoughts and turns toward the sound. As she slowly sits up in bed, she hears a knock come from the first floor.

She freezes.

Was that the door? Is it Tom? Did somebody go outside?

She hears it again and, amazed, she sits up. She places a hand on her belly and listens.

It comes again.

Malorie slowly swings her feet to the floor and rises before crossing the room. She stops at the door, one hand on her belly, one on the wood of the frame, and listens.

Another knock. This time it's louder.

She walks to the head of the stairs and stops again.

Who is it?

Beneath her pajamas, her body feels cold. The baby moves. Malorie feels a little faint. The birds are still making noise.

Is it one of the housemates?

She reenters her bedroom and grabs a flashlight. She walks to Olympia's room and shines the beam on her bed. She is sleeping. In the room at the end of the hall, she sees Cheryl on the bed.

Malorie walks slowly down the stairs to the living room.

Tom.

Tom is asleep on the carpet. Felix is on the couch.

"Tom," Malorie says, touching his shoulder. "Tom, wake up."

Tom rolls to his stomach. Then he looks up, suddenly, at Malorie.

"Tom," she says.

"Is everything okay?"

"Someone is knocking at the front door."

"What? Now?"

"Right now."

Another knock comes. Tom turns his face toward the hall.

"Holy shit. What time is it?"

"I don't know. Late."

"Okay."

Tom gets up quickly. He pauses, as if attempting to wake up entirely, leaving his sleep on the floor. He is fully clothed. Beside where he was sleeping, Malorie sees the crude beginnings of another helmet. Tom turns on the living room lamp.

Then the two are walking toward the front door. They pause in the hall. Another series of knocks come.

"Hello?" a man says.

Malorie grabs Tom's arm. Tom turns on the hall light.

"Hello?" the man says again.

More knocks follow.

"I need to be let in!" the man says. "I have nowhere else to go. Hello?"

Finally, Tom steps toward the door. From the end of the hall, Malorie sees a shape move. It is Don.

"What's going on?" he asks.

"Someone is at the door," Tom says.

Don, hardly awake, looks confused. Then he snaps, "Well, what are you going to do about it?"

More knocks.

"I need a place to go," the voice says. "I can't handle being alone out here anymore."

"I'm going to talk to him," Tom says.

"We're not a fucking hostel, Tom," Don says.

"I'm just going to talk to him."

Then Don is walking toward them. Malorie hears shuffling from upstairs.

"If anyone is there I could—"

"Who are you?" Tom finally calls.

There is a moment of silence. Then, "Oh, thank God someone is there! My name is Gary."

"He could be bad," Don says. "He could be *mad*."

Felix and Cheryl appear at the end of the hall. They look exhausted. Jules is here now, too. The dogs are behind him.

"What's going on, Tom?"

"Hey, Gary," Tom says, "tell us a little more about yourself?"

The birds are cooing.

"Who is this?" Felix asks.

"My name is Gary, and I'm forty-six years old. I have a brown beard. I haven't opened my eyes in a long time."

"I don't like the sound of his voice," Cheryl says.

Olympia is here now.

Tom calls, "Why are you outside?"

Gary says, "I had to leave the house I was staying in. The people there were no good. A situation arose."

"What the hell does that mean?" Don calls.

Gary pauses. Then, "They got violent."

"That's not good enough," Don says to the others. "Don't open this door."

"Gary," Tom calls, "how long have you been out there?"

"Two days, I think. Could be closer to three."

"Where have you been staying?"

"Staying? On lawns. Beneath bushes."

"Fuck," Cheryl says.

"Listen," Gary says. "I'm hungry. I'm alone. And I'm very afraid. I understand your caution but I've got nowhere else to go."

"You've tried other houses?" Tom says.

"Yes! I've been knocking on doors for hours. You are the first to answer."

"How did he know we were here?" Malorie asks the others.

"Maybe he didn't," Tom says.

"He knocked for a long time. He *knew* we were here."

Tom turns to Don. His expression is asking Don what he thinks.

"No way."

Tom is sweating now.

"I'm sure *you* want to," Don continues angrily. "You're hoping he has information."

"That's right," Tom says. "I am hoping he has ideas. I'm also thinking he needs our help."

"Right. Well, I'm thinking there could be seven men out there, ready to slit all our throats."

"*God,*" Olympia says.

"Jules and I were out there two days ago," Tom says. "He's right that the other houses are empty."

"So why doesn't he sleep in one of those?"

"I don't know, Don. Food?"

"And you guys were outside at the same time. And he didn't hear you?"

"Damn it," Tom says. "I have no idea how to answer that. He could have been a street over."

"You guys didn't try those houses. How do you know he's telling the truth?"

"Let him in," Jules says.

Don faces him.

"That's not how it works in here, man."

"Then let's vote."

"Come the fuck on," Don says, fuming. "If one of us doesn't want to open the fucking door, we shouldn't open the fucking door."

Malorie thinks of the man on the porch. In her imagination, his eyes are closed. He is trembling.

The birds still coo.

"Hello?" Gary says again. He sounds strained, impatient.

"Yeah," Tom says. "I'm sorry, Gary. We're still talking this over." Then he turns to the others. "Vote," he says.

"Yes," Felix says.

Jules nods.

"I'm sorry," Cheryl says. "No."

Tom looks to Olympia. She shakes her head no.

"I hate to do this to you, Malorie," he says, "but it's a tie. What are we going to do?"

Malorie doesn't want to answer. She doesn't want this power. This stranger's fate has been dumped at her feet.

"Maybe he needs help," she says. Yet, the moment after saying it, she wishes she didn't.

Tom turns to the door. Don reaches across and grabs his wrist.

"I don't want that door opened," he hisses.

"Don," Tom says, slowly pulling his wrist from Don's hand, "we voted. We're going to let him in. Just like we let Olympia and Malorie in. Just like George let you and me in."

Don stares at Tom for what feels to Malorie like a very long time. Will it come to blows this time?

"Listen to me," Don says. "If something bad comes from this, if my life is put in danger because of a fucking vote, I'm not going to stop to help you guys on my way out of this house."

"Don," Tom says.

"Hello?" Gary calls.

"Keep your eyes closed!" Tom yells. "We're letting you in."

Tom's hand is on the doorknob.

"Jules, Felix," Tom says, "use the broomsticks. Cheryl, Malorie, you'll need to get up close to him, feel him. Okay? Now, everybody, close your eyes."

In the darkness, Malorie hears the door open.

There is silence. Then Gary speaks.

"Is the door open?" he says eagerly.

"*Hurry,*" Tom says.

Malorie hears shuffling. The front door closes. She steps forward.

"Keep your eyes closed, Gary," she says.

She reaches for him, finds him, and brings her fingers to his face. She feels his nose, his cheeks, the sockets of his eyes. She touches his shoulders and asks for one of his hands.

"This is new to me," he says. "What are you searching—"

"*Shhh!*"

She feels his hands and counts his fingers. She feels the fingernails and the light hair on the knuckles.

"Okay," Felix says. "I think he's alone."

"Yes," Jules says. "He's alone."

Malorie opens her eyes.

She sees a man, much older than herself, with a brown beard and a tweed blazer over a black sweater. He smells like he's been outside for weeks.

"Thank you," he says, breathless.

At first, nobody responds. They only watch him.

His brown hair, combed over to the side, is unruly. He is both older and heavier-set than any of the housemates. In his hand is a brown briefcase.

"What's in there?" Don asks.

Gary looks to the case as though he'd forgotten he carried it.

"My things," he says. "What things I grabbed on my way out."

"What things?" Don asks.

Gary, looking both surprised and sympathetic, opens the case. He turns it toward the housemates. Papers. A toothbrush. A shirt. A watch.

Don nods.

As Gary closes the case he notices Malorie's belly. "Oh my," he says. "You're close, aren't you?"

"Yes," she says coolly, not knowing yet if they can trust this man.

"What are the birds for?" he asks.

"Warning," Tom says.

"Of course," Gary says. "Canaries in the mines. That's very clever of you. I heard them as I approached."

Then Tom invites Gary farther into the house. The dogs smell him. In the living room, Tom points to the easy chair.

"You can sleep there tonight," he says. "It reclines. Do you need something to eat?"

"Yes," Gary says, relieved.

Tom leads him through the kitchen and into the dining room.

"We keep the canned goods in the cellar. I'll get you something."

Tom quietly motions for Malorie to follow him into the kitchen. She does.

"I'm going to stay awake with him for a while," Tom says. "Get some sleep if you want to. Everybody's exhausted. It's okay. I'll get him some food, some water, and we'll talk to him tomorrow. All of us."

"There's no way I'm going to bed right now," Malorie says.

Tom smiles, tired.

"Okay."

He heads for the cellar. Malorie joins the others in the dining room. When Tom returns, he brings canned peaches.

"I never would have thought," Gary says, "that one day the world's most valuable tool would be a can opener."

Everybody is at the dining room table together. Tom asks Gary questions. How did he survive out there? Where did he sleep? It's clear that Gary is exhausted. Eventually, one by one, and beginning with Don, the housemates go to their bedrooms. As Tom walks Gary back into the living room, Malorie and Olympia rise from the table. On the stairs, Olympia puts her hand over Malorie's.

"Malorie," she says, "do you mind if I sleep with you tonight?"

Malorie turns to her.

"No," she says. "I don't mind at all."

twenty-eight

It is the next morning. Malorie gets up and gets dressed. It sounds like everyone is downstairs.

"Did you have electricity as well?" Felix is asking as Malorie enters the living room.

Gary is sitting on the couch. Seeing Malorie, he smiles.

"This," Gary says, fanning a hand toward her, "is the angel who felt my features when I entered. I have to admit, the human contact nearly made me cry."

Malorie thinks Gary talks a little like an actor. Theatrical flourishes.

"And so did a vote really decide my fate?" Gary asks.

"Yes," Tom says.

Gary nods.

"In the house I came from, no such courtesies were extended. If someone had an idea, they went with it, rather vigorously, whether or not everybody approved. It's refreshing to meet people who have retained some of the civility of our former lives."

"I voted against it," Don says abruptly.

"Did you?" Gary asks.

"Yes. I did. Seven people under one roof is enough."

"I understand."

One of the huskies gets up and goes to Gary. Gary rubs the fur behind its ears.

Tom begins explaining to him the same things he once explained to
Malorie. Hydroelectricity. The supplies in the cellar. The lack of a phone
book. How George died. After a while, Gary begins talking about a former housemate of his. A "troubled man" who didn't believe the creatures were harmful at all.

"He believed that the people's reaction to them was psychosomatic.
In other words, all this insanity fuss isn't caused by the creatures at all,
but rather by the dramatic people who see them."

Insanity fuss, Malorie thinks. Do these two dismissive words belong
to Gary's former housemate?

Or are they Gary's?

"I'd like to tell you guys about my experience at my former place,"
Gary continues. "But I warn you, it's a dark one."

Malorie wants to hear this. They all do. Gary runs his fingers through
his hair. Then he begins.

"There was no ad that we answered and we weren't as young as you
all. We had no communal sensibility, no group effort. My brother Duncan has a friend who took the Russia Report very seriously. He was
one of the early believers. It went well with his conspiracy theories and
paranoia that the government or *somebody* is out to get us all. As goes
myself, I *still* have moments where I can't believe it's happening. And
who can blame me? I'm over forty years old. So used to the life I was living, I never fathomed one like this. I resisted it. But Kirk, my brother's
friend, was certain of it from the very start. And nothing, it seemed,
would sway him. One afternoon Duncan called and told me Kirk suggested we gather at his place for a few days, or until we learned more
about this 'thing.'

" 'What thing?' I asked.

" 'Gary, it's all over the television.'

"'What thing, Duncan? The thing that happened in Russia? You can't be serious.'

"'C'mon,' Duncan said. 'We'll throw back some beers, eat some pizza, and humor him. You've got nothing to lose.'

"I told him no thank you. Hanging out with crazy Kirk as he analyzed sensational stories didn't sound like a good time to me. But I showed up soon enough.

"I'd heard the reports just like everybody in the country did. They started to worry me. There were just so many of them. Still, I foolishly attempted to maintain my disbelief. These kinds of things just don't happen. But then came a report that forced me to take action. It was the one about the sisters in Alaska. You might be wondering why it took me so long to be convinced. Alaska was relatively late, but Alaska was also an American report and I'm just provincial enough not to worry until it happens close to home. Even the reporter was clearly scared of what he was saying. Yes, even the man delivering the news did so trembling.

"You know the story. A woman saw her two elderly neighbors, sisters, leaving the house. She assumed they had gone for their daily walk. Three hours later, she heard on the radio that the sisters were in front of the hospital, crouched on the stone steps, trying to bite people as they passed. The woman drove to the hospital, fancying herself closer to the sisters than anyone else and likely able to help. But that wasn't the case. And the photos on CNN showed the woman with her face removed, literally on the sidewalk beside her bloody skull. Beyond her were the two old ladies, dead, shot by the police. That image chilled me. Such normal people. Such everyday environs.

"For Kirk, the Alaskan incident validated all paranoid fantasies. Despite my own growing fear, I wasn't ready to exchange the life I'd known for this new, militia-like existence he was espousing. I was prepared to drape the windows, lock the doors, and hide, but Kirk was already coming up with plans to combat what he believed was an 'invasion'—whether that be alien or otherwise was never clear. He talked about weapons, gear, and guns like a veteran soldier. Of course he wasn't one; he'd never enlisted in anything in his life."

Gary pauses. He seems to ponder.

"Soon the house was crowded with quasi-militant males. Kirk was enjoying his newfound position of general, and I watched a lot of the buffoonery from the sidelines. I made a habit of letting Duncan know he ought to keep his distance. A man like Kirk was liable to send his friends into harm's way. The men grew increasingly contentious, juiced with the fantasy of overthrowing the villains of Kirk's 'invasion.' Days passed, and yet nothing came of their boisterous claims that they would protect the city, eliminate the cause of this global madness, and secure their place in history as the band who fixed the 'big problem.' Yet, there was one man in the house who took action for what he believed. His name was Frank, and Frank believed that the creatures Kirk prepared for were no threat at all. Still, he came to the house, fearful, he admitted, of the inevitable lawlessness that could sweep the country.

"As Kirk planned useless daily drills, Frank became something of a shut-in, hardly leaving the bedroom on the second floor. And in there, he wrote. Day and night Frank wrote with pencil, pen, marker, and makeup. One day, walking the upstairs hall, I heard something behind his closed door. It was a furious sound, laborious, angry, unflagging in its pace. I eased the door open a crack and saw him hunched over a desk, whispering about the 'cultish, overreactive' society he loathed as he scribbled. I had no way of knowing what he was writing. But I wanted to find out.

"I talked to Duncan about it. My brother's face was painted with ridiculous camouflage. By then he was truly infected with Kirk's ravings. He didn't believe Frank was a threat. Frank who bugled phrases like *mass hysteria* and *psychosomatic idolatry* as Kirk and the others pantomimed target practice, weaponless, in the basement. Everyone dismissed Frank as a useless pacifist."

Gary runs his hands through his hair again.

"I set out to find out what Frank was up to in his room. I began looking for an opportunity to read his secret writings.

"What do you think would happen to a man who is already mad if he were to see the creatures outside? Do you think he'd be impervious to it, his mind already fractured? Or do you suppose his madness would reach another, higher echelon of insane? Perhaps the mentally ill will inherit this new world, unable to be broken any more than they already are. I don't know any better than you do."

Gary sips from a glass of water.

"My moment presented itself in this way. Kirk and the others were occupied in the basement. Frank was in the bath. I made my decision to snoop quickly. I entered his room and found his writings in the desk drawer. This was no little feat, as, by then, I was frightened of the man. The others may have dismissed him, found him laughable, but I suspected more brutish possibilities therein. I began reading. Soon I was overwhelmed with his words. No matter how long ago Frank had begun writing, it seemed impossible that he had already written this much. *Dozens* of notebooks, all in various colors, each more angry than the last. Tiny cursive couplets were followed by giant highlighted phrases, all declaring that the creatures were not to be feared. He referred to the rest of us as 'those with small minds' who 'needed to be exterminated.' He was dangerous, indeed. Suddenly, hearing him rise from the bath, I hurried out of his room. Maybe Duncan wasn't so wrong to fall in with Kirk. Those notebooks showed me there were much worse reactions to the new world than his."

Gary breathes deep. He wipes his lips with the back of his hand.

"When we woke up the next day, the drapes had been pulled down."

Cheryl gasps.

"The doors were unlocked."

Don starts to say something.

"And Frank was gone. He'd taken the notebook with him."

"Oh fuck," Felix says.

Gary nods.

"Was anybody hurt?" Tom asks.

Gary's eyes grow watery, but he maintains himself.

"No," he says. "Nobody. Which I'm sure Frank would have included in his notes."

Malorie brings a hand to her belly.

"Why did you leave?" Don asks impatiently.

"I left," Gary says, "because Kirk and the others talked at great length of tracking Frank down. They wanted to kill him for what he had done."

The room is quiet.

"I knew then I had to get out. That house was ruined. Plagued. Yours, it seems, is not. For this," Gary says, looking at Malorie, "I thank you for taking me in."

"I didn't let you in," Malorie says. "We all did."

What kind of man, she wonders, *would leave his brother behind?*

She looks to Don. To Cheryl. To Olympia. Has Gary's story endeared him to those who voted not to let him in? Or has it justified their fears?

Insanity fuss.

Tom and Felix are asking Gary questions about his story. Jules pipes in, too. But Cheryl has left the room. And Don, who has something to say about everything, isn't speaking much. He just stares.

A divide, Malorie thinks, *is growing.*

Exactly when it began doesn't matter to her. It's visible now. Gary brought with him a briefcase. A story. And, somehow, a divide.

twenty-nine

Malorie wakes with her eyes closed. It's not as difficult to do as it once was. Consciousness comes. The sounds, sensations, and smells of life. Sights, too. Malorie knows that, even with your eyes closed, there *is* sight. She sees peaches, yellows, the colors of distant sunlight penetrating flesh. At the corners of her vision are grays.

It sounds like she's outside. She feels cool open air on her face. Chapped lips. Dry throat. When is the last time she drank? Her body feels okay. Rested. There is a dull throbbing coming from somewhere to the left of her neck. Her shoulder. She brings her right hand to her forehead. When her fingers touch her face, she understands they are wet and dirty. In fact, her whole back feels wet. Her shirt is drenched in water.

A bird sings overhead. Eyes still closed, Malorie turns toward it.

The children are breathing hard. It sounds like they are working on something.

Are they drawing? Building? Playing?

Malorie sits up.

"Boy?"

Her first thought sounds like a joke. An impossibility. A mistake. Then she realizes it's exactly what's happening.

They're breathing hard because they're rowing.

"*Boy!*" Malorie yells. Her voice sounds bad. Like her throat is made of wood.

"Mommy!"

"What is going on?!"

The rowboat. The rowboat. The rowboat. You're on the river. You passed out. You PASSED OUT.

Hooking her lame shoulder over the edge, she cups a handful of water and brings it to her mouth. Then she is on her knees, over the edge, scooping handfuls in quick succession. She is breathing hard. But the grays have gone away. And her body feels a little better.

She turns to the children.

"How long? *How long?*"

"You fell asleep, Mommy," the Girl says.

"You had bad dreams," the Boy says.

"You were crying."

Malorie's mind is moving too fast. Did she miss anything?

"*How long?*" she yells again.

"Not long," the Boy says.

"Are your blindfolds on? *Speak!*"

"Yes," they say.

"The boat got stuck," the Girl says.

Dear God, Malorie thinks.

Then she calms herself enough to ask, "How did we get unstuck?"

She finds the Girl's small body. She follows her arms to her hands. Then she reaches across the rowboat and feels for the Boy.

They're each using one paddle. They're rowing together.

"We did it, Mommy!" the Girl says.

Malorie is on her knees. She realizes she smells bad. Like a bar. Like a bathroom.

Like vomit.

"We untangled us," the Boy says.

Malorie is with him now. Her shaking hands are upon his.

"I'm hurt," she says out loud.

"What?" the Boy asks.

"I need you two to move back to where you were before Mommy fell asleep. Right now."

The children stop rowing. The Girl presses against her as she goes to the back bench. Malorie helps her.

Then Malorie is sitting on the middle bench again.

Her shoulder is throbbing but it's not as bad as it was before. She needed rest. She wasn't giving it to her body. So her body took it.

In the fog of her waking mind, Malorie is growing colder, more frightened. *What if it happens again?*

Have they passed the point they are traveling to?

The paddles in her hands again, Malorie breathes deeply before rowing.

Then she starts to cry. She cries because she passed out. She cries because a wolf attacked her. She cries for too many reasons to locate. But she knows part of it is because she's discovered that the children are capable of surviving, if only for a moment, on their own.

You've trained them well, she thinks. The thought, often ugly, makes her proud.

"Boy" she says, through her tears, "I need you to listen again. Okay?"

"I am, Mommy!"

"And you, Girl, I need you to do the same."

"I am, too!"

Is it possible, Malorie thinks, *that we're okay? Is it possible that you passed out and woke up and still everything is okay?*

It doesn't feel true. Doesn't go with the rules of the new world. Something is out there on this river with them. Madmen. Beasts. Creatures. How much more sleep would have lured them all the way into the boat?

Mercifully, she is rowing again. But what lurks feels closer now.

"I'm so sorry," she says, crying, rowing.

Her legs are soaked with piss, water, blood, and vomit. But her body is rested. Somehow, Malorie thinks, despite the cruel laws of this unforgiving world, she's been delivered a break.

The feeling of relief lasts the duration of one row. Then Malorie is alert, and scared, all over again.

thirty

Cheryl is upset.

Malorie hears her talking to Felix in the room down the hall. The other housemates are downstairs. Gary has taken to sleeping in the dining room, despite the hard wood floors. Since his arrival, two weeks ago, Don has warmed up to him greatly. Malorie doesn't know how she feels about that. He's probably with Gary now.

But down the hall, Cheryl whispers hurriedly. She sounds scared. It feels like everybody is. More than usual. The mood in the house, once supported mightily by Tom's optimism, gets darker every day. Sometimes, Malorie thinks, the mood extends deeper than fear. That's how Cheryl sounds right now. Malorie considers joining them, perhaps even to comfort Cheryl, but decides against it.

"I do it every day, Felix, because I like to do it. It's my job. And the few minutes I step outside are precious to me. It reminds me that I once had a *real* job. One I woke up for. One I took pride in. Feeding the birds is the only thing I have that connects me to the life I used to live."

"And it gives you a chance to be outside."

"And it gives me a chance to be outside, yes."

Cheryl tries to control her voice, then goes on.

She is outside, she tells Felix, ready to feed the birds. She is feeling along the wall for the box. In her right hand are apple slices from a can in the cellar. The front door has closed behind her. Jules waits inside. Blindfolded, Cheryl walks slowly, using the house for balance. The bricks are coarse against her fingertips. Soon they will give way to a portion of wood paneling from which a metal hook protrudes. This is where the birds hang.

They are already cooing. They always do when she gets this close. Cheryl heartily volunteered to feed the birds when discussion of the chore came up. She's been doing it every day since. In a way, it feels like the birds are her own. She speaks to them, filling them in on trivial events from the house. Their sweet response calms her like music once did. She can gauge how close she is to the box, she tells Felix, by how loudly they sing.

But this time she hears something besides their coos.

At the end of the front walk she hears an "abandoned step." It's the only way she can explain it to Felix. It sounds to her like someone was walking, was planning to walk farther, then suddenly stopped.

Cheryl, always on high alert whenever she feeds the birds, is surprised to realize she is trembling.

She says, "Is anybody there?"

There is no answer.

She thinks of returning to the front door. She'll tell the others she's too freaked out to do this today.

Instead, she waits.

And there is no further sound.

In the box, the birds are active. She calls to them nervously.

"Hey hey, guys. Hey hey."

The quiver in her voice scares her. Instinctively, she lowers her head and raises the hand holding the apples to protect her, as though something were about to touch her face. She takes a step. Then another. Finally, she reaches the box. Sometimes, she tells Felix, the walk between the front door and the box is like floating in outer space. Anchorless.

Today she feels impossibly far from land.

"Hey hey," she says, opening the box's lid just enough to be able to drop a few of the apple slices. Normally she hears the pitter-patter of their tiny feet as they rush for the food. Today she does not.

"Eat up, guys. Aren't you hungry?"

She opens the lid the tiniest bit again and drops the remaining pieces inside. This, she tells Felix, is always her favorite part. When she closes the lid and presses her ear to the box, listening to their tiny bodies as they eat.

But they do not start eating. Instead, they anxiously coo.

"Hey hey," Cheryl says, trying to shake off the tremble in her voice. "Eat up, guys."

She takes her ear from the box, thinking her presence today is making them shy. As she does, she shrieks.

Something has touched her shoulder.

Spinning, blind, Cheryl waves her arms wildly. She touches nothing.

She can't move her legs. She can't run inside. Something touched her shoulder and she does not know what it was.

The voices of the birds no longer sound sweet. They sound like what Tom wanted them to be.

An alarm.

"Who's there?"

She worries someone will answer. She doesn't want someone to answer.

She decides to yell. One of the housemates can come get her. Pull her back to Earth. But as she takes a step, she hears a leaf crushed beneath her shoe. Frantically, she tries to recall the first time she arrived at the house. She looked at it through the window of her car. Was there a tree? Here by the front walk?

Was there?

Maybe it was only a falling leaf that grazed her.

It would be so easy to find out. If she could just open her eyes for a moment she could see she was alone. She could see it was just a leaf. Nothing more.

But she can't.

Shaking, she presses her back to the house and slowly slides toward the front door. Her head swivels left, then right, at the slightest sounds. A bird high in the sky. The rustling in a tree across the street. A small gust of warm wind. Sweating, she feels the brick at last and hurriedly makes it to the door.

"Jesus," Felix says. "Do you really think it could have been a leaf?"

She pauses. Malorie leans farther into the hall.

"Yes," Cheryl suddenly says. "I do. Playing it back. That's exactly what it was."

Malorie steps back into her bedroom and sits upon the bed.

Felix's story about the well and what he heard out there. Victor barking at the blanketed windows. Cheryl with the birds.

Is it possible, Malorie wonders, that the world out there and the things they hide from are closing in?

thirty-one

To Malorie, since the arrival of Gary, the house feels absolutely different, divided. It's a small change, but under these circumstances, any change is a big one.

And it's Don who worries her the most.

More often than not, when Tom, Jules, and Felix are talking in the living room, Don is in the dining room with Gary. He's expressed a heavy interest in the story about the man who took down the drapes and unlocked the doors. While washing clothes in the kitchen sink, halfway through the second-to-last jug of detergent, Malorie listens to two conversations at once. While Tom and Jules are turning long-sleeved shirts into dog leashes, Gary is explaining to Don the way Frank thought. Always the way Frank thought. Never quite what Gary thinks himself.

"I don't think it's a matter of one man being better prepared than another," Gary is saying. "I think of it more like a 3-D movie. At first, the audience thinks the objects are really coming at them. They hold their hands up for protection. But the intelligent ones, the ones who are very aware, know they were safe all along."

Don has come full circle with Gary. Malorie thinks she saw it when it happened.

Hey, I don't think that theory is any more cracked than ours, Don said to him once.

"It's hard," Don says now, "because we don't get any new reports."

"Exactly."

Yes, Don has gone from voting against letting Gary in, to being the one housemate who sits with him and talks. And talks. And talks.

He's skeptical, Malorie thinks. *That's his nature. And he's needed someone to talk to. That's all this means. He's different than you are. Don't you understand?*

But these thoughts, just as they are, aren't taking root. No matter how she perceives it, Gary and Don are talking about things like hysteria and the idea that the creatures can't cause harm to someone who is prepared to see them. Don, she knows, has long espoused a greater fear of man than creatures. Yet, he closes his eyes when the front door opens and closes. He does not look out the window. He has never *committed* to the idea that the creatures cannot hurt us. Could someone like Gary convince him at last?

She wants to talk to Tom about it. She wants to pull him aside and ask him to make them stop. Or at least go and talk with them. Maybe his words will influence their conversation. Make it sound safer.

Yes, she wants to talk to Tom about Don.

Division.

With trepidation, she crosses the kitchen and looks into the living room. Tom and Felix are reading a map on the floor. They are measuring distances according to the map's mileage scale. Jules is teaching the dogs commands.

Stop. Start again.

"We have to measure what is an average step for *you*," Felix says.

"What are you guys planning?" Malorie asks.

Tom turns to her.

"Distance," he says. "How many of my steps are in a mile."

Felix is using the measuring tape at Tom's feet.

"If I listen to music as I go," Tom says, "I could walk in rhythm with it. That way the steps we measure in here would be close to the ones I take out there."

"Like dancing," Felix says.

Malorie turns to see Olympia is now at the kitchen sink. She washes utensils. Malorie joins her and continues washing the clothes. After being confined to this house for almost four months, Olympia has lost a little of her shine. Her skin is pale. Her eyes deeper set.

"Are you worried?" Olympia suddenly asks.

"About what?"

"About making it."

"Making what?"

"Surviving our deliveries."

Malorie wants to tell Olympia that it's going to be okay but she struggles to locate the words. She is thinking about Don.

"I've always wanted a baby," Olympia says. "I was so excited when I found out. I felt like my life was complete. You know?"

This is not how Malorie felt but she says yes, she knows.

"Oh, Malorie, *who* is going to deliver our babies?"

Malorie doesn't know.

"Our housemates, I don't see—"

"But Tom's never done it before!"

"No. But he was a father."

Olympia stares at her hands, submerged in the bucket.

"I'll tell you what," Malorie says facetiously, "we'll deliver each other's."

"Deliver each other's!" Olympia says, smiling at last. "Malorie, you're too much!"

Gary enters the kitchen. He scoops a glass of water from a bucket on the counter. Then he scoops a second glass. Malorie knows it's for Don. As he exits, music suddenly comes from the living room. Malorie leans back so she can see in there. Tom holds the small battery-operated radio. It's one of George's cassette tapes. Felix, on his hands and knees, measures Tom's steps as he walks in rhythm to the song.

"What are they doing?" Olympia asks.

"I think they have somewhere specific in mind to go," Malorie says. "They're trying to come up with a better way of traveling outside."

Malorie quietly steps to the dining room's entrance. Peering in, she sees Don and Gary, their backs to her, sitting in dining room chairs. They are speaking quietly.

Again she crosses the kitchen. As she enters the living room, Tom is smiling. He has a leash in each hand. The huskies are playing with them, wagging their tails.

The discrepancy between the bright, progressive actions of those in the living room and the hushed conspiratorial tones of those in the dining room is all Malorie can think about.

She steps to the sink again and begins washing. Olympia is talking but Malorie is thinking of something else. She leans forward and is able to see Gary's shoulder. Beyond him, propped against the wall, is the only item he brought in with him from the outside world.

His briefcase.

He showed them the contents when he entered the house. Don asked him to. But did she get a good look at them? Did any of the housemates?

"And stop!" Tom says. Malorie turns to see the dogs and he are in the entranceway to the kitchen. The huskies both sit. Tom rewards them with raw meat.

Malorie keeps washing. She is thinking of the briefcase.

thirty-two

She has known this was coming. How could she not? All the signs have been there since they returned with the dogs. Tom and Jules have been training them ten, twelve hours a day. Using the house, then the yard. Seeing Eye dogs. The box of birds hanging outside works like an alarm. Just like Tom said it would. The birds cooed when Gary arrived. They sing when Cheryl feeds them. So, it was only a matter of time before Tom declared he was going to use the Seeing Eye dogs to enter the new world once again.

But this time it's worse. Because this time he's going farther.

They were gone two days for one block. When will we see them again if they go three miles?

Three miles. That's how far it is to Tom's house. That's where he wants to go.

"It's the only place I can be a hundred percent sure of," he said. "I've got supplies there. We need them. Band-Aids. Neosporin. Aspirin. Bandages."

Malorie's spirit rose with the mention of medicine. But Tom outside, and for that long, is too much for her to support.

"Don't worry," Felix said that same night. "We've mapped it out to a T. Tom and Jules are going to walk to the rhythm of a song. A single song. It's called 'Halfway to Paradise' by a guy named Tony Light. They'll bring the radio and play it over and over as they follow the directions we've figured out. We know how many steps it will take for each direction, for every portion of the trip."

"So you're planning on dancing there?" Gary said. "How nice."

"Not dancing," Tom said aggressively. "Walking to get help."

"Tom," Cheryl said, "you can practice this all you want, but if your steps are a half an inch longer out there, you're going to be off. You'll get lost. And how the fuck are you going to get back then? You won't."

"We will," Tom said.

"And it's not like we're helpless if we get lost," Jules added. "We need the supplies. You know this better than most, Cheryl. You took stock last."

Yes, this day has been coming. But Malorie doesn't like it at all.

"Tom," she said, pulling him aside, just before he and Jules left this morning. "I don't think the house could stand it if you didn't come back."

"We're going to come back."

"I understand that you think you will," Malorie said, "but I don't think you realize how much the house needs you."

"Malorie," he said, as Jules called that he was ready to go, "the house needs all of us."

"Tom."

"Don't let the nerves get to you like they did last time. Instead, lean on the fact that we came back last time. We'll do it again. And this time, Malorie, act as a leader. Help them when they get scared."

"Tom."

"You need the medicine, Malorie. Sterilization. You're close."

It was clear that Tom was on a path of his own, prepared to repeatedly risk his life in the name of advancing life in the house.

Last time they came back with children's shoes, she reminded herself.

And she reminds herself again of this, now. Now that Tom and Jules are gone, embarking on a three-mile walk into the most dangerous landscape the world has known.

They left this morning. Felix went over the map with them once more. Gary encouraged them. Olympia gave them a Petoskey stone she said had always been good luck for her. But Malorie did not say a word. As the front door closed for the second time on Tom, Malorie did not call to him. She did not hug him. She did not say good-bye.

It pains her now, only hours after their exit.

Yet, the few words Tom spoke to her before leaving are working. Without him here, the house needs a guiding force. A person who can remain calm among so much anxiety, so much justifiable fear.

But it's hard. The housemates are not in the mood for optimism.

Cheryl points out that the chances of encountering a creature are obviously much greater on a three-mile walk than they are over a two-block circle. She reminds those still in the house that nobody knows how animals are affected. What will happen to Tom and Jules if the huskies see something this time? Will they be eaten? Or worse?

Cheryl isn't the only one espousing dark possibilities.

Don is suggesting an alternate group prepare themselves to leave in the event Tom and Jules do not return. *We need more food,* he says. *Whether they make it back or not.*

Olympia says she has a headache. She says it means a big storm is coming. And a storm has to alter Felix's measurements when Tom and Jules are forced to find cover.

Cheryl agrees.

Don is heading into the cellar to take his "own look" at the stock, to find out exactly what they need and where to go to get it.

Olympia is talking about lightning and being out in the open.

Cheryl is debating with Felix about the map. She's saying maps don't mean anything anymore.

Don is talking about sleeping arrangements.

Olympia is describing a tornado from her youth.

Cheryl and Felix are getting heated.

Olympia sounds a little hysterical.

Don is getting mad.

Malorie, sick of the growing panic, speaks up at last.

"Everybody," she says, "we have things we could be doing. Right here in this house. We need to prepare dinner. The shit bucket hasn't been brought out all day. The cellar could be arranged better than it is. Felix, you and I could check the yard for tools, something we might have missed. Something we could use. Cheryl, you've got to feed the birds. Gary, Don, why not make phone calls. Call every combination of numbers. Who knows who you might reach. Olympia, it'd be really helpful if you washed the bedding. We did it a week ago, but with as little as we wash ourselves in this place, it's the little things, like cleaner sheets, that make it bearable."

The housemates look at Malorie like she's a stranger. For a moment, she feels embarrassed for asserting herself. But then, it works.

Gary quietly walks to the telephone. Cheryl goes to the cellar door.

You're close, Tom said to her before he left.

She thinks of this, as the housemates busy themselves with their chores, as Malorie and Felix go to get their blindfolds, she thinks of the things Tom and Jules might return with. Is there anything they could bring, *anything,* that would lead to a better life for her baby?

Picking up a blindfold, Malorie hopes.

thirty-three

The river is going to split into four channels, the man told her. *The one you want is the second one from the right. So you can't hug the right bank and expect to make it. It's tricky. And you're going to have to open your eyes.*

Malorie is rowing.

And this is how you'll know when that time comes, the man told her. *You'll hear a recording. A voice. We can't sit by the river all day. It's just too dangerous. Instead, we've got a speaker there. The recording will be playing on a loop. You'll hear it. It's loud. Clear. And when you do, that's when you'll have to open your eyes.*

The pain in her shoulder comes in waves. The children, hearing her groans, offer help.

In her first year alone with the children, Tom's voice came to her all the time. So many of his ideas were only spoken, never achieved. Malorie, with nothing but time on her hands, tried out many of them.

We ought to mic the yard, he once said.

Tom's idea of updating the alarm system from birds to amplifiers. Malorie, alone with two newborns, wanted those microphones.

But how? How would she get her hands on microphones, amplifiers, and cords?

We can drive somewhere, Tom once said.

That's madness, Don answered.

No, it's not. Drive slow. The streets are empty. What's the worst that can happen?

Malorie, rowing, remembers a definitive moment at the bathroom mirror. She'd seen other faces in the glass. Olympia. Tom. Shannon. All of them were pleading, telling her to leave the house, to do *something* more for the further safety of these kids. She was going to have to take a risk on her own. Tom and Jules weren't here to do it for her.

Tom's voice back then. Always Tom's voice. In her head. In the room. In the mirror.

Make a bumper around Cheryl's Wagoneer. Paint the windows black. Don't worry about what you run into. Just go. Drive five, six miles an hour. You have babies in the house now, Malorie. You have to know if something is out there. If something is near. The microphones will let you know that.

Leaving the bathroom, she went to the kitchen. There she studied the map Felix, Jules, and Tom once used to plan a route to Tom's house on foot. Their notes were still on it. Felix's calculations. Using the scale, she made her own.

She wanted Tom's advanced alarm system. She needed it. Yet, despite her newfound determination, she still didn't know where to go.

Late one evening, while the babies slept, she sat at the kitchen table and tried to remember her very first drive to the house. It had been less than a year ago. Back then, her mind was on the address from the ad. But what did she pass along the way?

She tried to remember.

A Laundromat.

That's good. What else?

Storefronts were empty. It looked like a ghost town and you were worried the people who placed the ad might no longer be there. You thought they'd either gone mad or packed up the car and driven far away.

Yes, all right. What else?

A bakery.

Good. What else?

What else?

Yes.

A bar.

Good. What did the marquee boast?

I don't know. That's a ridiculous question!

You don't remember the sadness you felt at the name of . . . the name of . . .

Of what?

The name of the band?

The band?

You read the name of a band slated to perform on a date already two weeks past. What was it?

I'll never remember the name of the band.

Right, but the feeling?

I don't remember.

Yes, you do. The feeling.

I was sad. I was scared.

What'd they do there?

What?

At the bar. What'd they do there?

I don't know. They drank. They ate.

Yes. What else?

They danced?

They danced.

Yes.

And?

And what?

How did they dance?

I don't know.

What did they dance to?

They danced to music. They danced to the band.

Malorie brought a hand to her forehead and smiled.

Right. They danced to the band.

And the band needed microphones. The band needed amplifiers.

Tom's ideas lingered in the house like ghosts.

Just like we did it, Tom might say. *Just like the time Jules and I took a walk around the block. You weren't able to partake in a lot of those activities, Malorie, but you can now. Jules and I rounded up dogs and later used them to walk to my house. Think about that, Malorie. It all kind of happened in a row, each step allowed the next step to happen. All because we weren't stagnant. We took risks. Now you've got to do the same. Paint the windshield black.*

Don had laughed when Tom suggested driving blind.

But it's exactly what she did.

Victor, *he* would help her. Jules once refused to let him be used like that. But Malorie had two newborns in a room down the hall. The rules were different now. Her body still ached from the delivery. The muscles in her back were always tight. If she moved too quickly, it felt like her groin might snap. She got exhausted easily. She never had the rest a new mother deserves.

Victor, she thought then, *he will protect you.*

She painted the windshield black with the paint from the cellar. She taped socks and sweaters to the inside of the glass. Using wood glue found in the garage, and duct tape from the cellar, she fastened blankets and mattresses to the bumpers. All this in the street. All this blindfolded. All this while enduring the pain of being a new mother, punished, it seemed, with every movement of her body.

She would have to leave them. She would go on her own.

She would drive a quarter of a mile in the opposite direction from which she arrived. She'd turn left and go four miles. Then a right, and another two and a half. She'd have to search for the bar from there. She'd bring food for Victor. He would guide her back to the car, back to the food, when she needed him to.

Five or six miles an hour sounded reasonable. Safe enough.

But the first time she tried it, she discovered just how hard it would be.

Despite the precautions, driving without seeing was horrifying. The Wagoneer bounced violently as she ran things over she'd never be able to identify. Twenty times she struck the curb. Twice she hit poles. Once, a parked car. It was pure, horrible suspense. With every click of the odometer, she expected a collision, an injury. Tragedy. By the time she returned home, her nerves were shattered. She was empty-handed and unconvinced she had the mettle to try it again.

But she did.

She found the Laundromat on the seventh try. And because she remembered it from her first drive to the house, it gave her the courage to try again. Blindfolded and scared, she entered a boot store, a coffee shop, an ice-cream parlor, and a theater. She'd heard her shoes echoing off the marble floor of an office lobby. She'd knocked a shelf of greeting cards to the floor. Still, she failed to find the bar. Then, on the ninth afternoon, Malorie entered an unlocked wooden door and immediately knew she had arrived.

The smell of sour fruit, stale smoke, and beer was as welcome as any she'd ever known. Kneeling, she hugged Victor around the neck.

"We found it," she said.

Her body was sore. Her mind ached. Her tongue was dry. She imagined her belly as a deflated, dead balloon.

But she was here.

She searched a long time for the wood of the bar. Banging into chairs, she knocked her elbow hard on a post. She tripped once, but a table saved her from falling to the floor. She spent a long time trying to understand equipment with her fingers. Was this the kitchen? Was this used to mix drinks? Victor tugged at her, playfully, and she turned, banging her stomach against something hard. It was the bar. Tying Victor's leash to what she believed was a steel stool, Malorie stepped behind the bar and felt for the bottles. Every movement was a reminder of how recently she'd given birth. One by one she brought the bottles to her nose. Whiskey. Something peach. Something lemon. Vodka. Gin. And, finally, rum. Just like the housemates once tried to enjoy the night Olympia arrived.

It felt good in her hands. Like she'd waited a thousand years to hold it.

She carried it with her around the length of the bar. Finding the stool, she sat down, brought the bottle to her mouth, and drank.

The alcohol spread through her. And for a moment, it lessened the pain.

In her private darkness, she understood a creature could be sitting at the bar beside her. Possibly the place was full of them. Three per table. Watching her silently. Observing the broken, blindfolded woman and her Seeing Eye dog. But right then, for that second, she just didn't care.

"Victor," she said, "you want some? You need some?"

God, it felt good.

She drank again, remembering how wonderful an afternoon at a bar could be. Forget the babies, forget the house, forget everything.

"Victor, it's good stuff."

But the dog, she recognized, was preoccupied. He was tugging at the leash tied to the stool.

Malorie drank again. Then Victor whined.

"Victor? What is it?"

Victor was pulling harder on the leash. He was whining, not growling. Malorie listened to him. The dog sounded too anxious. She got up, untied him, and let him lead the way.

"Where are we going, Victor?"

She knew he was taking her back to where they came in, by the door they had entered. They banged into tables along the way. Victor's feet slid on tiles and Malorie bashed her shin on a chair.

The smell was stronger here. The bar smell. And more.

"Victor?"

He'd stopped. Then he started scratching at something on the floor.

It's a mouse, Malorie thought. *There must be so many in here.*

She swept her shoe in an arc before it came up against something small and hard. Pulling Victor aside, she felt cautiously on the ground.

She thought of the babies and how they would die without her.

"What is it, Victor?"

It was a ring of some kind. It felt like steel. There was a small rope. Examining it blindfolded, Malorie understood what it was. She rose.

"It's a cellar door, Victor."

The dog was breathing hard.

"Let's leave it alone. We need to get some things here."

But Victor pulled again.

There could be people down there, Malorie thought. *Hiding. Living down there. People who could help you raise the babies.*

"Hello!" she called. But there was no response.

Sweat dripped from under the blindfold. Victor's nails dug at the wood. Malorie's body felt like it might snap in half as she knelt and pulled the thing open.

The smell that came up choked her and Malorie felt the rum come back up as she vomited where she stood.

"Victor," she said, heaving. "Something's rotting down there. *Something—*"

Then she felt the true scorching sensation of fear. Not the kind that comes to a woman as she drives with a blackened windshield, but the sort of fear that hits her when she's wearing a blindfold and suddenly knows there is someone else in the room.

She reached for the door, scared she might tumble into the cellar and meet with whatever was at the bottom. The stench was not old food. It was not bad booze.

"Victor!"

The dog was yanking her, hungry for the source of that smell.

"Victor! *Come on!*"

But he continued.

This is what a grave smells like. This is death.

Quickly, in agony, Malorie pulled Victor out of the room and back into the bar, then searched for a post. She found one made of wood. She tied his leash to it, knelt, and held his face in her hands, begging him to calm down.

"We need to get back to the babies," she told him. "You've *got* to calm down."

But Malorie needed calming herself.

We never determined how animals are affected. We never found out.

She turned back blindly toward the hall that led to the cellar.

"Victor," she said, tears welling. "What did you see down there?"

The dog was still. He was breathing hard. Too hard.

"Victor?"

She rose and stepped away from him.

"Victor. I'm just stepping over here. I'm going to look for some microphones."

A part of her started dying. It felt like she was the one going mad. She thought of Jules. Jules who loved this dog more than he loved himself.

This dog was her very last link to the housemates.

A torturous growl escaped him. It was a sound she'd never heard from him. Not from any dog on Earth.

"Victor. I'm sorry we came here. I'm so sorry."

The dog moved violently and Malorie thought he'd broken free. The wood post splintered.

Victor barked.

Malorie, backing up, felt something, a riser of some kind, behind her tired knees.

"Victor, no. *Please.* I'm so sorry."

The dog swung his body, knocking into a table.

"Oh God! VICTOR! Stop *growling*! *Stop! Please!*"

But Victor couldn't stop.

Malorie felt along the carpeted riser behind her. She crawled onto it, afraid to turn her back on what Victor had seen. Huddled and shaking, she listened to the dog go mad. The sound of him pissing. The sound of his teeth snapping as he bit the empty air.

Malorie shrieked. She instinctively reached for a tool, a weapon, and found her hands gripping the steel of some kind of small post

Slowly, she rose, feeling along the length of the steel.

Victor bit the air. He snapped again. It sounded like his teeth were cracking.

At the top of the steel rod, Malorie's fingers encircled a short, oblong object. At its end, she felt something like steel netting.

She gasped.

She was on the stage. And she was holding what she had come for. She was holding a microphone.

She heard Victor's bone pop. His fur and flesh had ripped.

"*Victor!*"

She pocketed the microphone and dropped to her knees.

Kill him, she thought.

But she couldn't.

Manically, she searched the stage. Behind her, it sounded like Victor had chewed through his own leg.

Your body is broken. Victor is dying. But there are two babies in boxes at home. They need you, Malorie. They need you they need you they need you.

Tears saturated and then spilled out through her blindfold. Her breath came in gasping heaves. On her knees, she followed a wire to a small square object at the far end of the stage. She discovered three more cords, leading to three more microphones.

Victor made a sound no dog should make. He sounded almost human in his despair. Malorie gathered everything she could.

The amplifiers, small enough to carry. The microphones. The cords. A stand.

"I'm sorry, Victor. I'm so sorry, Victor. I'm sorry."

When she rose, she thought her body couldn't take it. She believed that if she had one ounce less of strength, she'd fall down forever. Yet, she stood. As Victor continued to struggle, Malorie felt her way with her back against the wall. At last, she stepped down from the stage.

Victor saw something. Where was it now?

There was no stopping the tears. Yet, a stronger feeling took over: a precious calm. Motherhood. As if she were a stranger to herself, operating for the babies alone.

Crossing the bar, she came close enough to Victor to feel some part of him rub against her leg. Was it his side? His snout? Was he saying good-bye? Or had he thrown her his tongue?

Continuing through the bar, Malorie made it back to where they'd come in. The open cellar door was near. But she didn't know where.

"STAY AWAY FROM ME! STAY AWAY FROM ME!"

Struggling to carry the gear, Malorie stepped once and felt no ground beneath her shoe.

She lost her balance.

She almost fell.

And she righted herself.

Her voice sounded like a stranger's as she screamed before exiting the bar.

The sun was hot against her skin.

She moved quickly, back toward the car.

Her thoughts were electric. Events were happening too fast. She slipped off the concrete curb and smacked hard into the car. Frantic, she loaded the things in the back hurriedly. When she got behind the wheel, she wailed.

The cruelty. This world. Victor.

She had the key in the ignition and was about to turn it.

Then, her black hair wet with sweat, she paused.

What were the chances something had gotten into the car? What were the chances something was seated beside her in the passenger seat?

If something had, she'd be delivering it to the children.

To get home, she told herself (even the voice in her mind quivered; even the voice in her mind sounded like it was crying), *you absolutely have to look at the odometer.*

She flailed blindly about the car, her arms smacking the dashboard wildly, hitting the roof, thrashing against the windows.

She tore her blindfold off.

She saw the black windshield. She was alone in the car.

Using the odometer, she drove the same two and a half miles back, then four to Shillingham, then a quarter mile more to home, hitting every curb and sign on the way. Only five miles an hour; it felt like eternity.

After parking, she gathered what she'd found. Inside, the door secure behind her, she opened her eyes and rushed to the babies' bedroom.

They were awake. Red faced. Crying. Hungry.

Much later she lay awake shaking on the dank kitchen floor. Staring at the microphones and two small amplifiers beside her, remembering the sounds Victor made.

Dogs are not immune. Dogs can go mad. Dogs are not immune.

And whenever she thought she was going to stop crying, she started again.

thirty-four

Malorie is in the upstairs bathroom. It is late and the house is silent. The housemates are sleeping.

She is thinking of Gary's briefcase.

Tom told her to be more of a leader in his absence. But the briefcase is bothering her. Just like Don's sudden interest in Gary bothers her. Just like everything Gary says in his grandiose, artificial way.

Snooping is wrong. When people are forced to live together, their privacy is essential. But isn't this her duty? In Tom's absence, isn't it up to her to find out if her feelings are right?

Malorie turns her ear to the hall. There is no movement in the house. Exiting the bathroom, she turns toward Cheryl's room and sees the shape of her body, resting. Peering into Olympia's room, she hears her softly snoring. Quietly, Malorie descends the stairs, her hand on the railing.

She goes to the kitchen and turns the light on over the stove. It is dim and hums softly. But it's enough. Entering the living room, Malorie sees Victor's eyes looking back at her. Felix is asleep on the couch. The space on the floor usually occupied by Tom is vacant.

Passing through the kitchen, she approaches the dining room. The stove's muted light reaches just far enough so that she can see Gary's body lying on the floor. He's on his back, asleep.

She thinks.

The briefcase leans against the wall, within arm's reach of his body.

Softly, Malorie treads across the dining room. Floorboards creak under her weight. She stops and stares intently at his bearded, gaping mouth. He wheezes a bit, steady and slow. Holding her breath, she takes a final step toward him and stops. Hovering above him, she watches closely without moving.

She kneels.

Gary snorts. Her heart flutters. She waits.

To get the briefcase she must reach across his chest. Her arm dangles inches from his shirt as he slumbers. Her fingers grasp the handle when he snorts again. She turns.

He is staring at her.

Malorie freezes. She scans both of his eyes.

She exhales softly. His eyes are not open. Shadows fooled her.

Swiftly, she lifts the briefcase, rises, and leaves the room.

At the cellar door, she stops and listens. She hears no movement from the dining room. The cellar door opens quietly and slowly, but she can't help the whine of the hinges. It sounds louder than it usually does. As if the whole house is slowly creaking open.

And with just enough room to enter, she slips inside. The house is silent again.

She slowly descends the stairs down to the dirt floor.

She's nervous; it takes her too long to find the string for the lightbulb. When she does, the room gushes with bright yellow light. Too bright. Like it might wake Cheryl, sleeping two floors above.

Glancing around the room, she waits.

She can hear her own labored breathing. Nothing else.

Her body aches. She needs to rest. But right now, she wants only to see what Gary brought with him.

Stepping to the wooden stool, she sits.

She clicks opens the briefcase.

Inside she sees a worn toothbrush.

JOSH MALERMAN

Socks.

T-shirts.

A dress shirt.

Deodorant.

And papers. A notebook.

Malorie looks to the cellar door. She listens for footsteps. There are none. She pulls the notebook out from under the clothes and sets the briefcase on the ground.

The notebook has a clean, blue cover. The edges are not bent. It's as if Gary has kept it, preserved it—in the best condition he could.

She opens it.

And reads.

The handwriting is so exact that it frightens her. It's meticulously crafted. Whoever wrote it did so with passion. With pride. As she flips through the pages, she sees some sentences are written traditionally, from left to right, others are written in the opposite direction from right to left. Still others, deeper into the notebook, begin at the top of the page and walk down. By the end, the sentences spiral neatly, still perfectly crafted, creating odd designs and patterns, made of words.

To know the ceiling of man's mind is to know the full power of these creatures. If it's a matter of comprehension, then surely the results of any encounter with them must differ greatly between two men. My ceiling is different from yours. Much different from the monkeys in this house. The others, engulfed as they are in hyperbolic hysteria, are more susceptible to the rules we've ascribed the creatures. In other words, these simpletons, with their childish intellects, will not survive. But someone like myself, well, I've already proven my point.

Malorie flips the page.

What kind of a man cowers when the end of the world comes? When his brothers are killing themselves, when the streets of suburban America are infested with murder . . . what kind of man hides behind blankets and blindfolds? The answer is MOST men. They were told they would go mad. So they go mad.

Malorie looks to the cellar stairs. The light from the stove shows through the thin slit at the bottom of the cellar door. She thinks she should have turned it off. She thinks about doing it now. Then she flips the page.

We do it to ourselves we do it to ourselves we DO IT to OURSELVES. In other words (make note of this!): MAN IS THE CREATURE HE FEARS.

It's Frank's notebook. But why does Gary have it?

Because he wrote it of course.

Because, Malorie knows, Frank didn't tear down the drapes at Gary's old place.

Gary did.

Malorie stands, her heart racing.

Tom isn't home. Tom is on a three-mile walk to his house.

She stares at the foot of the cellar door. Light from the stove. She expects shoes to suddenly obscure it. She looks to the shelves for a weapon. If he comes, what can she kill him with?

But no shoes obscure the light, and Malorie brings the notebook closer to her face. She reads.

Rationally speaking, and in the interest of proving this to them, I've no choice. I will write this a thousand times until I convince myself to do it. Two thousand. Three. These men deny discourse. Only proof will change them. But how to prove it to them? How to make them believe?

I will remove the drapes and unlock the doors.

In the margins there are numbered notes and corresponding numbers are written painstakingly across the top. Here is note 2,343. Here is 2,344. Ceaseless, endless, brutal.

Malorie turns the page.

A noise comes from upstairs.

She looks to the door. She's afraid to blink, to move. She waits and stares.

Her eyes on the door, she reaches for the briefcase and slips the notebook back under Gary's things. Is it facing the right way? Was this how he had it?

She doesn't know. *She doesn't know.*

She closes the briefcase and pulls the lightbulb's string.

Malorie closes her eyes and feels the cool earth beneath her feet. She opens her eyes. Absolute blackness is cut only by the stove light from under the cellar door.

Malorie watches it, waiting.

She crosses the cellar, her eyes adjusting to the darkness as she climbs the stairs carefully and presses her ear against the door.

She listens, breathing erratically. The house is silent once again.

Gary is standing at the other end of the kitchen. He is watching the cellar door. When you open it, he will greet you.

She waits. And waits. And hears nothing.

She opens the door. The hinge creaks.

Briefcase in hand, Malorie's eyes dart into the kitchen. The silence is too loud.

But nobody is there. No one is waiting for her.

Hand on her belly, she squeezes herself through the doorframe and shuts the door behind her.

She looks to the living room. To the dining room.

To the living room.

To the dining room.

On the tips of her toes, she passes through the kitchen and enters the dining room at last.

Gary is still on his back. His chest rises and falls. He groans softly.

She approaches. He moves. She waits.

He moved . . .

It was only his arm.

Malorie watches him, staring at his face, his unopened eyes. Hastily, she kneels over his body, inches from his skin, and places the briefcase back against the wall.

Is this the way it was facing?

She leaves it. Standing, she rushes out of the room. In the kitchen, in the glow of the light, someone's eyes meet hers.

Malorie freezes.

It's Olympia.

"What are you *doing*?" Olympia whispers.

"Nothing," she says breathlessly. "Thought I left something in there."

"I had a terrible dream," Olympia says. Malorie is walking toward her, reaching for her. She leads Olympia back upstairs. They take them together. Once at the top, Malorie looks back down at the staircase.

"I have to tell Tom," she says.

"About my dream?"

Malorie looks at Olympia and shakes her head.

"No. No. I'm sorry. No."

"Malorie?"

"Yes."

"Are you okay?"

"Olympia. I need Tom."

"Well, he's gone."

Malorie stares at the foot of the stairs. The stove light is still on. Enough of it splashes across the living room's entrance that if someone were to enter the kitchen from the dining room, she'd be able to see their shadow.

She is staring fervently into the dim room. Waiting. For the shadow. Certain it's coming.

As she watches, she thinks of what Olympia just said.

Tom is gone.

She thinks of the house as one big box. She wants out of this box. Tom and Jules, outside, are still in *this* box. The entire globe is shut in. The world is confined to the same cardboard box that houses the birds outside. Malorie understands that Tom is looking for a way to open the lid. He's looking for a way out. But she wonders if there's not a second lid above this one, then a third above that.

Boxed in, she thinks. *Forever.*

thirty-five

It has been a week since Tom and Jules left for the three-mile walk with the huskies. More than anything, right now, Malorie wants them home. She wants to hear a knock at the door and to feel the relief of having them back again. She wants to hear what they encountered and see what they've brought back. She wants to tell Tom what she read in the cellar.

She did not go back to sleep last night. In the darkness of her bedroom, she thought only about Gary's notebook. She is in the foyer now. Hiding, it seems, from the rest of the house.

She can't tell Felix. He might do something. He would say something. Malorie wants Tom and Jules here in case he does. Felix would need them.

Who knows what Gary is capable of doing. *What he's done.*

She can't talk to Cheryl. Cheryl is fiery and strong. She gets angry. She would do something before Felix would.

Olympia would only be more scared.

She can't talk to Gary. She won't. Not without Tom.

But, despite the change in his affiliation, despite his unpredictable moods, Malorie thinks maybe she can talk to Don.

There is a goodness in him, she thinks. There always has been.

Gary has been the devil on Don's shoulder for weeks. Don *needed* someone like this in the house. Someone who sees the world more like him. But couldn't Don's skepticism prove to be helpful here? Hasn't he thought, in all his talks with Gary, that something might be wrong with the newcomer?

Gary sleeps with the briefcase within arm's reach. He cares about it. Cares about and believes the writings inside.

Everything in this new world is harsh, she thinks, but nothing so much as her discovering Gary's notebook while Tom is away.

He could be away for a long time.

Stop it.

Forever.

Stop it.

He could be dead. They could have been killed in the street right outside. The man you're waiting for could be dead a week, just a lawn away.

He's not. He'll return.

Maybe.

He will.

Maybe.

They mapped it out with Felix.

What does Felix know?

They all did it together. Tom wouldn't risk it unless he knew he had a chance to make it.

Remember the video George watched? Tom is a lot like George.

STOP!

He is. He idolized the man. And what about the dogs?

We don't know that dogs are affected.

No. But they could be. Can you imagine what it would be like? A dog going stark mad?

Please . . . no.

Necessary thoughts. Necessary visions. Tom might not come back.

He will he will he will . . .

And if he doesn't, you'll have to tell someone else.

Tom's coming back.

It's been a week.

HE'S COMING BACK!

You can't tell Gary. Talk to someone else first.

Don.

No. No. Not him. Felix. Don will kill you.

What??

Don has changed, Malorie. He's different. Don't be so naive.

He wouldn't hurt us.

Yes. He would. He'd take the garden axe to you all.

STOP!!

He doesn't care about life. He told you to blind your baby, Malorie.

He wouldn't hurt us.

He would. Talk to Felix.

Felix will tell everyone.

Tell him not to. Talk to Felix. Tom may not come back.

Malorie leaves the foyer. Cheryl and Gary are in the kitchen. Gary is at the table, sitting, scooping pears from a can.

"Good afternoon," he says, in that way he has of making it sound like he's responsible for the good afternoon.

Malorie thinks he can tell. She thinks he knows.

He was awake he was awake he was awake.

"Good afternoon," she says. She walks into the living room, leaving him.

Felix is sitting by the phone in the living room. The map is open on the end table.

"I don't understand," he says, confused. Felix does not look well. He hasn't been eating as much. The assurances he gave Malorie a week ago no longer exist.

"It's such a long time, Malorie. I know Tom would know what to do out there—but it's such a long time."

"You need to think about something else," Cheryl says, peering her head around the corner. "Seriously, Felix. Think about something else. Or just go outside without a blindfold. Either way you're driving yourself mad."

Felix exhales loudly and runs his fingers through his hair.

She can't tell Felix. He's losing something. He's lost something. His eyes are dull. He's losing sensibility, thought. Strength.

Without a word, Malorie leaves him. She passes Don in the hall. The words, what she's discovered, come to life within her. She almost speaks.

Don, Gary is no good. He's dangerous. He has Frank's notebook in his briefcase.

What, Malorie?

Just what I said.

You were snooping? Going through Gary's things?

Yes.

Why are you coming to me with this?

Don, I just need to tell someone. You understand that, don't you?

Why didn't you just ask Gary? Hey, Gary!

No. She can't tell Don. Don has lost something, too. He might get violent. Gary could, too.

One shove, she thinks, *and you lose the baby.*

She imagines Gary at the top of the cellar stairs. Her broken, bleeding body crumpled at the bottom.

You like reading in the cellar, DO YOU?? Then die down there with your child.

Behind her, she hears all the housemates are in the living room. Cheryl is talking to Felix. Gary is talking to Don.

Malorie turns toward their voices and approaches the living room.

She is going to tell them all.

When she enters the room, her body feels like it's made of ice. Melting. Like pieces of herself fall away and sink under the unbearable pressure of what's to come.

Cheryl and Olympia are on the couch. Felix waits by the phone. Don is in the easy chair. Gary stands, facing the blanketed windows.

As she opens her mouth, Gary slowly looks over his shoulder and meets her eyes.

"Malorie," he says sharply, "is something on your mind?"

Suddenly, clearly, Malorie realizes that everyone is staring at her. Waiting for her to speak.

"Yes, Gary," she says. "There is."

"What is it?" Don asks.

The words are stuck in her throat. They climb up like the legs of a millipede, reaching for her lips, looking to get out at last.

"Does anyone remember Gary's—"

She stops. She and the housemates turn toward the blankets.

The birds are cooing.

"It's Tom," Felix says desperately. "It *must* be!"

Gary looks into Malorie's eyes again. There is a knock at the front door.

The housemates move fast. Felix rushes to the front door. Malorie and Gary remain.

He knows he knows he knows he knows he knows.

When Tom calls out, Malorie is trembling with fear.

He knows.

Then, having heard Tom's voice, Gary leaves her and heads to the foyer.

Once the questions have been asked and the housemates have their eyes closed, Malorie hears the front door open. The cool air rushes in, and with it the reality of how close Malorie just came to confronting Gary without Tom in the house.

Dogs paws on the foyer tile. Boots. Something smacks against the doorframe. The front door closes quickly. There's the sound of the broomsticks scratching the walls. Tom speaks. And his voice is deliverance.

"My plan was to call you guys from my house. But the fucking phone was out."

"Tom," Felix says, manic but weak. "I knew you guys would do it. I knew it!"

When Malorie opens her eyes, she doesn't think about Gary. She doesn't see the perfectly manicured letters that wait in his briefcase.

She sees only that Tom and Jules are home again.

"We raided a grocery store," Tom says. The words sound impossible. "Someone had been there before. But we got a lot of good stuff."

He looks tired, but he looks good.

"The dogs worked," he says. "They led us." He is proud and happy. "But I got something from my house that I hope will help us even more."

Felix helps him with his duffel bag. Tom unzips it and removes something. Then he lets it fall to the foyer floor.

It's a phone book.

"We're going to call every number in here," he says. "Every single one. And somebody is going to answer."

It's only a phone book, but Tom has turned it into a beacon.

"Now," Tom says. "Let's eat."

The others excitedly prepare the dining room. Olympia gets the utensils. Felix fills glasses with water from the buckets.

Tom is back.

Jules is back.

"Malorie!" Olympia calls. "It's canned crabmeat!"

Malorie, caught somewhere between two worlds, enters the kitchen and begins helping with dinner.

thirty-six

Someone is following them.

There is no use asking herself how much farther they have to go. She doesn't know when she will hear the recorded voice that tells her she's arrived. She doesn't know if it still exists. Now, she only paddles, she only perseveres.

An hour ago, they passed what sounded like lions engaged in battle. There were roars. Birds of prey screech threats from the sky. Things growl and snort from the woods. The river's current is moving faster. She remembers the tent Tom and Jules found in the street outside their house. Could there be something like that, so astonishingly out of place, here, on the river? Could they crash into it . . . *now*?

Out here, she knows, anything imagined is possible.

But right now, it is something much more concrete that worries her.

Someone is following them. Yes, the Boy heard it, too.

A phantom echo. A second rowing, in step with her own.

Who would do it? And if they meant to harm her and the children, why didn't they do it when she was passed out?

Is it someone escaping their home as well?

"Boy," she says quietly, "tell me what you can about them."

The Boy is listening.

"I don't know, Mommy."

He sounds ashamed.

"Are they still there?"

"I don't know!"

"*Listen.*"

Malorie considers stopping. Turning. Facing the noise she hears behind them.

The recording will be playing on a loop. You'll hear it. It's loud. Clear. And when you do, that's when you'll have to open your eyes.

What follows them?

"Boy," she says again. "Tell me what you can about them."

Malorie stops rowing. Water rushes around them.

"I don't know what it is," he says.

Still, Malorie waits. A dog barks from the right bank. A second bark answers.

Wild dogs, Malorie thinks. *More wolves.*

She begins paddling again. She asks the Boy again what he hears.

"I'm sorry, Mommy!" he yells. His voice is cracked with tears. Shame.

He doesn't know.

It has been years since the Boy wasn't able to identify a sound. What he hears is something he's never heard before.

But Malorie believes he can still help.

"How far away are they?" Malorie asks.

But the Boy is crying.

"I can't do it!"

"*Keep your voice down!*" she hisses.

Something grunts from the left bank. It sounds like a pig. Then another one. And another.

The river feels too thin. The banks too close.

Does something follow them?

Malorie rows.

thirty-seven

For the first time since arriving at the house, Malorie knows something the others don't.

Tom and Jules have just returned. As the housemates prepared dinner, Tom brought the new stock of canned goods to the cellar. Malorie met him down there. Maybe Gary kept the notebook because he wanted to study Frank's writing. Or maybe he wrote it himself. But Tom needed to know. Now.

In the cellar light, he looked tired but triumphant. His fair hair was dirty. His features looked more aged than the first time she was down here with him. He was losing weight. Methodically, he removed cans from his and Jules's duffel bags and set them on the shelves. He began talking about what it was like inside the grocery store, the stench of so much rotten food, when Malorie found her opportunity.

But just when she did, the cellar door opened.

It was Gary.

"I'd like to help you if I can," he said to Tom from the top of the stairs.

"All right," Tom said. "Come on down then."

Malorie exited as Gary reached the dirt floor.

Now everybody is seated at the dining room table. And Malorie is still looking for her opportunity.

Tom and Jules describe their week slowly. The facts are incredible, but Malorie's mind is fixed on Gary. She tries to act normal. She listens to what they say. Each minute that passes is another in which Tom doesn't know that Gary may be a threat to the rest of them.

It almost feels like she and the others are intruding on Gary's space. Like Gary and Don had the decency to invite them into *their* dining room, their favorite place for exchanging whispered words. The two have spent so much time in here that it smells of them. Would they have joined the group if dinner was served in the living room? Malorie doesn't think so.

As Tom describes walking three miles blindfolded, Gary is affable, talkative, and inquisitive. And every time he opens his mouth Malorie wants to yell at him to stop. *Come clean first,* she wants to say.

But she waits.

"Would you say then," Gary says, his mouth full of crab, "that you are now convinced animals are not affected?"

"No, I wouldn't say that," Tom says. "Not yet. Maybe we just didn't pass anything for them to see."

"That's unlikely," Gary says.

Malorie almost screams it.

Tom then announces he has another surprise for everyone.

"Your duffel bag is a veritable clown car," Gary says, smiling.

When Tom returns, he's carrying a small brown box. From it, he pulls forth eight bicycle horns.

"We got these at the grocery store," he says. "In the toy aisle."

He hands them out.

"Mine has my name on it," Olympia says.

"They all do," Tom says. "I wrote them, blindfolded, with a Sharpie."

"What are they for?" Felix asks.

"We're inching toward a life of spending more time outside," Tom answers, sitting down. "We can signal one another with these."

Suddenly, Gary honks his horn. It sounds like a goose. Then it sounds like geese, as everyone honks their horns chaotically.

The circles under Felix's eyes stretch as he smiles.

"And *this*," Tom says, "is the grand finale." He reaches into his duffel bag and pulls forth a bottle. It's rum.

"Tom!" Olympia says.

"It's the real reason I wanted to go back to my house," he jokes.

Malorie, listening to the housemates laugh, seeing their smiling faces, can stand it no longer.

She stands up and slams her palms on the table.

"I looked through Gary's briefcase," she says. "I found the notebook he told us about. The one about tearing the blankets down. The one he said Frank took with him."

The room goes silent. Every housemate is looking at her. Her cheeks are red with heat. Sweat prickles her hairline.

Tom, still holding the bottle of rum, studies Malorie's face. Then he slowly turns to Gary.

"Gary?"

Gary looks to the tabletop.

He's buying time, Malorie thinks. *The fucker is buying time to think.*

"Well," he says, "I hardly know what to say."

"You looked through someone else's things?" Cheryl says, rising.

"I did. Yes. I know that violates the rules of the house. But we need to talk about what I found."

The room is silent again. Malorie is still standing. She feels electric.

"Gary?" Jules pushes.

Gary leans back in his chair. He breathes deep. He crosses his arms over his chest. Then he uncrosses them. He looks serious. Annoyed. Then he grins. He stands up and goes to the briefcase. He brings it back and sets it on the table.

The others are staring at the briefcase, but Malorie is watching Gary's face.

He snaps the case open, then pulls forth the notebook.

"Yes," Gary says. "I *do* have it on me. I do have Frank's notebook."

"Frank's?" Malorie repeats.

"Yes," Gary says, turning toward her. Then, maintaining his theatrical, gentlemanly way of speaking, he adds, "You little snoop."

Suddenly, everybody is talking at once. Felix is asking for the notebook. Cheryl wants to know when Malorie found it. Don is pointing his finger at Malorie and yelling.

In the chaos, Gary, still looking at Malorie, says, "You paranoid pregnant *whore*."

Jules is upon him. The dogs are barking. Tom gets between them. He is yelling at everyone to stop. Stop it. Malorie does not move. She stares at Gary.

Jules relents.

"She needs to explain this *right now*," Don explodes. He has leapt to his feet and is pointing angrily at Malorie.

Tom looks to her.

"Malorie?" he says.

"I don't trust him."

The housemates wait for more.

Olympia says, "What does the notebook say?"

"Olympia!" Malorie says. "The notebook is *right there*. Fucking read it for yourself."

But Felix already has it in his hands.

"Why do you have a souvenir from a man who put your life in danger?" he demands.

"That's *exactly* why I have it," Gary says insistently. "I wanted to know what Frank was thinking. I lived with him for weeks and never suspected he was capable of trying to kill us. Maybe I held on to it as a warning. To make sure I didn't start thinking like him. To make sure none of you did, either."

Malorie shakes her head vehemently.

"You told us Frank took the notebook with him," she says.

Gary starts to respond. Then he stops.

"I don't have a satisfactory response for that," Gary says. "Possibly I thought you would be frightened if you knew I had it on me. You can think what you will, but I'd rather you trusted me. I don't fault you for looking through a stranger's luggage, given the circumstances under which we're all living. But at least allow me to defend myself."

Tom is looking at the notebook now. The words crawl beneath his eyes.

Don takes it next. His angry expression slowly turns to confusion.

Then, as if Malorie's aware of something greater than what any vote might solve, she points a finger at Gary and says, "You can't stay here anymore. You have to *leave*."

"Malorie," Don says with little conviction, "come on. The man is explaining himself."

"Don," Felix says, "are you fucking nuts?"

The notebook still in his hands, Don turns to Gary.

"Gary," he says, "you must realize how bad this looks."

"I do. Of course I do."

"This isn't your writing? Can you prove that?"

Gary removes a pen from the briefcase and writes his name on a page in the notebook.

Tom looks at it for a second.

"Gary," Tom says, "the rest of us need to talk. Sit here if you want to. You'd hear us in the other room anyway."

"I understand," Gary says. "You're the captain of this ship. Whatever you say."

Malorie wants to hit him.

"All right," Tom says calmly to the others, "what do we do?"

"He has to go," Cheryl says without hesitation.

Then Tom begins the vote.

"Jules?"

"He can't stay here, Tom."

"Felix?"

"I want to say no. I want to say we can't vote to send someone outside. But there's just no reason to have that book."

"Tom," Don says, "we're not voting to send someone out who wants to go this time. We're voting on *forcing* someone to do it. Do you want that on your conscience?"

Tom turns to Olympia.

"Olympia?"

"Tom," Don says.

"You voted, Don."

"We can't force someone outside, Tom."

The notebook is resting on the table. It's open. The words are immaculately presented.

"I'm sorry, Don," Tom says.

Don turns to Olympia, hoping.

But she does not answer. And it doesn't matter. The house has spoken.

Gary rises. He picks up the notebook and places it back in the case. He stands behind his chair and raises his chin. He breathes deeply. He nods.

"Tom," Gary says, "do you think I might have one of your helmets? One neighbor to another."

"Of course," Tom says quietly.

Then Tom leaves the room. He returns with a helmet and some food. He hands it all to Gary.

"It just works like this then?" Gary says, adjusting the strap on the helmet.

"This is *terrible*," Olympia laments.

Tom helps Gary put the helmet on. Then he walks him to the front door. The housemates follow in a group.

"I think every house on this block is empty," Tom says. "From what Jules and I discovered. You have your pick of them."

"Yes," Gary says, nervously smiling beneath the blindfold. "That's encouraging I suppose."

Malorie, burning inside, watches Gary carefully.

When she closes her eyes, when they all do, she hears the front door open and close. And in between she thinks she hears his feet upon the lawn. When she opens them, Don is no longer standing in the foyer with the others. She thinks he has left with Gary. Then she hears something move in the kitchen.

"Don?"

He grunts. She knows it is him.

He mutters something before opening and slamming the cellar door.

Another profanity. Aimed at Malorie.

As the others silently scatter, she understands the severity of what they've done.

It feels like Gary is everywhere outside.

He's been banished. Ostracized.

Cast out.

Which is worse? she asks herself. *Having him here, where we could keep an eye on him, or having him out there, where we can't?*

thirty-eight

*D*oes Gary follow you?

The sounds of someone behind them, distant yet in earshot, continues.

He's trying to scare you. He could overtake you at any time.

Gary.

That was four years ago!

Could he have been waiting four years for revenge?

"Mommy," the Boy whispers.

"What is it?"

She fears what he is about to say.

"The sound, it's getting closer."

Where has Gary been for four years? He's been watching you. Waiting outside the house. He watched the kids grow. Watched the world grow colder, darker, until a fog came, one you foolishly thought would mask you. He saw through it. Through the fog. He's seen everything you've done. He's SEEN you, Malorie. Everything you've done.

"*Damn it!*" she yells. "*It's impossible!*" Then, turning her neck, the muscles resisting, she yells, "*Leave us alone!*"

A row isn't what it used to be. Not like it was when they started today. Then, she had two strong shoulders. A full heart of energy. Four years to propel her.

For all she's endured, she refuses to believe it's possible that Gary is behind her. It'd be such a cruel twist. A man out there all these years. Not a creature, but a *man*.

MAN IS THE CREATURE HE FEARS

The sentence, Gary's sentence, only six words, has been with her since the night she read it in the cellar. And isn't it true? When she heard a stick break through the amplifiers she retrieved with Victor, when she heard footsteps on the lawn outside, what did she fear most? An animal? A creature?

Or man?

Gary. Always Gary.

He could've gotten in at any time. Could've broken a window. Could've attacked her when she got water from the well. Why would he wait? Always following, always lurking, not quite ready to pounce.

He's mad. The old way.

MAN IS THE CREATURE HE FEARS

"Is it a man, Boy?"

"I can't tell, Mommy."

"Is it someone rowing?"

"Yes. But with hands instead of paddles."

"Are they rushing? Are they waiting? Tell me more. Tell me everything you hear."

Who follows you?

Gary.

Who follows you?

Gary.

Who follows you?

Gary Gary Gary Gary

"I don't think they're in a boat," the Boy suddenly says. He sounds proud for having finally been able to make a distinction.

"What do you mean? Are they *swimming*?"

"No, Mommy. They're not swimming. They're walking."

Far behind, she hears something she's never heard. It's like lightning. A new kind. Or like birds, all of them, in every tree, no longer singing, no longer cooing, but screaming.

It echoes, once, harsh, across the river, and Malorie feels a chill colder than any October air could deliver.

She rows.

thirty-nine

Don is in the cellar. Don is always in the cellar. He sleeps down there now. Does he dig a tunnel where the dirt shows? Does he dig a tunnel deeper, lower, farther into the earth? Farther away from the others? Does he write? Does he write in a notebook like the one Malorie found in Gary's briefcase?

Gary.

He's been gone five weeks. What has it done to Don?

Did he need someone like Gary? Did he need another ear?

Don sinks farther into himself like he sinks farther into the house, and now he is in the cellar.

He is always in the cellar.

forty

I t is what Malorie will later consider to be the last night in the house, though she will spend the next four years here. Her belly looks so big in the mirror that it scares her, looks like it could fall right off her body. She speaks to the baby.

"You're going to come out any day now. There are so many things I want to tell you and so many that I don't."

Her black hair is the longest it's been since she was a little girl. Shannon used to be jealous of it.

You look like a princess. I look like the princess's sister, she'd say.

Living off canned goods and well water, she can see some of her ribs, despite the bulge of her belly. Her arms are twig-thin. The features of her face are sharp and hard. Her eyes, deeper set in her skull, are striking, even to herself, in the mirror.

The housemates are gathered in the living room downstairs. Earlier today, the last names in the phone book were called. There are no more. Felix said they made close to five thousand calls. They left seventeen messages. That's it. But Tom is encouraged.

Now, as Malorie examines her body in the mirror, she hears one of the dogs growl downstairs.

It sounds like Victor. Stepping into the hall, she listens.

"What is it, Victor?" she hears Jules say.

"He doesn't like it," Cheryl says.

"Doesn't like what?"

"Doesn't like the cellar door."

The cellar. It's no secret Don wants nothing to do with the rest of the house. When Tom instigated his plan for calling the phone book, assigning each housemate a group of letters, Don declined, citing his "lack of faith" in the process as a whole. In the seven weeks since they shut the front door on Gary, Don hasn't joined the others for meals. He hardly speaks at all.

Malorie hears a kitchen chair slide on the floor.

"You okay, Victor?" Jules says.

Malorie hears the cellar door open, then Jules calls out.

"Don? You down there?"

"Don?" Cheryl echoes.

There is a muffled response. The door closes again.

Curious and anxious, Malorie pulls her shirt over her belly and heads downstairs.

When she enters the kitchen, she sees Jules is kneeling, consoling Victor, who now whines and paces. Malorie looks in the living room. There she sees Tom is looking at the blanketed windows.

He's listening for the birds, she thinks. *Victor is scaring him.*

As if sensing she is watching him, Tom turns toward Malorie. Victor is whining behind her.

"Jules," Tom says, entering the kitchen, "what do you think it is? What's scaring him?"

"I don't know. Obviously something's got him rattled. He was scratching at the cellar door earlier. Don is down there. But it's like pulling teeth to get him to talk. Even worse to get him upstairs."

"All right," Tom says. "Let's go down there then."

When Jules looks up at Tom, Malorie sees fear on his face.

What has Gary done to them?

He's introduced distrust, Malorie thinks. *Jules is afraid of confronting Don at all.*

"Come on," Tom says. "It's time we talk to him."

Jules stands up and puts his hand on the cellar doorknob. Victor begins growling again.

"You stay here, boy," Jules says.

"No," Tom says. "Let's bring him with us."

Jules pauses, and then opens the cellar door.

"Don?" Tom calls.

There is no answer.

Tom goes first. Then Jules and Victor. Malorie follows.

Despite the light being on, it feels dark down here. At first, Malorie thinks they are alone. She expected to see Don sitting on the stool. Reading. Thinking. Writing. She almost says that nobody is down here, then she shrieks.

Don is standing by the thin tapestry, leaning against the washing machine in the shadows.

"What's gotten into the dog?" he asks quietly.

Tom speaks carefully when he responds.

"We don't know, Don. It's like he doesn't like something down here. Is everything okay?"

"What's that supposed to mean?"

"You've been down here more than we have lately," Tom says. "I just want to know if everything is okay."

When Don steps forward, into the light, Malorie quietly gasps. He does not look good. Pale. Thin. His dark hair is dirty and thinning. The features of his face are claylike in texture. The dark circles beneath his eyes make it look like he's taken in some of the darkness he's been staring into for weeks.

"We called the whole phone book," Tom says, attempting, Malorie thinks, something bright in this damp, dark cellar.

"Any luck?"

"None yet. But who knows?"

"Yes. Who knows."

Then they are silent. Malorie understands that the divide she sensed growing between them is complete now. They are checking on Don. Checking *up* on Don. As if he lives somewhere else now. Repair feels impossible.

"Do you want to come upstairs?" Tom asks gently.

Malorie experiences a wave of light-headedness. She brings a hand to her belly.

The baby. She shouldn't have taken the cellar stairs. But she's as concerned about Don as anybody.

"What for?" Don finally answers.

"I don't know what for," Tom says. "It might do you some good to be around the rest of us for a night."

Don is nodding slowly. He licks his lips. He looks once around the cellar. To the shelves, the boxes, and the stool Malorie sat on, seven weeks ago, when she read the notebook in Gary's briefcase.

"All right," Don whispers. "Okay."

Tom puts a hand on Don's shoulder. Don begins crying. He brings a hand to his eyes to hide it.

"I'm sorry, man," he says. "I'm so confused, Tom."

"We all are," Tom says quietly. "Come upstairs. Everyone would love to see you."

In the kitchen, Tom pulls the bottle of rum from a cabinet. He pours a drink for himself and then one for Don. The two clink glasses, softly, then sip.

For a moment, it's like nothing has changed and nothing ever will. The housemates are together again. Malorie can't remember the last time she saw Don like this, without Gary crouched beside him, the demon on his shoulder, whispering philosophies, discoloring his mind with the same language she found in the notebook.

Victor rubs against Malorie's legs as he heads back into the kitchen. Watching him, she feels a second wave of dizziness.

I need to lie down, she thinks.

"Then you should," Tom says.

Malorie didn't realize she said this out loud.

But she doesn't *want* to lie down. She wants to sit with Tom and Don and the others and believe, for a moment, that the house could still be what it set out to be. A place for strangers to meet, to pool their resources, gather strength in numbers, to face the impossible, changing world outside.

Then, it's all just too much. A third wave of nausea hits and Malorie, standing, stumbles. Jules appears, suddenly, by her side. He is helping her up the stairs. As she enters her bedroom and lies down, she sees the others are in the room with her. All of them. Don, too. They are watching her, worried about her. *Staring.* They ask if she is okay. Does she need anything? Water? A wet cloth? She says no, or thinks she says no, but she is drifting. As she falls asleep, she hears a sound, coming through the vent, the sound of Victor again, growling, alone, in the kitchen.

The last thing she sees before closing her eyes are the housemates in a group. They are watching her closely. They look to her belly.

They know the moment has come.

Victor growls again. Don looks toward the stairs.

Jules leaves the bedroom.

"Thank you, Tom," Malorie says. "For the bicycle horns."

She thinks she hears the bird box, banging lightly against the house. But it is only the wind against the window.

Then she is asleep. And she dreams of the birds.

forty-one

The birds in the trees are restless. It sounds like a thousand branches shaking at once. Like there's a dangerous wind up there. But Malorie doesn't feel it down here on the river. No. There is no wind.

But something is disrupting the birds.

The pain in her shoulder has reached a level Malorie has never experienced before. She curses herself for not paying more attention to her body these last four years. Instead, she spent her time training the children. Until their abilities transcended the exercises she came up with.

Mommy, a leaf fell into the well!

Mommy, it is drizzling down the street and it heads our way!

Mommy, a bird has landed on the branch beyond our window!

Will the children hear the recorded voice before she does? They must. And when that happens, it'll be time to open her eyes. To look at where the river splits into four channels. She's to pick the second from the right. That's what she was told to do.

And soon she'll have to do it.

The birds in the trees are cooing. There is activity on the banks. Man, animal, *monster*. She has no idea.

The fear she experiences sits firmly upon the center of her soul.

And the birds in the branches directly above them are now cooing.

She thinks of the house. The last night she spent with the housemates, all of them together. The wind was loud against the windows. There was a coming storm. A big one. Maybe the birds in the trees know it. Or maybe they know something else.

"I can't hear," the Girl suddenly says. "The birds, Mommy. They're too loud!"

Malorie stops rowing. She thinks of Victor.

"What do they sound like to you?" she asks both children.

"Scared!" the Girl says.

"Mad!" says the Boy.

The closer Malorie listens to the trees, the worse it sounds.

How many are up there? It sounds like infinity.

Will the children hear the recording beneath the cacophony above?

Victor went mad. Animals go mad.

The birds do not sound sane.

Slowly, blindly, she looks over her shoulder toward what follows them.

Your eyes are closed, she thinks. *Just like your eyes were closed every time you got water from the well. Every time you attempted to drive to fetch the amplifiers. Your eyes were closed when Victor's weren't. What are you worried about? Haven't you been in close proximity before? Haven't you been so close to one that you believed you could smell it?*

She has.

You add the details, she thinks. *It's your idea of what they look like, and details are added to a body and a shape that you have no concept of. To a face that might have no face at all.*

The creatures of her mind walk horizonless, open fields. They stand outside the windows of former homes and gaze curiously at the glass. They study. They examine. They observe. They do the one thing Malorie isn't allowed to do.

They *look.*

Do they recognize the flowers in the garden as pretty? Do they understand which direction the river flows? Do they?

"Mommy," the Boy says.

"*What?*"

"That noise, Mommy. It sounds like someone talking."

She thinks of the man in the boat. She thinks of Gary. Even now, so far from the house, she thinks of Gary.

She tries to ask the Boy what he means, but the voices of the birds rise in a grotesque wave, nearly symphonic, shrieking.

It sounds like there are too many for the trees to hold.

Like they make up the entire sky.

They sound mad. They sound mad. Oh my God they sound mad.

Malorie turns her head over her shoulder again, though she cannot see. The Boy heard a voice. The birds are mad. Who follows them?

But it no longer feels like something is following them. It feels like that something has caught up.

"It's a voice!" the Boy yells, as if from a dream, his voice penetrating the impossible noise from above.

Malorie is sure of it. The birds have seen something below.

The communal birdsong swells and peaks before it flattens, twists, and the boundaries explode. Malorie hears it like she's *inside of* it. Like she's trapped in an aviary with a thousand madcap birds. It feels like a cage was lowered over them all. A cardboard box. A bird box. Blocking out the sun forever.

What is it? What is it? What is it?

Infinity.

Where did it come from? Where did it come from? Where did it come from?

Infinity.

The birds scream. And the noise they make is not a song.

The Girl shrieks.

"Something hit me, Mommy! Something fell!"

Malorie feels it, too. She thinks it's raining.

Impossibly, the sound of the birds gets louder. They are deafening, screeching. Malorie has to cover her ears. She calls to the children, begging them to do the same.

Something lands hard against her bad shoulder and she yelps, wincing in pain.

Wildly, her hand grasping her blindfold, she searches the boat for what struck her.

The Girl shrieks again.

"Mommy!"

But Malorie's found it. Between her forefinger and thumb is not a drop of rain but the broken body of a tiny bird. She feels its delicate wing.

Malorie knows now.

In the sky above, where she is forbidden to look, the birds are warring. The birds are killing one another.

"Cover your heads! Hold on to your blindfolds!"

Then, like a wave, they hit. Feathered bodies hail from above. The river erupts with the weight of thousands of birds splashing into the water. They hit the boat. They plummet. Malorie is struck. They hit her head, her arm. She's struck again. Again.

As bird blood courses down her cheeks, she can taste them.

You can smell it, too. Death. Dying. Decay. The sky is falling, the sky is dying, the sky is dead.

Malorie calls to the children, but the Boy is already speaking, trying to tell her something.

"Riverbridge," he is saying. "Two seventy-three Shillingham . . . my name is . . ."

"What?"

Crouched, Malorie leans forward. She presses the Boy's lips hard to her ear.

"Riverbridge," he says. "Two seventy-three Shillingham. My name is Tom."

Malorie sits up, wounded, clutching her blindfold.

My name is Tom.

Birds strike her body. They thud against the boat.

But she is not thinking of them.

She is thinking of Tom.

Hello! I'm calling you from Riverbridge. Two seventy-three Shillingham. My name is Tom. I'm sure you understand the relief I feel at getting your answering machine. It means you still have power. So do we . . .

Malorie starts shaking her head.

no no no no no no no no no no no

"NO!"

The Boy heard it first. Tom's voice. Recorded and played on a loop. Motion activated. For her. For Malorie. If ever she decided to take the river. Whenever that day would come. Tom, sweet Tom, speaking out here all these years. Trying to make contact. Trying to reach someone. Trying to build a bridge between their life in the house and a better one, somewhere else.

They used his voice because they knew you'd recognize it. This is it, Malorie.

This is the moment you're supposed to open your eyes.

How green is the grass? How colorful are the leaves? How red is the blood of the birds that spreads through the river beneath her?

"Mommy!" the Boy calls.

Mommy has to open her eyes, she wants to say. *Mommy has to look.*

But the birds have gone mad.

"Mommy!" the Boy says again.

She answers. She hardly recognizes her own voice.

"What is it, Boy?"

"Something is here with us, Mommy. Something is *right* here."

The rowboat stops.

Something has stopped it.

She can hear it move in the water beside them.

It's not an animal, she thinks. *It's not Gary. It's the thing you've been hiding from for four and a half years. It's the thing that won't let you look outside.*

Malorie readies herself.

There is something in the water to her left. Inches from her arm.

The birds above are growing distant. As if rising, rising, in a lunatic rush toward the ends of the sky.

She can *feel* the presence of something beside her.

The birds are growing quieter. Quieting. They fade. Rising. Gone.

Tom's voice continues. The river flows around the rowboat.

Malorie screams when she feels her blindfold being pulled from her face.

She does not move.

The blindfold stops an inch from her closed eyes.

Can she hear it? Breathing? Is that what she hears? *Is that it?*

Tom, she thinks, *Tom is leaving a message.*

His voice echoes across the river. He sounds so hopeful. Alive.

Tom. I'm going to have to open my eyes. Talk to me. Please. Tell me what to do. Tom, I'm going to have to open my eyes.

His voice comes from ahead. He sounds like the sun, the only light in all this darkness.

The blindfold is pulled an inch farther from her face. The knot presses against the back of her head.

Tom, I'm going to have to open my eyes.

And, so . . .

forty-two

. . . she does.

Malorie sits up in bed and grips her belly before she understands that she has been howling for some time already. The bed is soaking wet.

Two men rush into the room. It is all so dreamy

(*Am I really having a baby? A baby? I was pregnant this whole time?*)

and so frightening

(*Where's Shannon? Where is Mother?*)

that, at first, she does not recognize them as Felix and Jules.

"Holy *shit*," Felix says. "Olympia is already up there. Olympia started maybe two hours ago."

Up where? Malorie thinks. *Up where?*

The men are careful with her and help her ease to the edge of the bed.

"Are you ready to do this?" Jules asks anxiously.

Malorie just looks at him, her brow furrowed, her face pink and pale at once.

"I was sleeping," she says. "I was just . . . up where, Felix?"

"She's ready," Jules says, forcing a smile, trying to comfort her. "You look wonderful, Malorie. You look ready."

She starts to ask, "Up—"

But Felix tells her before she finishes.

"We're going to do this in the attic. Tom says it's the safest place in the house. In case something were to happen. But nothing's going to happen. Olympia's up there already. She's been going for two hours. Tom and Cheryl are up there with her. Don't worry, Malorie. We'll do everything we can."

Malorie doesn't answer. The feeling of something inside her that must get out is the most horrifying and incredible feeling she's ever known. The men have her, one under each arm, and they walk her out of the room, over the threshold, and down the hall toward the rear of the house. The attic stairs are already pulled down and as they steady her, Malorie sees the blankets covering the window at the end of the hall. She wonders what time of day it is. If it's the next night. If it's a week later.

Am I really having my baby? Now?

Felix and Jules help her up the old wooden steps. She can hear Olympia upstairs. And Tom's gentle voice, saying things like *breathe, you'll be fine, you're okay.*

"Maybe it won't be so different after all," she says (the men, thank God, helping her up the creaking steps). "Maybe it won't be so different from how I hoped it would go."

There is more room up here than she pictured. A single candle lights the space. Olympia is on a towel on the ground. Cheryl is beside her. Olympia's knees are lifted and a thin bedsheet covers her from the waist down. Jules helps her onto her own towel facing Olympia. Tom approaches Malorie.

"Oh, Malorie!" Olympia says. She is out of breath and only part of her exclaims while the rest buckles and contorts. "I'm so glad you're here!"

Malorie, dazed, can't help but feel like she's still sleeping when she looks over her covered knees and sees Olympia set up like a reflection.

"How long have you been here, Olympia?"

"I don't know. Forever, I think!"

Felix is talking quietly to Olympia, asking her what she needs. Then he heads downstairs to get it. Tom reminds Cheryl to keep things clean. They're going to be okay, he says, as long as they're clean. They're using clean sheets and towels. Hand sanitizer from Tom's house. Two buckets of well water.

Tom appears calm, but Malorie knows he's not.

"Malorie?" Tom asks.

"Yes?"

"What do you need?"

"How about some water? And some music, too, Tom."

"Music?"

"Yes. Something sweet and soft, you know, something to maybe"— *Something to cover up the sound of my body on the wood floor of an attic*— "the flute music. That one tape."

"Okay," Tom says. "I'll get it."

He does, stepping by her to the stairs that descend directly behind her back. She turns her attention to Olympia. She's still having trouble shaking the fog of sleep. She sees a small steak knife beside her on a paper towel, less than a foot away. Cheryl just dunked it into the water.

"Jesus!" Olympia suddenly hollers, and Felix kneels and takes her hand.

Malorie watches.

These people, she thinks, *the kind of person that would answer an ad like that in the paper. These people are survivors.*

She experiences a momentary surge of peace. She knows it won't last long. The housemates wisp through her mind, their faces, one by one. With each she feels something like love.

My God, she thinks, *we've been so brave.*

"*God!*" Olympia suddenly screams. Cheryl is quickly beside her.

Once, when Tom was up here looking for tape, Malorie watched from the foot of the ladder stairs. But she's never been up here herself. Now, breathing heavily, she looks to the curtain covering the lone window and she feels a chill. Even the attic has been protected. A room hardly ever used still needs a blanket. Her eyes travel along the wooden window frame, then along the paneled walls, the pointed ceiling, the boxes of things George left behind. Her eyes continue to a stack of blankets piled high. Another box of plastic parts. Old books. Old clothes.

Someone is standing by the old clothes.

It's Don.

Malorie feels a contraction.

Tom returns with a glass of water and the little radio they play cassettes on.

"Here, Malorie," he says. "I found it."

The sound of crackling violins escapes the small speakers. Malorie thinks it's perfect.

"Thank you," she says.

Tom's face looks very tired. His eyes are only half open and puffy. Like he slept for an hour or less.

Malorie feels a cramping so incredible that at first she thinks it isn't real. It feels like a bear trap has clamped down on her waist.

Voices come from behind her. Down the attic stairs. It's Cheryl. Jules. She's hardly aware of who's up here and who isn't.

"Oh *God*!" Olympia calls out.

Tom is with her. Felix is by Malorie's side again.

"You're going to make it," Malorie calls to Olympia.

As she does, thunder booms outside. Rain falls hard against the roof. Somehow the rain is the exact sound she was looking for. The world outside *sounds* like how she feels inside. Stormy. Menacing. Foul. The housemates emerge from the shadows, then vanish. Tom looks worried. Olympia is breathing hard, panting. The stairs creak. Someone new is here. It's Jules, again. Tom is telling him Olympia is farther along than Malorie is. Thunder cracks outside. As lightning strikes, she sees Don in relief, his features sullen, his eyes set deep above dark circles.

There is an unbearable pressing tightness at Malorie's waist. Her body, it seems, is acting on its own, refuting her mind's desire for peace.

She screams and Cheryl leaves Olympia's side and comes to her. Malorie didn't even know Cheryl was still up here.

"This is *awful*," Olympia hisses.

Malorie thinks of women sharing cycles, women in tune with one another's bodies. For all their talk about who would go first, neither she nor Olympia ever even joked that both of them might be in labor at the same time.

Oh, how Malorie longed for a traditional birth!

More thunder.

It is darker up here now. Tom brings a second candle, lights it, and sets it on the floor to Malorie's left. In the flickering flame she sees Felix and Cheryl but Olympia is difficult to make out. Her torso and face are obscured by flickering shadows.

Someone descends the stairs behind her. Is it Don? She doesn't want to crane her neck. Tom steps through the candlelight and then out of its range. Then Felix, she thinks, then Cheryl. Silhouettes are moving from her to Olympia like phantoms.

The rain comes down harder against the roof.

There is a loud, abrupt commotion downstairs. Malorie can't be sure but she thinks someone is yelling. Is her tired mind mistaking sounds? Who's arguing?

It *does* sound like an argument below.

She can't think about this right now. She won't.

"Malorie?" Malorie screams as Cheryl's face suddenly appears beside her. "Squeeze my hand. Break it if you need to."

Malorie wants to say, *Get some light in here. Get me a doctor. Deliver this thing for me.*

Instead she responds with a grunt.

She is having her baby. There is no longer *when*.

Will I see things differently now? I've seen everything through the prism of this baby. It's how I saw the house. The housemates. The world. It's how I saw the news when it first started and how I saw the news when it ended.

I've been horrified, paranoid, angry, more. When my body returns to the shape it was when I walked the streets freely, will I see things differently again?

What will Tom look like? How will his ideas sound?

"Malorie!" Olympia calls in the darkness. "I don't think I can do it!"

Cheryl is telling Olympia she can, she's almost there.

"What's going on downstairs?" Malorie suddenly asks.

Don is below. She can hear him arguing. Jules, too. Yes, Don and Jules are arguing in the hall beneath the attic. Is Tom with them? Is Felix? No. Felix emerges from the dark and takes her hand.

"Are you okay, Malorie?"

"No," she says. "What's going on downstairs?"

He pauses, then says, "I'm not sure. But you have bigger things to worry about than people getting in each other's faces."

"Is it Don?" she asks.

"Don't worry about it, Malorie."

It rains harder. It's as if each drop has its own audible weight.

Malorie lifts her head to see Olympia's eyes in the shadows, staring at her.

Beyond the rain, the arguing, the commotion downstairs, Malorie hears *something*. Sweeter than violins.

What is it?

"Oh fuck!" Olympia screams. "Make it *stop*!"

It's becoming harder for Malorie to breathe. It feels like the baby is cutting off her air supply. Like it's crawling up her throat instead.

Tom is here. He is at her side.

"I'm sorry, Malorie."

She turns to him. The face she sees, the look on his face, is something she will remember years after this morning.

"Sorry for what, Tom? Sorry this is how it's happened?"

Tom's eyes look sad. He nods yes. They both know he has no reason to apologize but they both know no woman should have to endure her delivery in the stuffy attic of a house she calls home only because she cannot leave.

"You know what I think?" he says softly, reaching down to grab her hand. "I think you're going to be a wonderful mother. I think you're going to raise this child so well it won't matter if the world continues this way or not."

To Malorie, it feels like a rusty steel clamp is trying to pull the baby from her now. A tow truck chain from the shadows ahead.

"Tom," she manages to say. "What's wrong down there?"

"Don's upset. That's all."

She wants to talk more about it. She's not angry at Don anymore. She's worried about him. Of all the housemates, he's stricken worst by the new world. He's lost in it. There is something emptier than hopelessness in his eyes. Malorie wants to tell Tom that she loves Don, that they all do, that he just needs help. But the pain is absolutely all she can process. And words are momentarily impossible. The argument below now sounds like a joke. Like someone's kidding her. Like the house is telling her, *You see? Have a sense of humor despite the unholy pain going on in my attic.*

Malorie has known exhaustion and hunger. Physical pain and severe mental fatigue. But she has never known the state she is in now. She not only has the right to be unbothered by a squabble among housemates, but she also very nearly deserves that they all leave the house entirely and stand out in the yard with their eyes closed for as long as it takes her and Olympia to do what their bodies need to do.

Tom stands up.

"I'll be right back," he says. "Do you need some more water?"

Malorie shakes her head no and returns her eyes to the shadows and sheet that is Olympia's struggle before her.

"We're doing it!" Olympia says, suddenly, maniacally. "It's happening!"

So many sounds. The voices below, the voices in the attic (coming from the shadows and coming from faces emerging from those shadows), the ladder stairs, creaking every time a housemate ascends or descends, assessing the situation up here and then the one (she knows there is a problem downstairs, she just can't care right now) going on a floor below. The rain falls but there *is* something else. Another sound. An instrument maybe. The highest keys of the dining room's piano.

Suddenly, strangely, Malorie feels another wave of peace. Despite the thousand blades that pierce her lungs, neck, and chest, she understands that no matter what she does, no matter what happens, the baby is coming out. What does it matter what kind of world she is bringing this baby into now? Olympia is right. It's *happening*. The child is coming, the child is almost out. And he has always been a part of the new world.

He knows anxiety, fear, paranoia. He was worried when Tom and Jules went to find dogs. He was painfully relieved when they returned. He was frightened of the change in Don. The change in the house. As it went from a hopeful haven to a bitter, anxious place. His heart was heavy when I read the ad that led me here, just like it was when I read the notebook in the cellar.

At the word "cellar" Malorie actually hears Don's voice from below.

He's yelling.

Yet, something beyond his voice worries her more.

"Do you hear that sound, Olympia?"

"What?" Olympia grumbles. It sounds like she has staples in her throat.

"That sound. It sounds like . . ."

"It's the rain," Olympia says.

"No, not that. There's something else. It sounds like we've already had our babies."

"What?"

To Malorie it *does* sound like a baby. Something like it, past the housemates at the foot of the ladder stairs. Maybe even on the first floor, the living room, maybe even—

Maybe even outside.

JOSH MALERMAN

But what does that mean? What is happening? Is someone crying on the front porch?

Impossible. It's something else.

But it's *alive*.

Lightning explodes. The attic is fully visible, nightmarishly, for a flash. The blanket covering the window remains fixed in Malorie's mind long after the light passes and the thunder rolls. Olympia screams when it happens and Malorie, her eyes closed, sees her friend's expression of fear frozen in her mind.

But her attention is drawn back to the impossible pressure at her waist. It seems Olympia could be howling for her. Every time Malorie feels the awful knife stabbing in her side, Olympia laments.

Do I howl for her, too?

The cassette tape comes to a stop. Then so does the commotion from below.

Even the rain abates.

The smaller sounds in the attic are more audible now. Malorie listens to herself breathing. The footsteps of the housemates who help them are defined.

Figures emerge. Then vanish.

There's Tom (she's sure).

There's Felix (she thinks).

There's Jules now at Olympia's side.

Is the world receding? Or am I sailing farther into this pain?

She hears that noise again. Like an infant on the doorstep. Something young and alive coming from downstairs. Only now it is more pronounced. Only now it doesn't have to fight through the argument and the music and the rain.

Yes, it is more pronounced now, more defined. As Tom crosses the attic, she can hear the sound between his footsteps. His boot connecting with the wood, then lifting, exposing the youthful notes from below.

Then, very clearly, Malorie recognizes what it is.

It's the birds. Oh my God. It's the birds.

The cardboard box beating against the house's outer wall and the soft sweet cooing of the birds.

"There is something outside the house," she says.

Quietly at first.

Cheryl is a few feet from her.

"*There is something outside the house!*" she yells.

Jules looks up from behind Olympia's shoulder.

There's a loud crash from below. Felix yells. Jules rushes past Malorie. His boots are loud and quick on the ladder stairs behind her.

Malorie frantically looks around the attic for Tom. He's not up here. He's downstairs.

"Olympia," Malorie says, more to herself. "We're alone up here!"

Olympia does not respond.

Malorie tries not to listen but she can't stop herself. It sounds like they're all in the living room now. The first floor for sure. Everybody is yelling. Did Jules just say "don't"?

As the commotion builds, so does the pain at Malorie's waist.

Malorie, her back to the stairs, cranes her neck. She wants to know what is happening. She wants to tell them to *stop*. There are two pregnant women in the attic who need your help. *Please stop.*

Delirious, Malorie lets her chin fall to her chest. Her eyes close. She feels like, if she were to lose focus, she could pass out. Or worse.

The rain returns. Malorie opens her eyes. She sees Olympia, her head bent toward the ceiling. The veins in her neck are showing. Slowly, Malorie scans the attic. Beside Olympia are boxes. Then the window. Then more boxes. Old books. The old clothes.

A flash of lightning from outside illuminates the attic space. Malorie closes her eyes. In her darkness, she sees a frozen image of the attic's walls.

The window. The boxes.

And a man, standing where Don was standing when she came up here.

It's not possible, she thinks.

But it is.

And, before her eyes are fully open, she understands who is standing there, who is in the attic with her.

"Gary," Malorie says, a hundred thoughts accosting her. "You've been hiding in the cellar."

She thinks of Victor growling at the cellar door.

She thinks of Don, sleeping down there.

As Malorie looks Gary in the eye, the argument downstairs escalates. Jules is hoarse. Don is livid. It sounds like they are exchanging blows.

Gary emerges from the shadows. He is approaching her.

When we closed our eyes and Tom opened the front door, she thinks, knowing it is true, *Don snuck him farther into the house.*

"What are you doing here?!" Olympia suddenly yells. Gary does not look at her. He only comes to Malorie.

"*Stay away from me!*" Malorie screams.

He kneels beside her.

"You," he says. "So vulnerable in your present state. I'd have thought you would have had more sympathy than to send someone out into a world like this one."

Lightning flashes again.

"*Tom! Jules!*"

Her baby is not out yet. But he must be close.

"Don't yell," Gary says. "I'm not angry."

"Please leave me alone. Please leave us."

Gary laughs.

"You keep saying that! You keep wanting me to leave!"

Thunder rolls outside. The housemates are getting louder.

"You never left," Malorie says, each word like removing a small rock from her chest.

"That's right, I never did."

Tears pool in Malorie's eyes.

"Don had the heart to lend me a hand, and the foresight to predict I might be voted out."

Don, she thinks, *what have you done?*

Gary leans closer.

"Do you mind if I tell you a story while you do this?"

"What?"

"A story. Something to keep your mind off the pain. And let me tell you that you're doing a wonderful job. Better than my wife did."

Olympia's breathing sounds bad, too labored, like she couldn't possibly survive this.

"One of two things is happening here," Gary says. "Either—"

"Please," Malorie cries. *"Please* leave me alone."

"Either my philosophies are right, or, and I hate to use this word, or I'm *immune.*"

It feels like the baby is at the edge of her body. Yet it feels too big to escape. Malorie gasps and closes her eyes. But the pain is everywhere, even in her darkness.

They don't know he's up here. Oh my God they don't know he's here.

"I've watched this street for a long time," Gary says. "I watched as Tom and Jules stumbled their way around the block. I was mere inches from Tom as he studied the very tent that sheltered me."

"Stop it. STOP IT!"

But yelling only makes the pain worse. Malorie focuses. She pushes. She breathes. But she can't help but hear.

"I found it fascinating, the lengths the man would go to, while I watched, unharmed, as the creatures passed daily, nightly, sometimes a dozen at once. It's the reason I settled on this street, Malorie. You have no idea how busy it can be out there."

please please please please please please please please PLEASE

From the floor below, she hears Tom's voice.

"Jules! I need you!"

Then a thundering of footsteps leading back down.

"TOM! HELP US! GARY IS UP HERE! TOM!"

"He's preoccupied," Gary says. "There's a real situation going on down there."

Gary rises. He steps to the attic door and quietly closes it.

Then he locks it.

"Is that any better?" he asks.

"What have you done?" Malorie hisses.

More shouting from below now. It sounds like everybody is moving at once. For an instant, she believes she has gone mad. No matter how safe she's been, it feels like there is no hiding from the insanity of the new world.

Someone screams in the hall below the locked attic door. Malorie thinks it's Felix.

"My wife wasn't prepared," Gary says, suddenly beside her. "I watched her as she saw one. I didn't warn her it was coming. I—"

"*Why didn't you tell us?!*" Malorie asks, crying, pushing.

"Because," Gary says, "just like the others, none of you would have believed me. Except Don."

"You're *mad*."

Gary laughs, grinning.

"What is happening downstairs?!" Olympia yells. "Malorie! What is *happening* downstairs?!"

"*I don't know!*"

"It's Don," Gary says. "He's trying to convince the others what I've taught him."

"IT'S DON!"

The voice from below is as clear as if it were spoken in the attic.

"DON PULLED THEM DOWN! DON PULLED THE BLANKETS DOWN!"

"They won't hurt us," Gary whispers. The whiskers of his moist beard touch Malorie's ear.

But she is no longer listening to him.

"Malorie?" Olympia whispers.

"DON PULLED THE BLANKETS DOWN AND OPENED THE DOOR! THEY'RE IN THE HOUSE! DID YOU HEAR ME? THEY'RE IN THE HOUSE!"

the baby is coming the baby is coming the baby is coming

"Malorie?"

"Olympia," she says, defeated, void of hope (is it true? is her own voice saying as much?). "Yes. They're in the house now."

The storm outside whips against the walls.

The chaos below sounds impossible.

"They sound like wolves," Olympia cries. "They sound like *wolves*!"

Don Don Don Don Don Don Don Don Don Don

tore the blankets down

let them in

someone saw them

let them in

someone went mad who was it?

Don let them in

Don tore down the blankets

Don doesn't believe they can hurt us

Don thinks it's only in our mind

Gary knelt by him in the chair in the dining room

Gary spoke to him from behind the tapestry in the cellar

Don pulled the blankets down

Gary told him they were fake, Gary told him they were harmless

may have gone mad who is it who has?

(*push, Malorie, push, you have a baby, a baby to worry about, close your eyes if you have to but push push*)

they're in the house now

and everyone in it

sounds like wolves.

The birds, Malorie thinks, hysterical, *were a good idea, Tom. A great one.*

Olympia is frantically asking her questions but Malorie can't answer. Her mind is full.

"Is it true? Is there really one in the house? That can't be true. We'd never allow it! Is there really one in the house? *Right now?*"

Something slams against a wall downstairs. A body maybe. The dogs are barking.

Someone threw a dog against the wall.

"DON TORE THE BLANKETS DOWN!"

Who has their eyes closed down there? Who has the presence of mind? Would Malorie? Would Malorie have been able to close her eyes as her housemates went mad?

Oh my God, Malorie thinks. *They're going to die down there.*

The baby is killing her.

Gary is still whispering in her ear.

"What you hear down there, that's what I mean, Malorie. They think they're supposed to go mad. But they don't have to. I spent seasons out there. I watched them for weeks at a time."

"Impossible," Malorie says. She doesn't know if this word is directed at Gary, the noise below, or the pain she believes will never pass.

"The first time I saw one, I thought I'd gone mad." Gary nervously laughs. "But I didn't. And when I slowly realized I was still of sound mind, I began to understand what was happening. To my friends. My family. To everybody."

"I don't want to hear any more!" Malorie screams. She feels like she may split down the center. There has been a mistake, she thinks. The baby that tries to escape her is too big and it will split her.

It's a boy, she believes.

"You know what?"

"Stop!"

"You know what?"

"No! No! No!"

Olympia howls, the sky howls, the dogs howl downstairs. Malorie believes she hears Jules specifically. She hears him racing a floor below. She hears him trying to tear something apart in the bathroom down there.

"Maybe I am immune, Malorie. Or maybe I'm simply *aware*."

She wants to say, *Do you know how much you could have done for us? Do you understand how much safer you could have made us?*

But Gary is mad.

And he probably always has been.

Don pulled the blankets down.

Gary knelt by him in the dining room.

Gary spoke to him from behind a tapestry in the cellar.

Gary the demon on Don's soft shoulder.

There is a thunderous knocking at the attic's floor door.

"LET ME IN!" someone screams.

It's Felix, Malorie thinks. *Or Don.*

"JESUS CHRIST LET ME IN!"

But it's neither.

It's *Tom*.

"*Open the door for him!*" Malorie screams at Gary.

"Are you sure you want me to do that? It doesn't sound to me like a safe idea."

"*Please please please! Let him in!*"

It's Tom, oh my God, it's Tom, it's Tom, oh my God, it's Tom.

She pushes hard. Oh *God* she pushes hard.

"Breathe," Gary tells her. "Breathe. You're almost there now."

"Please," Malorie cries. "*Please!*"

"LET ME IN! LET ME UP THERE!"

Olympia is screaming now, too.

"*Open the door for him! It's Tom!*"

The insanity from below is knocking on the door.

Tom.

Tom is insane. Tom saw one of the creatures.

Tom is insane.

Did you hear him? Did you hear his voice? That was the sound he makes. That was how he sounds without his mind, without his beautiful mind.

Gary rises and crosses the attic. The rain pounds on the roof.

The knocking on the attic floor door stops.

Malorie looks across the attic to Olympia.

Olympia's black hair mingles with the shadows. Her eyes blaze from within.

"We're . . . almost . . . there," she says.

Olympia's child is coming out. In the candlelight, Malorie can see it is halfway there.

Instinctively, she reaches for it, though it is an attic floor away.

"Olympia! Don't forget to cover your child's eyes. Don't forget to—"

The attic floor's door crashes open hard. The lock has been broken.

Malorie screams but all she hears is her own heartbeat, louder than all of the new world.

Then she is silent.

Gary rises and steps back toward the window.

There are heavy footsteps behind her.

Malorie's baby is emerging.

The stairs groan.

"Who is it?" she screams. "Who is it? Is everyone okay? Is it Tom? Who is it?"

Someone she cannot see has climbed the stairs and is in the attic with them.

Malorie, her back to the stairs, watches as Olympia's expression changes from pain to awe.

Olympia, she thinks. *Don't look. We've been so good. So brave. Don't look. Reach for your child instead. Hide its eyes when it comes out completely. Hide its eyes. And hide your own. Don't look. Olympia. Don't look.*

But she understands it's too late for her friend.

Olympia leans forward. Her eyes grow huge, her mouth opens. Her face becomes three perfect circles. For a moment Malorie sees her features contort, then shine instead.

"You're beautiful," Olympia says, smiling. It's a broken, twitching smile. "You're not bad at all. You wanna see my baby? Do you wanna see my baby?"

The child the child, Malorie thinks, *the child is in her and she has gone mad. Oh my God, Olympia has gone mad, oh my God, the thing is behind me and the thing is behind my child.*

Malorie closes her eyes.

As she does, the image of Gary remains, still standing at the edge of the candlelight's reach. But he does not look as confident as he professed that he should. He looks like a scared child.

"Olympia," Malorie says. "You've got to cover the baby's eyes. You've got to reach down. For your baby."

Malorie can't see her friend's expression. But her voice reveals the change within her.

"What? You're going to tell me how to raise my child? What kind of a *bitch* are you? What kind of a—"

Olympia's words morph into a guttural growl.

Insanity fuss.

Gary's diseased, dangerous words.

Olympia is baying.

Malorie's baby is crowning. She pushes.

With a strength she didn't know she possessed, Malorie inches forward on the towel. She wants Olympia's child. She will protect it.

Then, amid all this pain and madness, Malorie hears Olympia's baby's very first cry.

Close its eyes.

Then at last Malorie's child comes through and her hand is there to cup its eyes. Its head is so soft and she believes she's gotten to him in time.

JOSH MALERMAN

"Come here," she says, bringing the baby to her chest. "Come here and close your eyes."

Gary laughs anxiously from across the room.

"Incredible," he says.

Malorie feels for the steak knife. She finds it and cuts her own cord. Then she cuts two strips from the bloody towel beneath her. She feels his sex and knows it's a boy and has no one to tell this to. No sister. No mother. No father. No nurse. No Tom. She holds him tight to her chest.

Slowly, she ties a piece of the towel around his eyes.

How important is it that he sees his mother's face when he enters the world?

She hears the creature shift behind her.

"Baby," Olympia says, but her voice is cracked. She sounds like she's using the voice of an older woman. "My *baby,*" she crows.

Malorie slides forward. The muscles in her body resist. She reaches for Olympia's child.

"Here," she says blindly. "Here, Olympia. Let me have it. Let me see it."

Olympia grunts.

"Why should I let *you*? What do you want my child for? Are you *mad*?"

"No. I just want to see it."

Malorie's eyes are still closed. The attic is quiet. The rain lands softly on the roof. Malorie slides forward, still on the blood beneath her body.

"Can I? Can I just see her? It is a girl, right? Weren't you right about that?"

Malorie hears something so astonishing that she is halted midway across the floor.

Olympia is gnawing at something. She knows it's the child's cord.

Her stomach turns. She keeps her eyes closed tight. She's going to throw up.

"Can I see her?" Malorie manages to ask.

"Here. *Here!*" Olympia says. "Look at her. *Look at her!*"

At last, Malorie's hands are on Olympia's baby. It's a girl.

Olympia stands up. It sounds like she steps in a rain puddle. It's blood, Malorie knows. Afterbirth, sweat, and blood.

"Thank you," Malorie whispers. "Thank you, Olympia."

This action, this handing off of her child, will always shine to Malorie. The moment Olympia did right by her child despite having lost her mind.

Malorie ties the second piece of towel around the baby's eyes.

Olympia shuffles toward the draped window. To where Gary stands.

The thing waits behind Malorie and is still.

Malorie grips both babies, shielding their eyes even more with her bloody, wet fingers. Both babies cry.

And suddenly Olympia is struggling with something, sliding something.

Like she's climbing now.

"Olympia?"

It sounds like Olympia is setting something up.

"Olympia? What are you doing, Olympia? Gary, stop her. *Please,* Gary."

Her words are useless. Gary is the maddest of all.

"I'm going outside, sir," Olympia says to Gary, who must be near. "I've been inside a *long* time."

"Olympia, *stop.*"

"I'm going to step *OUTSIDE,*" she says, her voice at once like a child and a centenarian on her deathbed.

"*Olympia!*"

It's too late. Malorie hears the glass of the attic window shatter. Something bangs against the house.

Silence. From downstairs. From the attic. Then Gary speaks.

"She hangs! *She hangs by her cord!*"

Don't. Please, God, don't let this man describe it to me.

"She hangs by her cord! The most incredible thing I've *ever* seen! She hangs by her cord!"

There is laughter, joy in his voice.

The thing moves behind her. Malorie is at the epicenter of all this madness. Old madness. The kind people used to get from war, divorce, poverty, and things like knowing that your friend is—

"Hanging by her cord! By *her cord*!"

"Shut *up*!" Malorie screams blindly. "*Shut up!*"

But her words are choked, as she feels the thing behind her is leaning in. A part of it (*its face?*) moves near her lips.

Malorie only breathes. She does not move. The attic is silent.

She can feel the warmth, the heat, of the thing beside her.

Shannon, she thinks, *look at the clouds. They look like us. You and I.*

She tightens her grip over the babies' eyes.

She hears the thing behind her retract. It sounds as if it's moving away from her. Farther.

It pauses. Stops.

When she hears the wooden stairs creaking, and when she's sure it is the sound of someone descending, she releases a sob deeper than any she's ever known.

The steps grow quiet. Quieter. Then, they are gone.

"It's left us," she tells the babies.

Now she hears Gary move.

"Don't come *near* us!" she screams with her eyes closed. "Don't you *touch* us!"

He doesn't touch her. He passes by, and the stairs creak again.

He's gone downstairs. He's going to see who made it. Who didn't.

She heaves, aches from exhaustion. From blood loss. Her body tells her to sleep, *sleep.* They are alone in the attic, Malorie and the babies. She begins to lie back. She needs to. Instead, she waits. She listens. She rests.

How much time is passing? How long have I held these babies?

But a new sound fractures her reprieve. It's coming from downstairs. It's a noise that was made often in the old world.

Olympia hangs (*so he said so he said*) from the attic window.

Her body thumps against the house in the wind.

And now something rings from below.

It's the telephone. The telephone is ringing.

Malorie is almost mesmerized by the sound. How long has it been since she's heard something like it?

Someone is calling them.

Someone is calling *back*.

Malorie turns herself, sliding in the afterbirth. She places the girl in her lap, then gently covers her with her shirt. Using her empty hand, she feels for the head of the ladder stairs. They are steep. They are old. No woman who just gave birth should have to negotiate them at all.

But the phone is ringing. Someone is calling back. And Malorie is going to answer it.

Riiiiiiiiiiiing

Despite their towel blindfolds, she tells the babies to keep their eyes closed.

This command will be the most common thing she says to them over the next four years. And nothing will stop her from saying it, whether or not they're too young to understand her.

Riiiiiiiiiiiiiiing

She slides her ass to the edge of the floor and swings her legs over to rest her feet on the first step. Her body screams at her to stop.

But she continues down.

Down the stairs now. She cradles the boy in her right arm, her palm wrapped around his face. The girl is up inside her shirt. Malorie's eyes are closed and the world is black and she needs sleep so bad she might as well fall from the stairs and into it. Only she walks, she steps, and she uses the phone as her guide.

Riiiiiiiiiiiiiiiiiiiiiiing

Her feet touch the light blue carpeting of the second floor's white hall. Eyes closed, she does not see these colors, just like she does not see Jules lying facedown along the right wall, five bloody streaks trailing from the height of her head to where his hand lies pressed against the floor.

At the top of the stairs, she pauses. She breathes deep. She believes she can do it. Then she continues.

She passes Cheryl but does not know it. Not yet. Cheryl's head faces the first floor, her feet the second. Her body is horribly, unnaturally contorted.

Without knowing it, Malorie steps inches from her.

She almost touches Felix at the foot of the stairs. But she doesn't. Later, she will gasp when she feels the holes in his face.

Riiiiiiiiiiiiiiiiiiiiiiiiiiiiiing

She has no idea she passes one of the huskies. It is slumped against the wall; the wall is stained dark purple.

She wants to say, *Is anyone still here?* She wants to scream it. But the phone rings and she does not believe it will stop until she answers it.

She follows the sound, leaning against the wall.

Rain and wind come in through broken windows.

I must answer the phone.

If her eyes were to open, she would not be able to process the amount of blood marking the house.

Riiiiiiiiiiiiiiiiiiiiiiiiiiiiiing

She will see all of that later. But right now the phone is so loud, so close.

Malorie turns, puts her back against the wall, then slides, excruciatingly, to the carpet. The phone is on the small end table. Her body aches and burns, every part of it. Placing the boy beside the girl in her lap, she reaches out with her hand and fumbles for the phone that has been ringing without rest.

"Hello?"

"Hello."

It's a man. His voice sounds so calm. So horribly out of place.

"Who is this?" Malorie asks.

She can hardly understand that she is using a telephone.

"My name is Rick. We got your message a few days ago. I guess you could say we've been busy. What's your name?"

"Who is this?"

"Again, my name is Rick. A man named Tom left a message with us."

"Tom."

"Yes. He does live there, right?"

"My name is Malorie."

"Are you okay, Malorie? You sound broken up."

Malorie breathes deep. She doesn't think she will ever be okay again.

"Yes," she answers. "I'm okay."

"We haven't got much time right now. Are you interested in getting out from where you are? Somewhere safer? I'm assuming the answer is yes."

"Yes," Malorie says.

"Here's what you do then. Write this down if you can. Do you have a pen?"

Malorie says yes and reaches for the pen kept by Tom's phone book. The babies cry.

"It sounds like you have a baby with you?"

"I do."

"I imagine that's your reason for wanting to find a better place. Here's the information, Malorie. Take the river."

"What?"

"Take the river. Do you know where it is?"

"Y-yes. I do know where it is. It's right behind the house. Eighty yards from the well, I'm told."

"Good. Take the river. It's about as dangerous a thing as you can do, but I imagine if you and Tom have made it this long, you can do it. I found you guys on the map and it looks like you'll have to travel at least twenty miles. Now, the river is going to split—"

"It's going to what?"

"I'm sorry. I'm probably moving too fast. But where I'm directing you is a better place."

"How is that?"

"Well, we don't have windows for one. We have running water. And we grow our own food. It's as self-contained as you can find nowadays. There are plenty of bedrooms. Nice ones. Most of us think we've got it better now than we did before."

"How many of you are there?"

"One hundred and eight."

The number could be any for Malorie. Or it could be infinity.

"But let me tell you how to get here first. It would be a tragedy if the phone line went out before you knew where to go."

"All right."

"The river is going to split into four channels. The one you want is the second one from the right. So you can't hug the right bank and expect to make it. It's tricky. And you're going to have to open your eyes."

Malorie slowly shakes her head. *No.*

Rick continues.

"And this is how you'll know when that time comes," the man tells her. "You'll hear a recording. A voice. We can't sit by the river all day every day. It's just too dangerous. Instead, we've got a speaker down there. It's motion activated. We have a very clear understanding of the woods and water beyond our facility because of devices like it. Once the speaker is activated, the recording plays for thirty minutes, on a loop. You'll hear it. The same forty-second sound bite repeated. It's loud. Clear. And when you do, that's when you'll have to open your eyes."

"Thank you, Rick. But I just can't do that."

Her voice is listless. Destroyed.

"I understand it's terrifying. Of course it is. But that's the catch, I suppose. There's no other way."

Malorie thinks of hanging up. But Rick continues.

"We've got so many good things happening here. We make progress every day. Of course, we're nowhere near where we'd like to be. But we're trying."

Malorie starts to cry. The words, what this man is telling her—is it hope he gives her? Or is it some deeper variation of the incredible hopelessness she already feels?

"If I do what you're telling me to do," Malorie says, "how will I find you from there?"

"From the split?"

"Yes."

"We have an alarm system. It's the same technology used for triggering the recording you'll hear. Once you take the correct channel, you'll go another hundred yards. Then you'll trigger our notification alarm. A fence will be lowered. You'll be stuck. And we'll come looking for what got stuck in our fence."

Malorie shivers.

"Oh yeah?" she asks.

"Yes. You sound skeptical."

Visions of the old world rush through her mind, but with each memory comes a leash, a chain, and an instinctive feeling that tells her this man and this place might be good, might be bad, might be better than where she is now, might be worse, but she will never be free again.

"How many of you are there?" Rick asks.

Malorie listens to the silence of the house. The windows are broken. The door is probably open. She must stand up. Close the door. Cover the windows. But it all feels like it's happening to someone else.

"Three," she says, lifeless. "If the number changes—"

"Don't worry about it, Malorie. Any number you come with is fine. We have space enough for a few hundred and we're working on more. Just come as soon as you can."

"Rick, can you come help me now?"

She hears Rick take a deep breath.

"I'm sorry, Malorie. It's too much of a risk. I'm needed here. I realize that sounds selfish. But I'm afraid you'll have to get to us."

Malorie nods silently. Amid the gore, the loss, the pain, she respects that this man must stay safe.

Only I can't open my eyes right now and I have two newborns in my lap who have yet to see the world and the room smells of piss, blood, and death. Air comes in fast from outside. It's cold and I know that means the window is broken or the front door is open. So dangerously open. So, all this sounds good, Rick, it truly does, but I'm not sure how I'm going to get to the bathroom yet let alone onto a river for forty miles or whatever it was you said.

"Malorie, I'll check in on you. I'll call again. Or do you think you'll be coming right away?"

"I don't know. I don't know when I'll be able to come."

"Okay."

"But thank you."

It feels like the most sincere thank-you Malorie has ever spoken in her life.

"I'll call you in a week, Malorie."

"Okay."

"Malorie?"

"Yes?"

"If I don't call, it could mean the lines have finally died on our end. Or it could mean the lines at your place are out, too. Just trust me when I tell you we will be here. You come anytime. We will be here."

"Okay," Malorie says.

Rick gives her his phone number. Malorie, using the pen, blindly scribbles the numbers on a page in the open phone book.

"Good-bye, Malorie."

"Good-bye."

Just a simple, everyday talk on the phone.

Malorie hangs up. Then she hangs her head and cries. The babies shift in her lap. She cries for another twenty minutes, unbroken, until she screams when she hears something scratching at the cellar door. It is Victor. He is barking to be let out. Somehow, he was blessedly locked in the cellar. Maybe Jules, knowing what was coming, did it.

After rehanging the blankets and closing the doors, she will use a broomstick to search every inch of the home for creatures. It will be six hours before she feels safe enough to open her eyes, at which point she will see what went on in the house while she was delivering her baby.

But before then, with her eyes closed tightly, Malorie will stand up and step back through the living room until she reaches the top of the cellar stairs.

And there she will step by Tom's body.

She will not know it is him, believing it to be a bag of sugar that her foot nudges, as she kneels before the bucket of well water and begins the laborious job of cleaning the children and herself.

She will speak with Rick a number of times in the coming months. But soon the lines reaching the house will die.

It will take her six months to wash the house of the bodies and blood. She will find Don on the kitchen floor, reaching for the cellar. As if he raced there, mad, to ask Gary for his mind back. She will check for Gary. Everywhere. But she will never find a sign of him. She will always be aware of him. The possibility of him. Out there. In the world.

Most of the housemates will be buried in a semicircle around the well out back. She will forever feel the uneven lumps, the graves she dug and filled while blindfolded, whenever she gets water for herself or the children.

Tom will be buried closest to the house. The patch of grass to which she takes the children, blindfolded, as a means of getting them fresh air. A place where, she hopes, their spirits run freest.

It will be four years before she answers yes to whether or not she is coming soon to the place Rick described on the phone.

But now she just washes. Now she just cleans the babies. And the babies cry.

forty-three

om's recorded voice plays over again.

He is leaving a message.

" . . . Two seventy-three Shillingham . . . my name is Tom . . . I'm sure you understand the relief I feel at getting your answering machine . . ."

The blindfold is still held an inch from her closed eyes.

She raises a hand and brings her fingers to the black cloth. For a moment, both she and the creature hold the same blindfold. This creature, or ones like it, stole Shannon, her mother, her father, and Tom. This thing, and the things like it, have stolen childhood from the children.

In a way, Malorie is not afraid. They have done everything to her already.

"No," she says, tugging on the cloth. "This is mine."

For a moment, nothing happens. Then something touches her face. Malorie grimaces. But it is only the fold, returning to its place on her nose and temples.

You're going to have to open your eyes.

It's true. Tom's recorded voice means she has arrived where Rick said the channels split. He speaks as he once did, in the living room of the house, when he used to say, *Maybe they mean us no harm. Maybe they are surprised by what they do to us. It's an overlap, Malorie. Their world and ours. Just an accident. Maybe they don't like hurting us at all.*

But whatever their intentions are, Malorie has to open her eyes, and at least one is near.

She has seen the children do incredible things. Once, after flipping through the phone book, the Boy called out that she was on page one hundred and six. He was close. And Malorie knows she's going to need a feat like that, from them, right now.

There is movement in the water to her left. The creature is either no longer curious about the blindfold and is leaving, or it is waiting to see what Malorie does next.

"Boy?" she says, and she needs to say no more. He understands the question.

He is quiet at first. Listening. Then he answers.

"It's leaving us, Mommy."

Despite the distant, warring birds and Tom's beautiful, calming voice coming from the speaker, it feels like a moment of silence is occurring. Silence emanating from this thing.

Where *is* it now?

The rowboat, released, is being pulled along with the current. Malorie knows that the sound of the water ahead is the sound of the split. She doesn't have much time.

"Boy," she says, her throat dry. "Do you hear anything else?"

The Boy is quiet.

"Boy?"

"No, Mommy. I don't."

"Are you certain? Are you absolutely sure?"

She sounds hysterical. Whether or not she is ready, the moment has come.

"Yes, Mommy. We're alone again."

"Where did it go?"

"It went away."

"Which way?"

Silence. Then, "It's behind us, Mommy."

"Girl?"

"Yes. It's behind us, Mommy."

Malorie is quiet.

The children said the thing is behind them.

If there's one thing she can lean on in the new world, it's that she has trained them well.

She trusts them.

She has to.

Now they are level with Tom's voice. It sounds like he is in the boat with them.

She swallows hard.

She wipes tears from her lips.

She breathes deep.

Then she feels it. Just like when they let Tom and Jules back into the house. Just like when they thought they were letting Gary out.

The Moment Between.

Between deciding to open her eyes and doing it.

Malorie turns to face the channels and opens her eyes.

At first, she has to squint. Not from the sunlight, but from the *colors*.

She gasps, bringing a hand to her mouth.

Her mind is emptied of thoughts, worries, anxieties, and hopes. She knows no words to explain what she sees.

It's kaleidoscopic. Endless. *Magnificent.*

Look, Shannon! That cloud looks like Angela Markle from class!

In the old world, she could have looked at a world twice as bright and not had to squint. But now, the beauty hurts her.

She could look forever. Surely another few seconds. But Tom's voice urges her on.

As if in slow motion, she leans toward where his voice comes from, savoring his every word. It's like he's standing there. Telling her she's so close. Malorie understands that she cannot keep the colors she sees. She must close her eyes again. She must cut herself off from all this wonder, this world.

She closes her eyes.

She returns to the darkness she knows so well now.

She begins rowing.

As she approaches the second channel from the right, it feels like she is rowing with the years. The memories. She rows with the self she was when she found out she was pregnant, when she found Shannon dead, when she answered the ad in the newspaper. She rows with the self she was when she arrived at the house, met the housemates for the first time, and agreed to let Olympia in. She rows with the person she was when Gary arrived. She rows with herself, on a towel in the attic, as Don pulled the blankets from the windows downstairs.

She is stronger now. She is braver. By herself, she has raised two children in *this* world.

Malorie has changed.

The boat rocks suddenly as it touches one of the banks of the channel. Malorie understands they have entered it.

From here, she rows as the person she was when she had the children alone. Four years. Training them. Raising them. Keeping them safe from an outside world that must have grown more dangerous each day. She rows with Tom, too, and the dozens of things he said, the countless things he did and the hope that inspired her, encouraged her, and made her believe that it's better to face madness with a plan than to sit still and let it take you in pieces.

The boat is moving fast now. Rick said it was only a hundred yards to the trigger.

She rows with the person she was when she awoke today. The person who thought a fog might hide her and the children from someone like Gary, who could still be out there, still watching them move down the river. She rows with the self she was when the wolf struck. When the man in the boat went mad. When the birds went mad. And when the creature, the thing she fears above all things, toyed with her only form of protection.

The blindfold.

With the thought of the cloth, and all it's meant to her, Malorie hears what sounds like a loud metallic explosion.

The rowboat crashes into something. Malorie quickly checks the children.

It's the fence, she knows. They have triggered Rick's alarm.

Malorie, her heart pounding, no longer needing to row, turns her head toward the sky and yells. It is relief. It is anger. It is everything.

"We're here," she calls loudly. "*We're here!*"

From the banks, they hear movement. Something is coming fast toward them.

Malorie is gripping the paddles. It feels like her hands will always be in this position.

As she coils something touches her arm.

"It's all right!" a voice says. "My name is Constance. It's okay. I'm with Rick."

"Are your eyes open?!"

"No. I'm wearing a blindfold."

Malorie's mind is flooded with distantly familiar sounds.

This is what a woman sounds like. She hasn't heard another female voice since Olympia went mad.

"I have two children with me. It's just the three of us."

"Children?" Constance says, suddenly excited. "Grab my hand, let's get you out of the boat. I'll take you to Tucker."

"Tucker?" Malorie pauses.

"Yes, I'll show you—it's where we live. Our facility."

Constance helps Malorie grab the children first. Their hands are clasped together as Malorie is pulled out of the boat.

"You'll have to excuse me for carrying a gun," Constance says timidly.

"A gun?"

"You can only imagine the sorts of animals that have triggered our fence. Are you hurt?" Constance asks.

"I am. Yes."

"We have medicine. We have doctors."

Malorie's lips crack painfully as she smiles bigger than she has in more than four years.

"Medicine?"

"Yes. Medicine, tools, paper. So much."

They begin walking, slowly. Malorie's arm clutches Constance's shoulders. She cannot walk by herself. The children grip Malorie's pants, following blindfolded.

"Two kids," Constance says, her voice soothing. "I can only imagine what you've been through today."

She says *today* but both know she means for years.

They are walking uphill and Malorie's body throbs with pain. Then the ground beneath them changes, suddenly. Concrete. A sidewalk. Malorie hears a light clicking sound.

"What is that?"

"That noise?" Constance asks. "It's a walking stick. But we don't need it anymore. We're here."

Malorie hears her knock quickly on a door.

What sounds like heavy metal creaks open and Constance guides them inside.

The door slams shut behind them.

Malorie smells things she hasn't smelled in years. Food. *Cooked* food. Sawdust, as though someone is building something. She can hear it, too. The low hum of a machine. Several machines whirring at once. The air feels clean and fresh, and the sound of conversations echoes far away.

"It's okay to open your eyes now," Constance says kindly.

"*No!*" Malorie shouts, gripping the Boy and Girl. "Not the children! I'll do it first."

Someone else approaches. A man.

"My *God*," he says. "Is it really you? *Malorie?*"

She recognizes a man's dull, husky voice. Years ago, she heard this voice on the other end of a phone. She has debated, with herself, for four long years, whether or not she'd hear his voice once more.

It is Rick.

Malorie tugs at her blindfold and slowly opens her eyes, squinting against the harsh white light of the facility.

They are in a large hallway flooded with light. It is so bright that Malorie can barely keep her eyes open. It's an enormous school. The ceilings are high, with domed light panels that make Malorie feel as though she's outside. Tall walls reach to the ceiling and are crowded with bulletin boards. Desks. Glass cases. There are no windows, but the air feels fresh and crisp, like the outdoors. The floor is clean and cool, the hallway is brick, and very long. Turning back to Rick, she stares at his withered face and understands.

His eyes are open but they do not focus on any one thing. They loll in his head, glassy and gray, and lost their glimmer years ago. His full head of brown hair hangs long and shaggy over his ears but does not hide a deep and faded scar near his left eye. He touches it apprehensively, as if feeling Malorie's gaze. She notices his wooden walking stick, worn and awkward, bent from some broken tree limb.

"Rick," she says, pulling the children close behind her, "you're blind."

Rick nods.

"Yes, Malorie. Many of us here are. But Constance can see as clearly as you can. We've come a long way."

Malorie slowly looks around at the walls, taking it all in. Handwritten banners mark the progress of their recovery, and flyers declare daily assignments for farming, water purification, and a medical evaluation timesheet, filled with appointments.

Her eyes stop above her, and in brass letters embedded in a brick arch, she reads:

"The man—" Rick pauses. "The one on the recording—he isn't with you, is he?" Rick says.

Malorie feels her heartbeat quicken and swallows with difficulty.

"Malorie?" he says, concerned.

Constance touches Rick's shoulder and softly whispers, "No, Rick. He isn't with them."

Malorie steps back, still gripping the children, moving toward the door.

"He's dead," she answers rigidly, scanning the hall for others. Not trusting. Not yet.

Rick begins to tap his walking stick, moving closer to Malorie, reaching out to touch her.

"Malorie—we've contacted many people over the years, but fewer than you might think. Who knows how many of us are alive out there? And who knows how many are sane? You're the only person we expected to be coming down the river. That doesn't mean nobody else could, of course, but after careful thought, we decided Tom's voice would not only alert you to the fact that you'd arrived, but it would also let strangers know a civilization of some kind was near, if they were to get stopped by the fence first. Had I known he was no longer with you, I'd have insisted we use something else. Please, accept my apology."

She watches him closely. His voice sounds hopeful, optimistic even. She hasn't heard a tone of voice like his in a long time. Still, his face wears the stress and age of living in this new world just like hers does. Like the housemates once looked, years ago.

As he and Constance begin to explain how the facility operates, the fields of potatoes and squash, their harvest of berries in the summer, a means of purifying rainwater, Malorie sees a shadowy figure move behind Rick's head.

A small group of young women emerge from a room wearing plain, light blue clothing. They tap walking sticks, their hands waving in front of them. The women move quietly, ghostly, past Malorie, and she can feel her stomach sink as she sees their cavernous, hollow eyes. She feels light-headed, sick, like she might throw up.

Where the women's eyes should be are two enormous, dark scars.

Malorie clutches the children tighter. They bury their heads against her legs.

Constance reaches toward her, but Malorie pulls away, frantically searching for her blindfold on the ground, dragging the children with her.

"She's seen them," Constance says to Rick.

He nods.

"Stay away from us!" Malorie pleads. "Don't *touch* us. Don't come *near* us! What is going *on* here?!"

Constance looks over her shoulder and sees the women exiting the hall. The room is quiet except for Malorie's panting breaths and quiet sobs.

"Malorie," Rick begins, "it's how we *used* to do things. *We had to.* There was no other choice. When we arrived here, we were starving. Like forgotten settlers in a foreign, hostile land. We didn't have the amenities we have now. We needed food. So we hunted. Unfortunately, we didn't have the security we have now, either. One night, while a handful were out, searching for food, a creature got in. We lost many people that night. A mother, who one moment was completely rational, snapped and killed four children in a fit of rage. It took us months to recover, to rebuild. We vowed to never take that risk again. For the good of the whole community."

Malorie looks to Constance, who has no scars.

"It wasn't a matter of choice," Rick continues. "We blinded ourselves with whatever we had—forks, kitchen knives, our fingers. Blindness, Malorie, was the absolute protection. But that was the old way. We don't do that anymore. After a year, we realized we'd fortified this place enough to lighten this awful burden on our shoulders. So far, we've had no security lapses."

Malorie thinks of George and his video, the failed experiments. She remembers how she almost blinded her children in an act of sacrificial desperation.

Constance can see. She isn't blind. Had you found the courage four years ago, Malorie thinks, *who knows what would have happened to you. To the children.*

Rick leans on Constance for support.

"If you had been here, you would understand."

Malorie is frightened. But she *does* understand. And in her desperation, she wants to trust these people. She wants to believe she has led the children somewhere better.

Turning, she catches a reflection of herself in an office window. She hardly resembles the woman she once was, when she checked the flatness of her belly in the bathroom, as Shannon shouted about the news on the television in the other room. Her hair is thin, matted, and caked with dirt and the blood of so many birds. Her scalp, raw and red, is visible in patches. Her body is gaunt. The bones in her face have shifted—her delicate features have been replaced with sharp and angular ones—her skin tight and sallow. She opens her mouth slightly to reveal a chipped tooth. Her skin is bloodied, bruised, and pale. The deep gash from the wolf mars her swollen arm. Still, she can see that something powerful burns within the woman in the glass. A fire that has propelled her for four and a half years, that demanded she survive, that commanded her to make a better life for her children.

Exhausted, free from the house, free from the river, Malorie falls to her knees. She pulls away the blindfolds from the children's faces. Their eyes are open, blinking and straining against the bright lights. The Boy and Girl stare in awe, quiet and unsure. They do not understand where they are and look to Malorie for guidance. This is the first place they have seen outside the house in their entire lives.

Neither cries. Neither complains. They stare up at Rick, listening.

"Like I said," Rick says cautiously, "we're able to do a lot of things here. The facility is much bigger than this hall implies. We grow all of our own food and have managed to capture a few animals. There's chickens for fresh eggs, a cow for milk, and two goats we'll be able to breed. One day soon we hope to go in search of more animals, to build a little farm."

She breathes deep and looks at Rick for the first time with hope.

Goats, she thinks. *Other than fish, the children have never seen a living animal.*

"At Tucker, we're completely self-sufficient—we've got a whole medical team dedicated to rehabilitating those who are blind. This place should bring you some peace, Malorie. It does for me every day."

"And you two," Constance says, kneeling by the children. "What are your names?"

It's as if this is the first time the question has ever mattered to Malorie. Suddenly there is room in her life for such luxuries as names.

"This," Malorie says, placing a bloodied hand on the Girl's head, "this is Olympia."

The Girl looks at Malorie quickly. She blushes. She smiles. She likes it.

"And this," Malorie says, pressing the Boy to her body, "is Tom."

He grins, shy and happy.

On her knees, Malorie hugs her children and cries hot tears that are better than any laughter she's ever felt.

Relief.

Her tears flow freely, softly, as she thinks of her housemates working together to bring water from the well, sleeping on the living room floor, discussing the new world. She sees Shannon, laughing, finding shapes and figures in the clouds, curious with warmth and kindness, doting on Malorie.

She thinks of Tom. His mind always working, solving a problem. Always *trying*.

She thinks of his love for living.

In the distance, farther down the long school hall, others emerge from different rooms. Rick places a hand on Constance's shoulder as they begin to walk farther into the facility. It's as if this whole place knows to give Malorie and her children a moment to themselves. As if everyone and everything understands that, at last, they are safe.

Safer.

Now, here, hugging the children, it feels to Malorie like the house and the river are just two mythical locations, lost somewhere in all that infinity.

But here, she knows, they are not quite as lost.

Or alone.

acknowledgments

While writing *Bird Box,* I heard mention of a mythological creature known as the Lawyer. Because this news came to me from a good friend, I happily agreed to meet one. On the way, I confessed to said friend that I had no idea what someone like myself would do with a Lawyer. "I've got nothing to law!" But my friend assured me—and he was right to. Wayne Alexander did more than "law," as he read this tale and told me an abundance of his own, each more compelling than the last.

Soon, Wayne informed me of a second fabled being: the Manager. I was inclined to confess, "But I've nothing to manage!" Undeterred, Wayne introduced me to a duo, Managers—Candace Lake and Ryan Lewis who, like Wayne, did much more than their professional title implied. Not only did we read *Bird Box* together, but we began toying with it, our e-mails tallying a higher word count than the book itself. Along the way, we became friends (Ryan's phone in particular has become something of a notebook for me, flooded with ideas as small as "Hey! Janitor closets are kinda scary!" and as lofty as "What do you think of a thousand-page movie script?")

Eventually, Candance and Ryan began speaking of yet a third, impossible entity: the Agent. "But I've nothing to agent!" Mercifully, they ushered me toward one. Kristin Nelson quickly taught me that, though it's delightful to have one thousand ideas, it's just as worthy to make one of them presentable. We went deeper with *Bird Box*. Kristin and I fed the book, starved it, then fed it again. We dressed it up in funny clothes, sometimes keeping only a glove or only the hat. Other times it would sing to us, not unlike Tom's birds, letting us know when it was content.

And when *Bird Box* was ready, Kristin made mention of a fourth and final shadowy personage: the Editor. This time I was *scared*. "But I *do* have something to edit! *Oh no!*" In my imagination, the Editor meditated in a mountain-cave, espoused the rules of grammar, and frowned upon speculative fiction. But, of course, it didn't turn out that way. Lee Boudreaux is as much an artist as the writers she works with. And the ideas she suggested were great, original, and even scary.

Lee and all of Ecco, THANK YOU. And Harper Voyager in the UK, THANK YOU.

And, Dave Simmer, my friend, thank you, too, for introducing me to the Lawyer, and for opening that mythical door to begin with.